# A VOID OF MAGIC

SANDY WILLIAMS

*To all my readers who are fans of commas.*

# 1

FOR THE FIRST TIME EVER, I WISHED I WERE SITTING THROUGH one of Dr. Campbell's lectures. Boring was good. Boring was safe. Boring meant I wouldn't say the wrong thing and start an interspecies war.

Nora Lehr, the only daughter of Octavian Lehr, who was the alpha of the Appalachian pack and quite possibly the strongest werewolf on the continent, turned away from the arched window. I met her gaze from behind my parents' scuffed-up desk.

"Could you say that again, please?" I asked, polite as a neighbor asking for a cup of sugar.

Nora's amber eyes narrowed. When I didn't look away, she clenched her teeth in that oh-so-familiar way that took me straight back to high school. Spiders crawled up my spine, not because I was intimidated—her dominant-gene juju didn't work on hotel property—but because I could practically hear the warning my mom had given me over and over again: *Don't antagonize the paranorms, Kennedy. They'll eat you on the way to school.*

They *could* eat me, but they wouldn't. I'd learned that in sixth grade PE.

Nora slipped into her signature alpha stance, chin lifted, shoulders straightened. Her posturing had always annoyed the hell out of me. Five years away from home hadn't changed that.

"On May sixteenth," Nora said, leaving a deliberate gap between each word. "The Rain will host my wedding in the hillside gardens. The reception will immediately follow in the Silver Ballroom. You will reserve half the rooms and five suites. I'm prepared to pay all costs now. In cash."

I held her gaze for another three seconds, then set my pen on the desk, taking the time to make sure the Hotel Rain logo was faceup. In other words, stalling, because that wasn't what I needed Nora to repeat. It was the earlier part, the part where she mentioned the name of the groom, that had almost made me snort coffee out my nose.

I couldn't let her see I was rattled though. *Don't show weakness in front of the paranorms, Kennedy. They're always ready for an easy snack.*

I took a few extra seconds to make sure the pen lined up precisely parallel to the edge of the desk.

I adjusted it half a millimeter.

Then half a millimeter more.

"You will do this, Kennedy Rain."

If I'd been a wolf, my hackles would have risen. Nora expected obedience. The aggravating thing was, she usually got it. People—or rather, paranorms and the very tiny group of humans who were aware of their existence—knew her father was in charge of the strongest pack in the US. But even men and women who had no clue about the paranormal world went out of their way to follow her orders. Not only had she been born with the alpha gene, she'd been born beautiful too.

"My parents—"

"Would sign the contract." Nora cut me off. "It doesn't violate the treaty."

Technically no, but good God. Her father would flip. Jared's master would flip. The hotel, its workers, and my family would be caught in the middle, treaty or no treaty. This was not something I could authorize.

And it wasn't something I should be discussing. I should be across town in Campbell's class while my parents handled this lunacy.

My parents *excelled* at handling lunacy.

I tilted my head, studying Nora's too-perfect posture. Was that why she was here? She thought I'd be easier to convince? That I was the weakest link in the family? She should know better.

I glanced at my cell phone. Mom still hadn't answered my last text. I didn't know where she and Dad had run off to, just that they were on a much-needed vacation somewhere with very poor cell service. The only communications I'd received from them since they left were a handful of texts saying they were having a good time and staying busy.

The last time I'd received a handful of messages saying they were busy, they'd been on a second honeymoon.

Or a third or fourth one. I didn't ask for details. I didn't want the details I already had. The only reason they were permanently etched into my brain was due to a tragically timed pocket dial—one of them had apparently rolled over in bed.

My roommate, laughing, had told me I should be grateful they still loved each other. I'd thrown my phone at her head.

I wanted to throw it at Nora's head now. She didn't have her supernatural reflexes here. I bet I could hit her.

"Put the date on the schedule, Kennedy," she said.

I rolled my eyes toward the computer screen. May 16 was, unfortunately, wide open.

"Can't you just marry somebody else?"

Nora's smooth expression finally cracked, making her look

more human than stepping into the hotel's Null-zone had. "You are not serious."

*She* couldn't be serious. This had to be one of her stunts, a way to piss off Lehr and test just exactly how much he'd let his daughter get away with.

I stood. "Have you thought this through? Jared's what? Three centuries old? You can't have anything in common, and if you—"

"He's two centuries old," Nora snapped. "And we have everything in common. You don't know him."

"I know he's a vampire."

"He's a person."

"He's Arcuro's scion. His second-in-command. His freaking henchman. Your dad will kill both of you."

"I'll handle my father."

"Really?" I crossed my arms. "I doubt that. I've met your dad. He's kind of a hard-ass, Nora."

"My father—"

"You can't have a wedding here." I rolled the chair under the desk, intending to walk around it and show Nora the door. Before I took a step in that direction, she grabbed the briefcase she'd brought with her and slammed it on the desk.

"Just put us on the damn schedule." Her eyes punched the air with so much fury it felt like the Null had shattered. If I hadn't been used to her flare-ups, I might have been intimidated.

She opened the briefcase, took something out, then dropped it on the desk. "Contract. Guest list. Payment."

Against my better judgment, I glanced down. My gaze went straight to the money.

"Um." I cleared my throat. "I don't think we accept cash deposits."

I met her gaze. She met mine. The German clock on the wall—a gift from one of our overseas guests—ticked in the silence. If my parents had chosen that moment to come home, my mom would have ordered me out of the room. She would have told me I was provoking a paranorm and that my job as a Rain was to keep the wolves, the vampires, and the other supernatural beings who might walk through our doors calm and happy.

That wasn't because the family business was supposedly in hospitality; it was because we weren't supposed to rock the boat. Stability in the paranormal world was paramount, and this hotel—*our* hotel—would become a battleground if war broke out between the species.

The briefcase of money lay open between Nora and me. My credit cards were almost maxed out—I wanted to look at it again—but I'd stopped deferring to paranorms years ago. I might not live in The Rain anymore or be immersed in the world of vamps and wolves and all things other, but I wasn't about to back down. Besides, The Rain wasn't the place Nora thought it was. It wasn't an oasis. It was just another tool Arcuro and Lehr used to increase their power and influence.

"Please." It sounded like Nora was pulling out a tooth, but since I was fairly certain she'd never uttered that word before, I took it as a submission.

And as a sign of something else.

"You're really in love with him, aren't you?"

Her nostrils flared, and I swear to God her eyes turned glassy.

"I wouldn't be here if I wasn't."

"And your father doesn't know? Arcuro doesn't know?"

"Not yet." Fear flickered in her eyes.

Damn it. Damn it. Damn it. I've always been a sucker for tragic love stories. If she and Jared were serious about each other, it could turn out to be *Romeo and Juliet* to the extreme.

I sighed. "I'll put you on the schedule, but my parents will take you off."

"They won't." She lifted her chin, sounding one thousand percent confident. *Welcome back, spoiled little rich were.*

I countered her chin lift with a raise of an eyebrow. "Don't tell me you printed up save-the-date cards already."

She gave me a smug smile. "You should check the hotel's financial records."

---

CHECK THE FINANCIAL RECORDS? What did she mean by that?

I didn't get a chance to ask. Nora left as quickly as if she had her supernatural speed back, leaving me with my eyebrow still raised. It didn't lower until I frowned at the computer. I wasn't there to dig around in The Rain's business operations. I wasn't there to get involved at all. I'd made that mistake before, and it had more than bitten me in the ass.

A tap came from the door.

"Ms. Rain?" Wheelan, the hotel inspector, peeked inside the cracked-open door. "I was told to find you here."

I hid a scowl behind a plastered-on smile. He shouldn't have been sent up here to our private study. Neither should have Nora. We should be meeting downstairs in the main office where my parents conducted most of the hotel's business. Sullens, the front-desk supervisor I'd met that morning, was being a jerk.

"All done with the—" My question became trapped in my throat when his gaze dropped to the still-open briefcase. Covering my mouth to cough, I ever so subtly tossed Nora's papers inside, then slammed it shut. I didn't *think* he saw the money.

"You need a signature?" I asked.

"Well." Wheelan lowered himself into the chair, then placed a folder on the desk. When I'd spoken to him earlier, he'd been cordial. There weren't any remnants of a smile on his face anymore. He looked closed off, like a man who was bearing bad news and bracing for someone to go apeshit on him.

"Is there a problem?"

He opened the folder. "A few problems, actually."

Great.

"Your hotel has been around a long time. My records don't show the date of the first build, but it appears the north and west wings, the restaurant, and the ballroom were all added later than the lobby. The north wing, in particular, is a problem. Do you know when it was built?"

Way before I was born. The Rain was one of the oldest hotels in North America, if not the oldest. It started as a tavern sometime in the eighteenth century, and its early history was… hazy. At some point, paranorms discovered the tavern and much of the land around it nullified all magic and supernatural abilities. That made The Rain the only place on Earth where vampires could see the sun rise and where werewolves could escape the influence of the full moon. It reminded them of what it was like to be human, and for wolves who had turned violent, it was their best chance at resetting their minds, their best chance at survival. But, of course, the vampires and were-wolves fought over the right to stay here, so my ancestors expanded, building by building, to accommodate more of them.

"I'm not sure," I said. "Forty or fifty years ago?"

"That would make sense. Asbestos wasn't banned until later."

"Asbestos?"

"It causes cancer."

"Oh," I said. Then, after a short hesitation, I added, "Crap."

"That's not the only violation." He turned the folder around, then slid it toward me. I flipped through the paperwork, glancing at the highlighted infractions: aluminum wiring in the older wings, blocked and locked emergency exits, a lack of a fire-suppression system.

I looked up. "We have a sprinkler system."

He pulled the folder back. "Yes, but not the right kind. You don't have enough water pressure for it to function effectively during an emergency."

"We'll just avoid emergencies then."

Wheelan looked at me from under his bushy eyebrows. "These aren't minor violations, Ms. Rain."

Note to self: he had no sense of humor. "I understand."

"If somebody gets sick and they trace it back to the asbestos, the lawsuit would bankrupt you."

No one was going to get sick. None of the guests, at least. If a vampire or werewolf was exposed, the second they stepped out of the Null, their bodies would heal any damage that had been done.

"These issues should have been found and resolved years ago," Wheelan said. "I can't find a record of a previous inspection. Do you happen to have a copy in your files?"

As far as I knew, we'd never had someone inspect the place. A human snooping around our business wasn't a great idea, but Wheelan had already started his work when I'd arrived, and I hadn't been able to think of an excuse to get him to leave.

"I'll look for the report," I said. "Can you tell me why you came for an inspection now?"

"A concerned guest submitted a complaint."

It had to be Nora, damn it. I was going to kill her. As long as she was on Rain property, I had a chance to do it.

"I'll email you and your parents a copy of the report." He closed the file and tapped it on the desk to straighten the papers. "Do you know when they'll return?"

"The sooner the better," I muttered.

"Excuse me?"

"A few more days," I said. "I'll let them know your concerns."

"They're more than just concerns. If you can't show that you're making significant progress on rectifying each item, you won't be able to keep your insurance. A grievance will be filed with the county. You'll be shut down."

That wouldn't happen. The paranorms' I'm-superior-to-you bullshit got on my nerves, but they had resources and power, and they would provide a buffer between us and any legal problems that might arise.

If, of course, they weren't the ones creating the problems.

"We'll make sure it's taken care of," I said.

"I hope so. I'll be back next week."

I stood when he did. "Next week?"

"You have to show significant progress. Contact your parents. Fix what you can. If you're denied coverage, you can protest. That will buy you more time for repairs. Some of them won't cost much. Start with those."

I nodded. He was trying to be helpful, and this wasn't his fault. It wasn't mine or my parents'. We'd kept The Rain quiet and off the radar of human authorities. *Nora* had decided to take this action. But it was a blatant bluff. She would have to back off, or she would risk us losing The Rain.

After walking him to the elevator at the end of the hall, I said goodbye, then I returned to the study to call my parents. It wasn't until I picked up my phone that I noticed the time.

I choked off a curse. My shift at Parlay started in just over an hour. The restaurant was a forty-five-minute drive. Totally doable if traffic didn't suck, but traffic always sucked.

I shoved my phone into my pocket, the inspector's report into my purse, then after the briefest hesitation, grabbed the suitcase. This was the study in our should-have-been-private residence on the top floor of the original inn, but I wasn't going to leave *some*teen thousand dollars sitting in the open. We had a safe in the main office. I could shove it in there.

I fished my keys out of my purse to lock up. A literal key. Most hotels had cards today. They had flat-screen TVs in every room. They had Wi-Fi. I'd had to beg my parents to get wired internet when I was in junior high. They'd only agreed because I needed it for school. It wasn't that they didn't care about The Rain—Mom had lived here all her life, and Dad loved it and her enough to marry into this madness—but modernizing cost money.

Nora's advice to check the financial records echoed in my mind. Running a hotel of this size and age was expensive. Money had always been tight. We had a steady income from the vampires and werewolves who stayed here, but we didn't charge an exorbitant amount for a room and hadn't raised prices in decades. Convincing the paranorms to accept any change at The Rain was all kinds of tricky.

I reached the elevator at the end of the hall. It opened before I pushed the call button, revealing a man inside.

*Whoa.*

Some men were attractive. This guy was stop-what-you're-doing-and-stare gorgeous. He wore jeans that hugged muscular thighs and a brown jacket that did nothing to diminish the size of his chest and shoulders. He would have chiseled abs under that white shirt and biceps too big to wrap my hands around.

A slow, knowing smile spread across his face.

"Kennedy Rain."

The mini-me doing flips in my stomach stopped midair. The arrogance in the way he said my name, like he knew exactly how he affected women, slammed a door on my libido.

"Can I help you?" My voice went flat.

The elevator door started to close. He stopped it with a hand, and his eyes roamed down to my feet, then back to my face.

"You've grown up," he said.

"I assume you haven't." I was pretty sure he was a were-wolf. They aged slowly, and I'd recognize him if we'd met before. He had the kind of presence a girl would remember.

His overconfident smile remained in place. "We need to talk, Ms. Rain. Your office?"

The door tried to shut again. He kept it open.

"The office is downstairs," I said.

"This one's closer."

"This one's private."

"It wasn't too private for the inspector," he said smoothly. "And it wasn't too private for Nora."

No doubt his presence was about Nora, the longtime bane of my existence. Add that interest to his arrogance and the fact that he was allowed in the doors during the vampires' occupancy, and he had to be a werewolf with a ton of power.

"You're Lehr's new second," I said.

His smile was all charm. "My reputation precedes me."

"Not really," I said. "I just heard some asshole took out Wallace a year ago. You fit the description."

The door attempted to slide shut again. This time, it beeped a warning it was obstructed. I was pretty sure it was supposed to beep the first time it failed to close.

"We can make this meeting brief, Ms. Rain, or we can make it as long as you want."

Powerful paranorms were such a pain in the ass. Like Nora, this guy was way too used to getting his way.

"I'm running late."

"Then by all means"—he waved a hand to the interior of the elevator—"enter."

There was plenty of space to step inside, but all of it belonged to him. I'd be a sheep in his territory.

"I forgot something," I said.

"You have your purse and a briefcase full of money. What else could you possibly need?"

A separate elevator would be nice.

After a quick calculation, I decided our conversation would be shorter if I stepped inside. Squaring my shoulders, I entered the elevator as if his presence had no effect on me. It helped that I had a lifetime of experience dealing with paranorms. They might lose their supernatural abilities when they entered the Null, but their personalities remained the same: superior and smug.

Lehr's second let the door groan shut. The elevator gave a shimmy before it started down.

This was the only elevator on the property, and it was ancient. That fact had never bothered me before, but the wolf seemed to suck in all the air. He was watching me, measuring me, stalking me without moving even one of those very nice muscles.

"I'm Blake," he said. "You should visit your parents more often. Things have changed in the years you've been gone."

I ignored the pressure in my chest, the little ball of guilt I couldn't quite shake.

"I do visit." At least, I had a few times. Every time I did, I regretted it, so I made sure I was too busy to come home. It helped that my architectural degree was time-consuming and college was expensive. I had to work to pay for my books, my apartment, and the minimum balances on my credit cards. When my student loans came due, it was going to hurt.

Blake gave one of those easy, nonchalant shrugs that somehow made a guy ten times more attractive, and awareness prickled across my skin. I swear the elevator descended even more slowly than usual.

"Let me help you out, Ms. Rain," he said. "You hand me the briefcase. I'll return it to Lehr, and you won't have to worry about repercussions from this little incident."

"I'm pretty sure this is Nora's money."

"It's pack money." He held out his hand. Did he know what it was for? Nora had said her father didn't know about Jared, and this was his second. He reported directly to Lehr.

When I didn't respond, he lowered his outstretched hand. It didn't feel like a capitulation though. It was more like he was scouting the territory to determine a new line of attack.

"You don't want to be involved in this."

"Involved in what?" I asked, extra innocent. That didn't go over well. His eyes narrowed, and he faced me fully.

"Nora is making a mistake," he said. "I know you agree with me."

"Last I checked, wolves didn't have mind-reading abilities."

"We have body-reading talents."

*So* much innuendo there. I didn't let it affect me.

"Not on Rain property," I said.

He snorted. "Some things aren't smothered by the Null, and I don't think you're an idiot. You can't give Nora what she wants."

"You should take up *this issue* with her." Speaking in ambiguities was fun.

He moved closer, apparently not entertained with the conversation, and damn, he smelled good, like a forbidden romp in the woods.

"Don't make a mistake as well, Ms. Rain."

My thumb slid over the briefcase's smooth handle. If I handed over the briefcase, Nora would be his problem, not mine. Not my parents'. We didn't owe Nora anything, and I'd told her the wedding wouldn't happen. Five years ago, I'd vowed never again to get involved in paranormal politics. I could keep that promise right now.

I was oh so close to handing it to him, but a smile slid into his eyes. It was like he could read my thoughts, see that he'd won. To him, it was *inevitable* the little human would give him what he wanted.

*If you give a wolf a cookie, he'll walk all over your ass.*

My quote. Not my parents'.

"No." I stared straight ahead and tried to ignore the way he studied me. This wasn't me getting involved; it was me not caving in to wolf arrogance.

We were *still* descending.

The sign to the right of the door caught my attention. Last inspection: 1995. It figured.

I made a mental note to add elevator upgrades to the inspector's long, long list of required repairs.

We finally reached the ground floor, and the doors screeched open. I would have immediately exited, but I didn't want Blake at my back, so I looked at him and waited.

He looked at me and waited.

If we were outside the Null, the stare down might have been impossible. Alpha werewolves made it feel as if the world's gravity doubled. You wanted to look down. You wanted to drop to your knees. You wanted to do whatever it took to please them. Only strong paranorms could resist submitting.

Or humans who'd learned not to take crap from any wolf.

"Do you need an escort to the door?" I asked.

"Give me the briefcase."

"I thought wolves had good hearing. I told you no."

He closed the distance between us. I had to tilt my head back to maintain eye contact, but there was no way in hell I'd lower my gaze. No trampling me like a carpet. He could wipe his paws off on somebody else.

The elevator chimed and started to close. Blake reached past me to stop it with a hand; then he remained there, his arm blocking the exit.

God, he was huge. Even though he didn't have his super-natural strength or speed, he could still snap me in two with his pinkies. His scent washed over me again, and the already small elevator compartment seemed to shrink.

"Get out, Blake, or I'll have you removed."

I swear yellow flashed in his irises. He didn't like being defied. How far would he push this though? He could yank the briefcase from my hand—no problem—but I was a Rain. I had the protection of the treaty my ancestors had signed with the paranorms two centuries ago. Blake could intimidate and threaten and manipulate as much as he wanted, but if he went too far, he would violate the agreement.

Blake took another small step forward. He lifted his hand...

...and tweaked my nose.

"You're cute," he said. "See you again soon."

## 2

THE BASTARD *TWEAKED* MY NOSE!

He'd tweaked it like I was a two-year-old!

I wanted to storm after him, tell him I wasn't a child. I wasn't *cute*. I didn't have to put up with his crap. He'd left the door wide open, practically daring me to follow.

But I wasn't an idiot. The Rain was built on the northern edge of our property. Ten feet away from the front porch, he'd have his abilities back. His pheromones would make him even more attractive, and meeting his gaze—i.e. not submitting—would be harder. Not impossible, but I wasn't there to get tangled up with a paranorm. The smart thing was to let it go.

"Handled brilliantly," someone commented.

I looked to my left, and my mood soured further.

Sullens stood near the lobby's fireplace, which rose to the ceiling in the center of the room like a stone tower. British accents were supposed to make men sound sexy. Sullens's made him sound pretentious. The extra millimeter he raised his nose didn't help either.

"You should have warned me he was coming," I said. "You should have warned me about Nora too."

"You don't operate The Rain."

I had no idea why he hated me. I'd met him a few hours ago, and as far as I knew, the only thing I could have possibly done to offend him was to walk in the door.

Maybe that was it. With my parents gone, Sullens acted as if he were in charge of The Rain. He wasn't. He couldn't be. He was a paranorm, and not only was the stability of The Rain important, but so was its neutrality. It was a precarious balance, running The Rain. That's why I had been called in to deal with the inspector. My parents couldn't give control to any paranorm. Even when I was a kid, they put me in charge on the few occasions they went out of town. I thought it had been fun, like playing pretend, and the staff went along with it, humoring me and asking my opinions on silly, inconsequential things. They'd been like family. They'd watched me grow up.

And then, when I'd needed their support, not one of them had stood up for me. They'd treated me like I'd broken a sacred tradition.

"The inspector?" Sullens asked.

The report was in my purse. I wanted to hand it to Sullens and forget about it. He could cross most of the items off the list. Some of the others, though, would need my parents' approval and a significant amount of money. If Sullens read the report and mentioned the cost of repairs or the threat to The Rain to anyone else, the news could spread to the vampires and wolves.

*Never threaten the paranorms' safe haven, Kennedy.* That was another one of my parents' sayings, and they never had to qualify it. Anxious vampires and werewolves were dangerous. The other species wouldn't be overjoyed about it either.

"He gave me his report," I said. "It's fine."

"The briefcase?" His gaze dropped to my hand.

"It's not a problem either."

"You're sure?"

"I'm taking care of it." I headed to my parents' office to stash the briefcase. My gaze drifted up to the stacked clocks on the wall. I ignored the lower one, which showed the rise and fall of the sun, and stared at the one above it. Intricately carved fey created the frame. They appeared to pass the clock's hands between them, hands that pointed to 4:02 p.m.

Damn it, I couldn't be late to work again.

Cursing under my breath, I shouldered open the office door. I intended to shove the cash into our safe, but I kept screwing up the combination.

I tried it one more time, making sure I was careful to stop exactly at the right numbers. When it didn't work yet again, I gave up. I didn't have time to mess with it, but I couldn't just leave a briefcase full of money sitting in the office. I'd have to drop it off at the bank.

That meant I had exactly fifty-two minutes to make the forty-minute drive to work. The bank was on the way. As long as it didn't take more than twelve minutes to drop off the cash, I'd be fine.

I could do it. I'd just have to drive fast.

---

THE BANK TOOK TOO LONG. My boss cut my hours because I was late, and now it was almost midnight and what was I doing? Driving the dark foothills of the Appalachians on my way back to The Rain because the second I got off work, Sullens had called. There was an emergency at the hotel. My presence was required.

I glanced at my phone as I turned in to The Rain's parking lot. I'd had a voice mail from my mom that hadn't pinged until after I'd hung up with Sullens. She'd said their cell service was spotty, and if I needed something, I should text. But my problems—the inspector and Nora and the new trouble I was about to walk into—were too complicated to send in a message, so when I pulled into a parking spot and turned off my car, I tried calling again.

It went straight to voice mail.

Annoyed, I shortened what could have been a chapter in a novel to one line of text that said Nora had paid us a shit ton of money to marry Jared at the hotel. It was an easy way of saying the paranormal world was poised to implode. That should get her to call.

Locking my car, I made my way to The Rain's front porch. Something crunched under my shoes when I reached for the door handle.

I looked down. Small shards of a dark brown glass glittered under the porch light. It looked like someone had done a piss-poor job of cleaning up a broken beer bottle. Add that to my list of things to upgrade—a better trained staff.

I made a note to myself to find a broom later, then I pushed open The Rain's front doors. They were tall and wooden and carved with trees and a large chalice, which split down the middle when they opened. I stepped inside and let the feel of my home wrap around me.

I'd always thought The Rain smelled like a promise. Its light, almost citrusy scent reminded me of my childhood. I'd curl up in one of the big chairs clustered in the lobby and watch the vampires and the werewolves arrive. They'd intrigued me. I'd watched their faces when the Null extinguished their magic. Relief and joy and hope humanized their expressions. I'd loved being a part of that, part of the place that renewed their spirits, but time scraped away at that fairy tale layer by layer until my senior year, when I'd come to terms with the fact that The Rain wasn't a refuge; it was just another way for powerful paranorms to increase their control over the weaker ones.

Tonight, The Rain felt stifling. A few guests sat on the stone bench that circled the central fireplace. Others lounged on the two clusters of chairs and couches near the front windows, and a few others hovered closer to the entrance to the attached restaurant. Vampires, all of them. More than I expected. Their sleep schedules always became erratic when they entered the Null. They didn't want to miss a dawn, but it was hard to change their internal clocks. The fact that so many were gathered in the lobby now meant they were there for the show.

There wouldn't be a damn show. I'd handle this problem in a quiet and civil manner.

Sullens separated from a small group standing near the reception desk. I could feel his distaste grow with every step he took toward me.

"Where?" I asked before he could talk down to me.

He pointed to the restaurant.

Ignoring the stares of the staff and guests, I strode across the worn carpet.

My great-great ancestors had knocked out the eastern wall of The Rain over a hundred years ago to add on a restaurant. It seated close to eighty people and had a bar along the back wall that curved out into the lobby. Even at this hour, a good number of paranorms usually sat at the tables, but now only three people were there: a woman with a bloody towel pressed against her neck, a staff member who stood glowering with hands stuffed in his pockets, and the broad-shouldered bartender who loomed between them like an impenetrable brick wall.

A grin leaped to my face. "Garion!"

The bartender didn't smile outright, but his expression softened and a familiar, affectionate light flickered in his eyes.

I gave the immovable man a hug. I thought he'd be gone like most of the others who'd worked here before I left. He couldn't have much time left in his contract. Every paranorm hired stayed for five years. Then they left so that others had the opportunity to fill their positions. They weren't allowed back without the approval of Lehr or Arcuro, who controlled and patrolled the territory around our property.

"It's good to see you," I said. Garion was the only paranorm I'd grown close to the year I'd moved away. I'd had more than enough of the paranormal world. Nora and I had been at each other's throats at school, and after the staff turned their backs on me when I'd needed their support, I hadn't made any effort to get to know the new hires.

Garion's mouth finally tilted into a smile. "If you visited more often, you wouldn't miss me."

"I've been—"

"Busy," he said. "Busy and avoiding us. I understand."

Maybe he did. He'd seen the way I withdrew from everything paranormal before I left home, and while the other employees started to leave me alone, he hadn't. He'd tried to keep my spirits up. I'd tried—and failed—to resent him for it.

"Who are you?" the woman to Garion's left demanded.

Right. The reason I was there. I was representing The Rain, and greeting an old friend with a smile and a hug wasn't exactly the right way to react when a woman had her neck chewed on.

"I'm sorry it took me so long to arrive," I said. "Are you okay?"

"No, I'm not okay. *He* bit me." She jabbed her finger at the man standing to Garion's right. "And *he* won't give me my phone." She jabbed her finger at Garion.

Garion handed me the phone. "She wants to call the police."

"And an ambulance. I'm *bleeding.*"

My stomach dropped. My eyes widened. I blinked and tried to control my expression, but this was worse than I thought. When Sullens had called, he'd said that an employee had bitten someone. I'd assumed that someone was another paranormal, but I was wrong. A paranorm wouldn't call the police or an ambulance.

"I didn't know," the staff member—the vampire—said.

Maybe he hadn't. Humans rarely came to The Rain. Sure, it happened every now and then, but nothing about this girl said *Hey, I'm not a paranorm*, and there weren't any rules about the staff fraternizing with the guests. She couldn't be much older than me—late twenties, maybe—and she was pretty. Her brown hair was ridiculously shiny, beautiful and with waves that looked natural but couldn't possibly be. She had a creamy complexion that was so flawless it could have belonged to a vampire, and her bright blue eyes were wide and... surprisingly steady.

It was that steadiness that made me pause, that made a spark of suspicion ping-pong in my chest. She was hurt and bleeding and angry, but she hadn't lost one ounce of self-confidence.

"What's your name?" I asked.

"What's yours?" she countered.

"I'm Kennedy Rain."

Her gaze seemed to zero in on me. "You own this place."

"My parents do. Let me see your neck," I said.

"Let me see my phone."

I chewed the inside of my cheek. My gut said something was off. Had she deliberately provoked the vampire? Had someone put her up to this?

If I accused her and was wrong, I'd come off as an insensitive bitch, so I took the safe route and said, "I just want to check your injury. Make sure you don't still need an ambulance."

"I want him fired."

"Let me see it," I said again, keeping my voice calm.

She huffed out a breath and removed the towel.

Holy crap, it was bad. I didn't know what I'd expected.

Vampires didn't grow fangs in The Rain, so of course there wouldn't be two neat puncture wounds. But I hadn't expected to see the circle of teeth marks. He'd more than broken her skin; he'd almost ripped out a chunk of flesh.

"Melissa," she said.

I met her gaze, hoping my face didn't show my shock at the wound.

"My name is Melissa, and I'm going to sue the shit out of this hotel." No outrage, no lingering pain in her voice. Just a steady statement of fact.

I put another mark under the Deliberately Provoked column.

"What do you think you would get from a lawsuit?" I asked.

"I'm injured and emotionally distraught. I'd get a fortune." She said that with a perfectly straight face.

"Of course, we'd have to fight the charges. The legal fees would cut into your payout." I said that with a perfectly reasonable tone.

She sat on the barstool and crossed her long legs, which were barely covered by her short black skirt. "If I had money now, I could pay for stitches. Cosmetic surgery. Probably a rabies shot, too." She glared at the vampire behind me.

"I understand," I said. "Can I ask what brought you to The Rain? Have you booked a room?"

I knew the answer to the last question would be no. We rarely booked rooms to anyone who wasn't a vampire or wolf. Occasionally, we had a witch, an elemental, a fey, or one of the other rarer paranormal species stay for a meeting with someone they were in conflict with. Sometimes, they stopped by just because they could. The Rain might not be important to the sanity and mental health of the other paranorms, but if someone was in a power struggle with a wolf or vampire, they would talk to my parents. They'd try to get my parents to offer a night's stay, or they'd try to get the wolf or vampire banned. Sometimes, they offered astronomical sums to buy The Rain. If they controlled the only Null-zone on the planet, they'd have serious clout in the paranormal world.

Unfortunately, my parents always refused those offers.

"No room," Melissa answered. "You don't have an online booking tool, and no one answered the phone when I called."

"So you're here for…?"

"The atmosphere." She looked up at the heavy wooden beams supporting the roof, then down to the stained cement floor. "The reviews say this place is haunted. They didn't mention anything about being infested with vampires though."

I snapped my mouth shut, cutting off my planned response. Was she admitting she provoked the vampire? Or was that just an offhand remark? I glanced at Garion, then at the vampire who'd bitten her. Both men stood still, their expressions completely deadpan.

I wet my lips, then addressed the other issue she'd mentioned.

"Reviews?"

"Yeah. Reviews." She dabbed at her neck with the bloody towel, looked at it with disgust, then tossed it onto the counter. "You really should pay attention to your online reputation. Only ghost hunters and people interested in paranormal shit would drive all the way out here for this. Honestly, I don't know how you stay in business."

"We're not haunted," I said. I didn't even know if it was possible. If ghosts existed, would they return to human form when they stepped onto our property? Or would they go *poof* like a vampire in the sun and disappear into heaven or hell?

"You're interested in paranormal stuff?" I asked.

"It's a hobby," she said.

Garion's mouth tightened before he walked around to the other side of the bar.

I really didn't know what to do about that. I hadn't checked The Rain's reviews since I was a kid, and at that time, we hadn't had any. We hadn't even had an online presence. But at some point in the past few years, The Rain started showing up on the internet. We couldn't get the maps and search services to erase us, so we just let it be. No one wanted to book a room at an obscure hotel with no website.

Except ghost hunters and hobbyists apparently. This was exactly the type of attention my parents had wanted to avoid.

Melissa put her arms on the bar and leaned toward Garion, accentuating the cleavage peeking out of her low-cut, white silk blouse. "Pour me a whiskey sour, sweetie."

Garion looked at me. I made a "go ahead" motion, and he turned to the back wall to grab a bottle. He poured the drink, then slid the glass toward her.

She smiled. "Ten thousand will do."

It took a second for her words to click.

"You want ten thousand dollars?" I couldn't quite keep the derision from my voice.

The vampire beside me laughed.

Melissa met his gaze, took a sip of her drink, then said, "Fifteen."

"You're dead——"

I cut off the vampire's lunge. He nearly knocked me down, but I grabbed the counter, and the second he realized he'd almost trampled me, he caught my elbow, made sure I'd found my balance, then took two steps backward. That retreat was the closest thing I'd get to an apology.

"Give us a second," I said to Melissa. Then I motioned for the vampire to follow me.

"What's your name?" I asked when we were a safe distance away.

The skin around his eyes tightened. He'd backed off when he'd nearly plowed me over, but that didn't mean he liked me.

It didn't mean he would recognize my authority. It didn't mean anything more than the fact that I was a Rain and protected by the treaty. Plus, aside from Garion, I couldn't shake the feeling that Sullens wasn't the only employee who didn't want anything to do with me.

That was fine. I didn't really want anything to do with them either.

"Isaiah," he said. "I thought she was a vampire. She told me to bite her. I barely scraped my teeth across her throat, but she wanted more, and I just… bit."

"She'll create trouble."

"I will not pay her a cent."

"I'm not asking you to."

Some of the vehemence left his eyes. "What are you asking then?"

I looked away, my conscience scratching at my spine. If Melissa knew about vampires and had deliberately provoked him, would she be satisfied with money? Would she try to extort more? And that's assuming we could even come up with that amount.

"I can have someone take care of her," he said when I didn't respond soon enough. It took too long to realize what he meant.

"No!" My voice carried. Melissa looked my direction, her head tilted.

"No," I said again, quieter this time. "She will not be hurt any more than she already is. Can you make her forget this happened?"

I hated myself for asking. I hated that I'd been put into this position where I was forced to ask. Often, I hated that I'd been born into this life and would, one day in the far, far future, have to run The Rain.

"If I leave the Null, my contract will be void," Isaiah said.

"It's either that or you find fifteen grand."

"Or I make a phone call. It will be fine. People go missing all—"

"Finish that sentence and you're fired."

His mouth snapped shut. His gaze traveled down to my feet, then back up as if he were seeing me for the first time. Finally, he said, "You don't have the authority to—"

"Can you do it?" I demanded.

He took a step toward me. The tendons in his neck stood out. "I won't."

"I'll call Arcuro then," I said. "He can send someone to heal her neck and wipe her memories."

Isaiah went absolutely still. Arcuro terrified him, and rightly so. He was one of the Aged, not as old as the vampires' reclusive king but more powerful than ninety-nine percent of the other vampires on the planet. He was strong. He was deadly. And if he had to take care of this matter, he'd have someone waiting to murder Isaiah the second he stepped out of the Null.

"You would not," Isaiah said.

"Try me." My voice was low and steady.

*Never play poker with a paranorm, Kennedy. They'll taste the truth on their tongues.*

I gritted my teeth hard. The last thing I wanted to do was contact Arcuro. Okay, the second to the last thing. It was a better option than having Melissa killed.

Isaiah's face twitched. "I have three years left in my contract. If I step off the property, I might never be allowed back."

I had no idea how old he was, no idea how much he'd needed the Null when my parents hired him. He might have been days away from greeting the sun, a common way older vampires chose to die when they became bored or disenchanted with their existences. If he left The Rain, he might never see another dawn.

I didn't care. I couldn't care. I wouldn't make the mistake of sympathizing with paranorms again.

"Her memories can't be erased," Isaiah finally said, his shoulders slumping. "Not by me or anyone I know. It's been too long, and she's too cognizant. Only one of the Aged can do it."

Damn it. That wasn't what I wanted to hear. I'd wanted—

"God, you guys are killing me." Melissa strode confidently toward us. "It's late. I'm tired. I'm going home. Here." She shoved a napkin into my hand. "Send the money to that account in three days or I'm contacting my lawyer."

The napkin had her first and last name—Melissa Geary—written above a Venmo username. I slipped it into my pocket, waited until she exited The Rain, then said to Isaiah, "Go take a break."

He looked like he wanted to bury my remains under The Rain's floorboards. I felt the same way about him.

He muttered something about me having no business being there. I wished that were true.

After Isaiah left, I slid onto a barstool.

"You okay?" Garion asked.

"Fine," I snapped.

He scowled as he made the bloody rag disappear into a trash can, and I mentally winced. He didn't deserve my hostility.

"I thought you'd be gone by now," I said, softening my tone. "Is there an exception to the five-year contract for… berserkers?"

He sniffed and gave me his best you-don't-amuse-me look, which of course meant he was thoroughly entertained.

I crossed my arms and studied him more closely. "Bunny shifter?"

He chuckled, shaking his head. "Still wrong, Kennedy. Let it go. You'll never guess what I am."

I'd bet I already had. I'd guessed hundreds of different species in the time that I'd known him. Half of them I wasn't even sure existed. Garion never gave any indication that I'd come close to the right answer, no tightening of the lips or eyes, no twitch or tic I could detect. He was the only paranorm who didn't have his species listed next to his name on his employment contract. Ever since seeing that, I'd been trying to figure him out. Most of our employees were vampires and wolves, but we'd hired witches, elementals, fey, even a Valkyrie in the past. They'd all been listed. It had killed me that Garion was the only one with a big, fat blank next to his name.

"One day, I'm going to figure you out."

"Go to bed, kid, before I have to tell your parents you're up past your bedtime."

I gave him a glare, but it wasn't very threatening, considering I yawned in the middle of it. Rest was exactly what I needed. I would have preferred to sleep at my apartment rather than here, but there was no way I'd be able to make that drive again tonight.

## 3

A LOUD BANG JERKED ME AWAKE. MY BEDROOM LIGHT FLASHED on. I shot upright in bed.

"Good," Nora said. "You're awake."

My brain ricocheted around in my skull before I recognized my room. My *old* room. I was at The Rain, not my apartment outside of Knoxville.

I forced my sleep-crusted eyes to focus on the werewolf standing at the foot of the bed. "What the hell are you doing here?"

Nora walked to my dresser. "I need a favor."

"How did you get in? I locked the door." I was *certain* I'd locked it. Right before I crashed into bed, then tossed and turned until dawn, my mind too occupied to shut off and let me sleep until a couple of hours ago.

She opened a drawer. "I'm a werewolf, Kennedy. A locked door isn't going to keep me out."

"If you broke—"

"I didn't break it." She rummaged through my drawer like she owned the dresser.

"What do you want?" I demanded.

"I told you, I need a favor." She threw a pair of jeans at my face.

"Your favor is me not telling your father you gave me half a million dollars to marry a vampire." I chucked the jeans back at her.

She didn't bother to catch them. She stood there, arms crossed and hip cocked.

"Get out," I said.

"Get *up*. It's ten a.m. This is laziness."

"This is Saturday."

"You want the inspector to disappear, don't you?" Nora asked.

My eyes narrowed. "So you did report The Rain."

"No, but I can make the problem go away."

I didn't believe her denial. Also…

"What do you mean by go away?" If I had to talk a second paranorm out of committing murder today, the government was going to have to start paying me a salary.

Nora scowled. "I'm not a heathen, Kennedy."

"No, you're a wolf, and wolves and vampires and all paranorms have a way of making your problems disappear permanently."

"We don't randomly kill people."

"This wouldn't be random, would it? And did you send Melissa?"

"Send who?"

"Melissa." I stood up. I wasn't very formidable with a bad case of bed hair and a wrinkled nightshirt, but too much was being thrown at me too fast. Too *suspiciously* fast. My thoughts last night had swung between my parents setting up a series of trials to see how I handled them to a global conspiracy to take down the entire Rain family to an elaborate scheme plotted by Nora and Jared to ensure we had no choice except to host their wedding. The last one was by far the most plausible.

"I don't know who you're talking about."

"It's something you would do."

"What's that supposed to mean?" she demanded.

"It means you get mean when you don't get your way."

She snorted. "I see what this is. It's another one of your blame-the-paranorm-for-all-your-woes days. You haven't changed at all."

"Neither have you. You're still trying to piss off your dad. You still think the whole world should bow down to you."

"You're always—" She cut herself off. It looked like it was painful, holding back what she wanted to say. This was the second time in twenty-four hours she'd basically backed down to me. It was a rare enough occurrence that I was beginning to wonder if she wasn't as dominant a wolf as she used to be.

She mumbled something that sounded like *He was wrong*, then turned and left the room.

I shouldn't go after her. I should mind my own business and go back to sleep, but she was the only paranorm I knew who had strong connections and was powerful in her own right. If I couldn't solve the inspector problem or the issue with Melissa on my own, Nora could help.

If she chose to.

*Damn it.*

"Nora!" I called, hurrying through the living room, then out the door she'd left open.

"Nora," I called again. She was already at the elevator, waiting for it to arrive.

She didn't turn around. Typical.

"If you wait for me to get dressed, we can talk."

The elevator chimed and opened. Nora stepped inside, then turned around and looked at me. I thought she was going to let the doors close without responding, but just before they slid shut, she said, "Meet me at my car."

"That wasn't what I... offered." The doors closed. She didn't hear me.

Fine. It was better for her to leave. My parents would deal with this when they returned. I'd shown up as required. Getting any more involved was a bad idea.

I went back to my room, dressed, combed out the tangles in my hair, and brushed my teeth. I had a paper I needed to write and a shift at the restaurant tomorrow morning that my boss hadn't canceled. In other words, I had a life, and it ran much more smoothly when I stayed away from The Rain.

Grabbing my keys, I locked up our suite, took the elevator to the lobby, and walked out The Rain's front door.

A human who didn't know about the existence of para-norms wouldn't have noticed the change in the air. It wasn't anything obvious. It was subtle, like the atmosphere had shim-mered into a more vivid, more volatile world. And Nora, standing at the edge of our parking lot, had shifted with it, not into her wolf form but into an even more beautiful, more confident version of herself. Her posture changed. She looked like she had the poise of a queen; I felt like I had the poise of a pig.

"You're still here," I said, my voice flat.

"Get in." She walked to the driver's side door of a silver convertible that had to cost more than my college education.

"Uh, no. I might dent the leather."

"I'll bring you back," she said.

"I'm going home."

Hints of gold flickered in Nora's amber eyes. "This is your home, Kennedy."

I didn't like that statement, that reminder of my inheri-tance, my future responsibilities. The Rain might nullify a paranorm's powers, but it smothered my freedom. I'd had to keep the paranorms' secrets and maintain the peace and stability of their world, and I'd had to do it while Nora went through some kind of teenage rebellion. She had been pissed her father insisted on her going to school, so she did everything she could to push back against him. That pushback included making my life hell. She found ways of tormenting me that went right up to the edge of breaking the treaty. Her father wouldn't back down though. Nora was a naturally born were-wolf, something that was extremely rare, and Lehr thought it important for her to be around humans.

"It's not my home now," I said.

Her mouth flattened. "Fine. This was a bad idea anyway."

She opened her door.

"Whose idea was it?" I asked.

She just gave me a look, then sat behind the wheel.

It had to be Jared's. I'd crossed paths with him once, and it wasn't something I wanted to do again. Old vampires were scary. They were calculating. They could take offense at anything while at the same time thinking the most morose things were funny.

But old vampires were also powerful. Jared wouldn't have any problem erasing Melissa's memories. *If* she was human. I'd call in that favor after I tracked her down. For now…

I sighed. I'd probably regret this.

I walked around to the passenger seat and climbed inside. "How long will this take?"

She stared out the windshield. "An hour. Maybe two."

That was a long drive. Then again, I had no clue where Jared lived.

"And you think you can get the inspector to go away *without killing him*?" I didn't really think Nora would do that. Dead bodies tended to draw attention the paranorms didn't want —*most* paranorms at least—and since she wasn't a vampire, I didn't have to worry about her getting thirsty and making a Slurpee out of his neck. Besides, Wheelan wasn't her type. Her type was…

Well, her type was Jared—tall, hot, and dangerous.

And powerful. He could make both Wheelan and Melissa forget they had ever heard of The Rain.

Nora grabbed her sunglasses from the dash, popped them on her face, then started the engine.

---

AN UNEXPECTED BENEFIT of riding in Nora's convertible was the absence of conversation. To hear each other, we would have had to yell over the wind and road noise, so a solid thirty minutes passed before I broke our stalemate.

"Are we almost there?" I yelled. She'd said this would take an hour or two. If we turned around right now, that would be one hour in the car.

"Yes," she said. We were nearing the expensive, west side of Knoxville with its multimillion-dollar houses and luxury shopping centers. It was exactly the kind of place I'd expect an old, rich vampire to live.

Nora took the first exit for Beardan, sliding into the traffic on the feeder.

"You never let our power influence you," Nora said.

I frowned. I didn't know where she was going with that. "I lived at The Rain."

"Even outside the Null. You never let us push you around."

"Speaking of yourself in the plural now? How very alpha of you."

"See?" She glanced away from the road long enough to give me a scowl. "You should be afraid of me, especially away from The Rain, but you aren't. You should try to please me, but you don't."

"I'm sorry. I didn't realize this was a class election." She'd been class president. And homecoming queen. And a general pain in the ass.

Her hands tightened on the wheel. "You don't have to be so snide."

Snide? I snorted. Sometimes, Nora sounded as old as her dad. She wasn't. She was my age. Naturally born wolves matured at the same rate as humans until sometime in their twenties when it slowed down to a crawl. Nora could expect to be gorgeous for the next hundred years of her life.

She stared out at the road. "Most humans feel the urge to please me. The pack has no choice except to do what I want. It's not their fault—I am what I am—but even if I asked for honest opinions, I couldn't trust they'd give one. I can trust your opinion though."

From someone else, that might have been a compliment. From Nora, it was... Well, I wasn't sure what it was except unexpected.

"I always appreciated that," she added. "I respected it."

Unexpected and weird.

Maybe I wasn't giving her enough credit. We'd graduated almost five years ago. I'd left town. She hadn't. And if she had the same entourage of friends as she had in high school, then yes, she was one hundred percent right—they'd tell her what she wanted to hear. It took a strong-willed person to disagree with a werewolf, or it took someone like me, a human who knew what Nora was and how she could influence you.

She glanced at me again, then she turned onto Tulip Avenue, a new, upscale shopping center with a decent view of the Cumberland Mountains to the south.

*Shopping center.* Not residential area or mansion or luxury apartment complex.

"What are we doing here?" Both sides of the road were filling with high-end clothing stores and cafés that charged upward of $10 for a cup of coffee.

"I'm not canceling the wedding," she said. She pulled into a parking spot in front of a bridal boutique.

I stared at the frilly display. "You're kidding me. *This* is your favor?"

She turned off the engine and removed her sunglasses. "I need an opinion I can trust."

"You can't trust me! I'll make sure you look like a hag."

She arched a perfectly sculpted eyebrow. "Look at me, Kennedy. It's impossible to make me look like a hag."

"So let me get this straight. I go in there with you, tell you every dress looks awful, and you'll make sure Wheelan forgets about The Rain?"

"Yes." She opened her door and got out of the car.

This was so much better than having to talk to Jared in person. Oddly though, I didn't feel completely relieved. I felt worried. If she went in there and found the perfect dress, it would be that much bigger a blow when she finally realized The Rain wouldn't solve her wedding problem.

I climbed out of the car and beat her to the door. "Nora, this is a bad idea."

"All I'm asking is for your opinion."

"My opinion is that you're not thinking this through. Lehr and Arcuro hate each other. They're going to be at each other's throats when they find out. Literally, Nora. You're going to cause a war."

Her cool gaze swept the sidewalk, and the humans who were nearby got the unspoken message to move on and mind their own business.

"What may or may not happen doesn't concern you."

"Seriously?" I said. "You believe that? When your people fight, everyone suffers. My parents will have to play mediator. The Rain will be caught in the middle of the slaughter, so don't pretend this only affects you. If you marry Jared, you're—"

She was in my face before I saw her move.

"Enough, Kennedy."

The threat in her voice slithered over me. My heart rate kicked up. I started to sweat despite being in the shade of the boutique's awning. Nora's alpha gene gave her the ability to make the air feel heavy and solid. It pressed down, urging me to drop my gaze.

No way was that happening. Deliberately, I slowed my breathing and lifted my chin a notch.

Nora's eyes almost glowed, but holy hell, she looked away first. She'd backed down to me.

*Again.*

What the hell was wrong with her?

"I should have free choice in who I marry," she said.

"So should I, but it's not that easy for either of us."

When she met my gaze again, curiosity flickered in her eyes.

Damn it. Those words had slipped out, but The Rain wasn't the magical place of my childhood. I'd stopped dreaming of weddings and families and white picket fences a long time ago. Instead, I woke up with nightmares of boyfriends finding out about the paranorms, the hotel, and my future role in that world.

I cleared my throat. Then, to redirect the conversation, I said, "You have no intention of telling your father, do you?"

She backed up half an inch. "Just help me with this."

"Don't you have friends?"

"I told you"—she put another inch of distance between us —"I'm the alpha's daughter. They'll tell me what I want to hear. You won't."

She opened the door and entered the boutique.

## 4

"YOU ARE STUNNING," LISA, THE BOUTIQUE'S OWNER, SAID. She circled Nora, fluffing out layers of lace and silk and gazar.

*Gazar.* That was a word I hadn't known before today.

Nora looked at me in the mirror.

I looked at the time on my phone and muttered, "It's perfect."

It wasn't. The layers in the skirt made the dress look like a tiered cake. Nora could pull it off—she could pull off a plastic trash bag—but the sweet look didn't suit her.

"Next one, please," she said to Lisa.

"Of course, Ms. Lehr." Lisa helped her take off the dress. Underneath it, Nora wore a strapless bra and lace panties, and of course she looked like a runway model. If someone had photographed her in each of the dozen dresses she'd tried on, every one of the pictures would have been on the cover of a magazine. It was ridiculous and unfair. I wouldn't make the front page of a dying e-zine.

"One more dress," I said when Lisa left.

Nora's eyebrows arched.

"I have a life, and we're way past the two hours you said this would take."

"Your life is mundane. School, studies, and a minimum wage job where you pander for tips."

I glared. "Have you been following me?"

"I have people who look into things for me."

"Well, not all of us have people. Or rich daddies."

Lisa hung the dress on a wall hook with a loud *tsk*. She was a fan of loud *tsks*. At least, she was with me. In her defense, I hadn't done much to help her sell a dress. My sarcasm was more transparent than the most sheer veil in the place, and I'd been a little more than obvious with my opinions on the prices of the gowns. I was actually surprised—and disappointed—she hadn't booted me out of the store yet.

While she and Nora discussed the next masterpiece she'd try on, I walked to the display of veils and tiaras. The tiaras were in a glass cabinet and ranged in price from the mid-hundreds to the disgustingly high thousands. Same with the veils. I wanted to touch the long white fabric, but I was worried that privilege would cost me a grand.

"I gave you money," Nora said, like I shouldn't have any financial issues.

"You gave my parents money," I said, "and that's going to be returned as soon as they come home."

Nora faced the mirror and ran her fingers through her long hair. "When will they be back?"

"Tomorrow."

"Where did they go?"

"Just a quick vacation."

I could feel Nora watching me in the mirror. Paranorms were good at sniffing out human lies, but I wasn't exactly lying. They'd told me they were going away for their anniversary for a few days. I was passing along a factual answer. It didn't matter if I doubted it.

"That's unusual, isn't it?" Nora asked.

With a steady gaze, I said, "Wanting to get away from you people is completely normal."

Another *tsk* from Lisa, who was showing Nora a dress that I could already tell would be a big fat no. I should have started counting Lisa's *tsks* an hour ago. She had to be up somewhere beyond a dozen already.

Nora shook her head. "Bring me the Rosefeldt."

"Of course, Ms. Lehr." Lisa left the dressing room.

"The Rosefeldt?" This was the first time Nora had requested a specific dress.

"You don't want to run The Rain, do you?" She fingered the material of one of the bridesmaids dresses Lisa had set aside earlier. That happened to put her in full view of the boutique's front windows. Nora didn't care who saw her though. Earlier, I'd handed her a sleek, silky robe to put on, and she'd sniffed and set it aside.

"It's, literally, the last job on Earth that I want."

"You'd rather wait tables for humans who may or may not make it worth your time."

"I have to pay my bills. Do you work?"

"For the pack."

"What do you do?"

"Accounting."

"You have a degree?"

"I have a brain," she said. She took the bridesmaid dress off the rack and held it up. It was orange. I felt sorry for her bridesmaids, whoever the hell they might be.

"Your dad pays you?"

She gave a pretty little snort. "He pays me an allowance. The cash is clean, if that's what you're worried about."

"I don't have to worry because you're taking it back."

She held out the dress. "Try this on."

I laughed. "Absolutely not."

"You're the perfect size."

"No."

"It will give you something to do while you wait."

"I'm not that bored." Actually, I was. "I need you to find someone for me." I'd been thinking about this since the second dress she'd tried on. Paranorms had resources that I didn't. If Melissa was human and serious about black-mailing The Rain, Nora could find her more quickly than I could.

"Who?" she asked, sounding disinterested.

"Melissa Geary. I have her Venmo account name. I need to know if someone sent her to The Rain and if she knows about"—I waved my hand in her general direction—"all of you."

"Done." She held out the dress.

My eyes narrowed—that was a little too easy—but I took the dress and stepped inside a smaller dressing room.

"Who's your maid of honor?" I asked, slipping out of my jeans.

"I haven't decided yet."

"Who's in the running?" Basically, *who are your friends?*

"A few people from the pack. A human or two. Possibly one of Jared's people."

One of his vampires, most likely. Someone he'd bonded. Supposedly, it was a mutually beneficial relationship, but I'd always thought it sounded like servitude.

"I have the Rosefeldt, Ms. Lehr."

I stepped into the orange dress and pulled it on. It was sleek and shimmery and reached almost to my knees. The spaghetti straps showed my red bra, and my curves were exag-gerated—my hips much more than my breasts, of course—but it did give me better-than-usual cleavage. That was the only upside though.

I stepped out of the dressing room, intending to tell Nora

that this dress was just mean, but she was already in the Rose-feldt, and all my disparaging comments died.

It was *the* dress. It didn't just fit perfectly; it wrapped Nora in an atmosphere that was as ethereal as a wolf loping beneath a full moon. The lace bodice dipped low between her breasts and showed off her trim waist before a layer of tulle took over. The see-through fabric was long and delicate and barely hid the wild vines embroidered into the underskirt.

She would look poised and preternatural walking down an aisle. Otherworldly and beautiful.

Nora looked at my reflection in the mirror and raised her eyebrows in question.

"You look hideous," I made myself say.

She smiled. Gah, that made her look even more exquisite.

"Jared will like it," she said.

"He's male. He'll like it *off* you."

She practically beamed.

Lisa placed both her hands on her hips. "I told you this was the one."

Yes, it was definitely the one. It was also the one Nora had requested by name.

"You already knew this was the dress."

"I'd hoped," Nora said.

"You'd hoped? We've been here three hours."

"I had to learn your faces."

I gave her a new face to learn. It didn't affect her, but Lisa *tsked* again and left the dressing area.

"Sunset isn't your color," Nora said, scrutinizing my dress.

"I really do have things to do." Returning to the dressing room, I shut the door. I would have said this trip was a waste of time except that Nora was helping me out with two problems. Honestly, I was getting the better end of this deal. It was too easy, really, which made me think Nora was responsible for both the inspection and Melissa despite her claims otherwise.

It was warm in the changing room, so I dug around in my purse for a hair tie and ended up activating my cell phone's screen. I had a message from my mom. It said, *When?*

I had to read my previous text to figure out what she was talking about. The last thing I'd written was that Nora wanted to marry Jared at The Rain.

*When?* That was my mom's response? Not *Hell no, that's not happening?*

Halfway into typing a sarcastic response, my phone died.

Damn it. I needed a new one. My battery had stopped holding a charge a few months ago, but I didn't have the extra money to upgrade.

I chucked it into my purse, then started to take off the ugly dress. Sunset my ass. The thing was orange.

"You're supposed to be stopping the wedding," a voice rumbled above the door.

I yelped and yanked the dress straps back up. The low and sensual voice belonged to Blake. He was just outside the stall. He rested one arm along the top of the door and peered down at me.

"What are you doing here?" I demanded. "And do you mind?"

"You're helping Nora plan her wedding."

"I'm not." I reached down, grabbed my T-shirt, then straightened and called out, "Nora!"

"Oh, Nora ran the second she sensed me." He smiled. "Yes, she left you to a wolf."

I tried to snatch my jeans off the top of the door, but Blake's heavily muscled arm kept them in place.

"Give me my jeans."

"Most women want me to *take* their jeans." His slow appraisal made heat strike through my core. Ugh! I hated para- norms and their pheromones.

I jerked on my jeans again. This time, he removed his arm, and they slapped me in the face.

"I'm going to kill her," I muttered.

"I'm afraid I'd have to stop you, her being my alpha's daughter and all."

I glared. "I'm going to change. You're going to go away."

He looked entertained by my declarations.

Cocking my hip, I crossed my arms and waited.

"Orange isn't your color," he said, then he turned his back to my door.

"Good thing I'm not in the wedding!" I shimmied out of the *orange* dress and pulled on my T-shirt.

He tilted his head slightly. "In the wedding that's not going to happen?"

"It's not happening at The Rain." That was about all I could control. If Nora wanted to elope off to Vegas or somewhere else, I couldn't stop her.

I pulled on my jeans one second before Blake turned around.

"Has Nora mentioned Jared?"

I tried to shove open the door, but Blake blocked it. "She mentioned she wants to marry him."

"When did she see him last?"

"I don't know. Why don't you ask her?" I wanted to kick the door open and knock Blake on his ass, but wolves were stalwart. I was trapped until he decided to move.

"In case you haven't noticed, Nora's avoiding me."

"Aren't you dominant? Can't you just voodoo yourself into her head?"

"She's blocking me," he said. "She's blocking everyone. It's become a problem. Lehr's ignored it for weeks, but he's running out of patience. He wants to know what's bothering his daughter."

"Why haven't you told him?"

Blake sobered. The change in his demeanor was so complete and sudden it raised the hair on the back of my neck.

He opened the dressing room door. I didn't dare step out though. His easy arrogance might have grated against my nerves, but I wanted it back. This version of him was too serious. Too intense.

"Nora is my friend," he said. "I'm hoping I don't have to tell Lehr. I'm hoping either she or Jared will come to their senses. If they don't, Lehr will go after Arcuro. He'll accuse him of sending his scion to seduce Nora. There won't be a wedding because there will be war."

The walls of my dressing stall pressed in, and even though Blake hadn't moved, he was too close. The whole paranormal world felt too close. I wished I were wrong about the war, about the conflict and the consequences that could spill across the continent. For the past five years, I'd almost succeeded in pretending their world didn't exist, but every damn time I went home, I was reminded it wasn't a dream or a fairy tale. This was serious shit, and my family had a history of intervening to dispel it. We kept the peace. We kept things stable.

My parents couldn't get back quickly enough.

"I need to talk to Jared," Blake said.

"Then talk to him."

"He's missing."

"The Aged don't just go missing."

"That's the term his people used when I tracked them down."

Jesus. He was tracking down Jared's vampires? That wasn't good. There were likely other *missing* vampires now.

I cleared my throat. "She hasn't mentioned where he is."

"I know where he is," Blake said. "He's at The Rain."

A laugh burst from my lungs, but Blake's expression didn't twitch. He was serious.

I crossed my arms and gave him a look that said, *Really? You're going to go there?*

"It's the only place that makes sense," Blake said.

It made the opposite of sense. "You were there yesterday. Did you see him?"

His intense brown eyes remained steady. "I saw a lot of vampires who would do anything to gain the favor of one of the Aged."

"He's not at The Rain." I grabbed my purse off the floor, then turned back to the door.

"Can you prove that?" Blake asked, peering down at me. Had he moved closer? It felt like he had. My whole body hummed, reacting to the pheromones and power that came from his being a dominant werewolf. He didn't need the magic —he was ridiculously good-looking even without it. Most girls would pull him into the dressing room and shut the door.

I met his gaze, leaned closer, and said, "Move."

The corner of his mouth crept up, likely because he knew I wasn't completely unaffected by his presence. Fortunately, he stepped aside, allowing me just enough room to squeeze out of the dressing stall.

"This wouldn't be the first time a Rain helped a paranorm," he said.

I stiffened. He hadn't been Lehr's second five years ago, but he must have been ranked high enough in the pack to have heard some of the rumors.

"My parents follow the rules." They did. I didn't. That's why I'd finished my senior year at a boarding school.

I fished my keys out of my purse and continued to the shop's front door, very aware of Blake following close behind me. I reached for the handle, but his hand closed over mine before I could open it.

"Turnover is Monday," he said. "When the wolves check

in, we'll find Jared. When we do, it will be bad for him and Nora. But it won't be good for you either. Do you understand?"

I met his gaze, not letting his nearness or his threat intimidate me. "Someone would have told me if he was at The Rain."

His head cocked into a very wolfish slant. "Are you certain? Jared has vampires loyal to him. He might be using an alliance with Nora to weaken his master and take over."

"Or he might love her."

Blake's eyes narrowed like I was a bunny that might need to be eaten. "Are you going to be a problem?"

"Are you?" I looked pointedly at his hand.

He removed it, but he did it slowly, letting his fingers trail past my wrist before letting me go.

The bell above the door jingled when I pushed it open. It was only after I'd stepped onto the sidewalk that I remembered I hadn't driven there.

## 5

I STARED AT THE NOW EMPTY PARKING SPOT WHERE NORA'S convertible had been. "I'm really going to kill her."

Blake eased into my line of sight. "I thought we went over this, sweetheart."

I glared. "Don't mock me."

"Me? Mock you? Never." He moved away to lean against the thin trunk of a decorative tree.

Damn him, he hadn't backed off just now in the shop. He'd let me go so he could come out here and gloat.

Gritting my teeth, I scanned the street for a bus stop. Of course there wasn't one. This part of town was too snooty for that. It wouldn't help anyway because I needed to get my car from The Rain. How the hell was I going to get there? I couldn't afford an Uber. It would cost my whole next paycheck.

My gaze rested on the Aston Martin parked beside an old Ford truck that looked like it was one shallow pothole away from falling apart. That car had to cost twice as much as Nora's. It wasn't fair that paranorms had so much money to throw around.

I looked at Blake. "You're giving me a ride home."

"Am I?"

God, he was smug. He'd known he was the logical choice.

It took effort, but I made sure my expression was completely indifferent and said, "Yep."

He could turn me down. I didn't think he would. The Rain wasn't that far out of the way of Lehr's estate.

"You think you're safe with me?" he asked.

I studied him before I answered. He was Lehr's second-in-command, a strong, dominant wolf who could control his instincts. He wouldn't violate the treaty—he'd enforce it—and despite his threat to make my life hell, he wouldn't do it. He'd figure out Jared wasn't at The Rain, and as soon as my parents came home, I'd be done with this mess. He'd forget about me.

"I'm completely safe with you." My smile might have been a little pompous. I suspected Blake was annoyed I wasn't swooning at his feet, and it was satisfying to taunt him. Karma, baby.

"We'll see," he said, light glinting in his eyes.

*Never pique the interest of a paranorm, Kennedy. It makes you stand out in the flock.*

I ignored my mom's often repeated warning. "Let's go."

He nodded, acknowledging my words, then he placed a hand on my lower back and led me forward. It was so casual and smooth I didn't think anything of it until I'd taken two steps.

I sidestepped out of reach. "Watch the hand."

"You're on the wrong side."

At first, I thought that was another offhand remark about helping Nora with her wedding. Then I realized where he had been leading me.

I stared at the dilapidated Ford.

"You're kidding."

He strode past me and opened the passenger door. It creaked so loudly I stood there waiting for it to fall off.

"You wanted a ride, didn't you?" he asked.

I eyed the ripped seat cushion and the wires sticking out from under the dash. "I'm reconsidering my request."

"Ah," he said, sounding oh so sage and knowledgeable. "You're scared."

"Of that thing? Absolutely." The truck had to be ten times older than my second-hand car. The sides of the bed were dented and rusted, and I swear the only thing holding it together was the rope strung between the back ends where the tailgate was missing. "It will violate the treaty."

Blake laughed, and anything else I might have said got caught in my throat. That was a real laugh, not something measured and mocking. It made him seem normal. It made him seem human.

Maybe this was a bad idea, but I couldn't back down now. I held my breath as I slipped past him and into the vehicle that was sure to become my coffin.

Blake closed my door, then walked to the driver's side. Another wave of uneasiness washed over me. The truck smelled a little bit of oil, a little bit of gasoline, and quite a bit of Blake. Awareness of him, of how dominant and *male* he was, sharpened my senses even before he took his seat behind the wheel. I rarely encountered wolves outside The Rain, and none of them generated charisma and power the way Blake did.

He grabbed his keys from a cubby in the dashboard and inserted one into the ignition. The engine turned over half a dozen times before it clanked to life, and the whole truck quivered as he put it into gear.

My car was an old Camry with chipping paint and a huge dent in the passenger-side door. I was self-conscious about the way it looked, but I was downright embarrassed to be in Blake's truck. It was *loud*. The sides of the truck bed shook and swayed as we shuddered down the road. There was no way this thing could stay together past fifty miles per hour.

Blake turned onto the feeder. I watched the speedometer. The numbers were hard to read underneath the fogged plastic window. I think we were inching up past forty-five.

Still, I might have managed to survive the drive in silence if it hadn't started to rain. Blake grabbed a pair of pliers and twisted a knobless screw beside the wheel. The windshield wipers turned on. They screeched in protest to the left, then screeched in protest to the right.

"Why?" I yelled to be heard over the din.

"Why what?"

"Why *this*?" I threw my hands out to gesture to the wreck of a truck.

His grin made me regret asking.

"I want people to know when I'm coming."

"So they have time to run?"

A one-shouldered shrug. "I like a good chase, but it also tells them to get shit done before I pull up."

My stomach did an annoying little flip. He was completely at ease, cool, and with a lazy, Han Solo type of charisma. I'd always been attracted to guys who could pull off that vibe. That's why wolves—especially *this* wolf—were dangerous. Underneath that easy self-possession was an alert and ruthless killer.

I didn't smell oil or gas anymore. Just him.

"If you're afraid of succumbing to my charms," Blake said, "you can roll the window down."

I eyed the handle on the inside of the door. He literally meant *roll*. God, this thing was ancient.

"Don't need to," I said in a you-don't-affect-me kind of way. I would have scooted closer to my door, but I wasn't sure the thing would stay attached if we picked up more speed.

With a too-perceptive smile, Blake merged onto the highway.

I looked at the dash for what I was sure would be my time of death. The only thing there was a monstrosity of a radio with clunky metal buttons, knobs for tuning and volume, and the most antiquated input device on the planet: either a cassette tape or 8-track slot. I didn't know the freaking difference.

I pinched the bridge of my nose. Forty-five minutes. That's about how long it would take to get to The Rain. If this thing didn't shake apart going down the highway, I could survive that long.

Blake reached for the cubby in the dash. He took something out, slipped it over his ear. I hadn't heard anything ring, but his smile had evaporated. His expression was stern now, businesslike and… different. I'd glimpsed this side of him twice now, once right before he tweaked my nose—the jerk—and again in the bridal shop when he'd claimed Jared was hiding at The Rain.

This was the alpha in him, rising to the surface.

"No," he said to whoever was on the call. The finality of that single syllable wedged itself into my chest. It was ridiculous, considering the command wasn't directed at me, but it felt like a physical thing, something that demanded the world bend to his will.

He looked at me, and I made sure my expression was nonchalant. He was assessing me though, and I felt his gaze on my skin.

Note to self: never again get into a vehicle with a hot werewolf.

Whatever he was searching for, he must have found it because his mouth tilted up and he nodded.

"I'm not far," Blake said. He took off his earpiece, tossed it into the cubby, then exited the highway.

"This isn't the way to…" His short phone conversation fully sank in. "No. Absolutely not."

He merged onto the feeder. "It won't take long."

"I don't want anything to do with wolf business."

"You can handle it."

"I don't want to handle it. I don't want to handle any of this."

He glanced at me, and again, his eyes were assessing, like he was understanding something about me.

I didn't need him to understand anything except that he needed to take me to The Rain first.

"Blake—"

"Kennedy."

I pressed my lips together. He was doing his alpha thing, holding my gaze, saying my name, emanating a contagious confidence that said I had nothing to worry about.

"You're safe with me, remember?"

"I'm not worried about my safety." I crossed my arms, sank back into my seat, and stared out the windshield, trying to ignore the crack that ran right through my line of sight. Wolf business. Vampire business. Any kind of paranormal business. It always became something messy and complicated.

Blake turned onto an unpaved road.

Potholes and the piece-of-crap truck did *not* go together, at least not with me sitting shotgun. I grabbed the handle above the door as the truck lurched and clanked and sputtered. Wolves probably didn't have to worry about whiplash, but I did, and by the time we came to a stop beside a dry creek bed, my right arm felt bruised from shoulder to wrist from banging against the door and window.

Blake put the truck into park, then stared out the windshield. I did, too. Three people were in the clearing: two men and a woman. The woman was agitated. She paced and ran her hand through hair that looked like it hadn't been washed in weeks. Her feet were bare, and in sweatpants and a too-large white T-shirt, she looked like she'd just woken from a long sleep in a pile of dirt and leaves.

My pulse pounded loud enough Blake had to be able to hear it. I knew what this was.

The wolves called it moon sickness. I called it having-too-many-assholes-in-your-head. Some wolves couldn't handle the cacophony of the pack. They communicated with images, not words, and it took mental fortitude to partition their thoughts, to know which impressions belonged to them and which ones belonged to others. A strong alpha could help weaker wolves, training them to recognize their thoughts and to push all the other noise to the background. Not all wolves could be helped, though. They grew unstable. Violent. Eventually, they had to be put into chains during the full moon. When they couldn't control themselves beyond that night, they had to be killed.

There was only one thing that could stop the progression into violence: a stay at The Rain.

I glared at Blake, making sure my expression said *I told you I shouldn't be here.* He looked at me, and the way his mouth tightened suggested he might have agreed.

"Stay here." Blake turned off the ignition, tossed the keys back into the cubby, then climbed out of the truck.

The woman turned on her companions. The truck was so old, decrepit, and un-soundproofed, I clearly heard her snarl.

"Control yourself," Blake commanded. I barely recognized him now. It was like he'd slipped out of one skin and into another. He was intense. Focused. The wolves were attuned to him. Even the forest seemed to recognize his presence, going still and quiet around him.

For the woman, the forced peace lasted only a moment.

"I *am*," she hissed. Though she was in distress, she didn't look weak. She looked like she could rip the heads off mountain lions.

One of the men stepped forward. "If Lehr would let her—"

"It's been decided." Blake's words were sharp. Final.

The male lowered his gaze.

"Keisha," Blake said. "We can chain you. That's all I can offer."

"I will not be chained like an animal!" Saliva flew from her lips. She was out-of-her-mind feral.

*I can help.*

Some muscle in my throat locked up, forbidding me from voicing that thought. I'd helped five years ago. I'd bypassed the rules of the paranormal world and smuggled unsanctioned wolves and vampires into The Rain. It had ended badly.

I couldn't get involved in this.

I *wouldn't* get involved.

I bit my lower lip and used the pain as a reminder that I couldn't make this better. Anything I did would backfire. It would make things worse.

I closed my eyes and drew in a deep breath, clinging to my resolve. This was Blake's problem to deal with, not mine.

My gaze focused out the window again… and I froze. Keisha's attention was locked onto me. Her eyes were a bright yellow.

"Keisha," Blake growled.

She didn't so much as glance his way.

Shit. She wasn't responding to a dominant wolf.

"Charles," Blake said. "She shouldn't be this far gone. What happened?"

Both male wolves averted their gazes.

"What happened?" he said, each syllable rumbling from his chest.

"There were hikers," the second male said. "We kept her away from the trails, but they went off path."

"We stopped her though," Charles said. "She didn't hurt

anyone. Blake, it's just two days. She'll be fine after—"

"You can do it or I can," Blake said.

Sweat beaded on Charles's forehead. He seemed lost, looking back and forth between Keisha and Blake. The tension beside the creek grew potent, almost solidifying the air. A primitive instinct gripped me, telling me not to move, not to breathe. Keisha still hadn't looked away from me, and even from this distance, a mad hunger shone in her eyes.

"I can't," Charles said. "Please—"

"Go then." Blake's order was a sharp slap, a command that should have been immediately followed.

Keisha spun toward Blake.

They changed, all four wolves at once. It was like a series of buildings imploding. Their human bodies crashed inward, but instead of a cloud of smoke and debris, *wolf* exploded outward.

Keisha and Charles attacked Blake, the darkest of the group. The fourth wolf hung back, snarling and crouching and ready to strike.

Blake defended himself: quick, agile, lethal. He wasn't the largest of the four, but he was the fastest. He avoided Keisha's and Charles's jaws, darting in and out with precision, his teeth gleaming red with blood and flesh.

A targeted strike ripped out Keisha's throat.

Charles howled. He twisted back to his feet, saw Blake snarling over Keisha's body.

Charles snapped his teeth and paced, his eyes never leaving Blake's. Blake's growl deepened, and he lunged forward. It was a sharp, short movement, a demand that Charles back down.

Charles stopped pacing, faced Blake, and crouched low.

Blake struck first. A pain-filled yelp pierced the air, and it was over.

My heart started slamming against my chest, just now catching up with what had happened.

Seconds. That's how long it had taken Blake to take two lives.

Instinct kicked in, telling me to get the hell out of there. I fought against it. Running from wolves was stupid. Instead, I let the fear weaving between my ribs turn into something else. I was angry Blake had brought me there, angry that he had killed, and angry I had sat there and done nothing.

Moving behind the wheel, I grabbed the keys off the dash and shoved them into the ignition. The truck screeched and groaned, went *phut, phut, phut*, and didn't start.

Blake's wolf sprinted toward me. My door swung open, a human Blake suddenly appearing. Startled, I struck out with the edge of my hand, aiming for his throat.

He raised his arm and blocked it.

I followed up with a palm strike I'd learned as a kid in Judo, but I was in a bad position, and a werewolf, even one in his human form, would always have the advantage over me, especially outside The Rain.

He caught my wrist. "Raj will drive you home."

"I can drive myself."

"Raj will drive you home," Blake repeated. His yellow-edged eyes captured me as effectively as the hand he'd locked around my wrist. I couldn't look away. That might have been a good thing though. If I had, my gaze would have gone to his bare chest. I was extremely aware he was naked. So was the wolf standing behind him. Both men were muscular and masculine, and if this had been another situation, my heart would have been thudding for a completely different reason.

"I don't know him," I said, my hand tightening into a fist.

"You don't know me, Ms. Rain." He released my wrist, then stepped closer, his smooth chest only a few inches away. His scent invaded the cab when he reached into the back seat. I didn't breathe until he stepped back, clothes in hand. He tossed a pair of athletic pants to Raj.

"Take her home," he said. "Then report to Lehr."

Blake strode away, a second pair of pants draped over his shoulder. His back was just as powerfully built as his front, but a deep gash tore through his right shoulder blade. Blood leaked down his spine.

"Move," Raj said.

I was still in the driver's seat, still had one hand white-knuckling the steering wheel.

Blake had given him an order. Raj wouldn't ignore it.

Bastard.

I moved back to the passenger seat before Raj forced me over. Then I stared out the windshield at Blake, who was frowning down at Charles's and Keisha's dead forms. This wasn't the first time I'd seen a paranorm kill. I'd been young when it first happened, and it had shaken my view of the world I lived in.

The truck started just fine for Raj. He backed it up and turned it around. He didn't glance my way during the drive, and I didn't glance his although he pulled at my attention like a magnet. He wasn't as dominant as Blake, but even a submissive wolf could influence a human's emotions. I'd grown a resistance to it when I'd been in school with Nora. Now I was out of practice and had to put effort into controlling my thoughts. Raj wanted me to fear him, to submit and shut up.

I dug my fingernails into my palms and said, "That didn't have to happen."

His dark eyes remained locked on the road.

"One stay at The Rain, and she would have been fine."

The squeaks and bangs of the Ford reverberated inside the cab. A hard jostle knocked my elbow into the door. I focused on that sharp, fleeting pain. Raj's lack of response was predictable. He was just another paranorm following centuries-old rules and traditions, and God help anyone who had the audacity to break or bend them.

THE CLOUDS THAT HAD BEEN SEESAWING BETWEEN RAIN AND NO rain finally made up their minds. They parted, allowing the last rays of the day's sunlight to dance in the water drops painting the window.

I wished they had gathered and stormed. That would have matched my mood better.

I sat in The Rain's library, curled up in my chair by a window, only it didn't feel like my chair anymore. When I'd lived here, this had been my spot. It's where I studied, where I lounged, where I generally hung out if I wasn't snooping around. It's where I'd found a certain kind of contentment at being a part of a magical place—or rather, an antimagical place, but there was a beauty and enchantment in that too. Years had passed though, and the chair had lost my shape and scent. It felt wrong to sit there, like it belonged to everyone except me.

The library was empty. The two vampires who had been there when I entered left as soon as the weather cleared. They'd returned to the pool and gardens and trails with the other guests—the places where they spent the majority of their time, soaking in the warmth of the sun and the colors of the world beneath it.

I set the copy of *Dune* I'd been thumbing through on the round table beside my chair, then ran my hands over my face. The faint smell of books, the familiar setting, and the fireplace on the opposite wall should have made the library cozy and comfortable, but it wasn't settling me like it usually did.

Raj had finally spoken just before I climbed out of the truck. He'd said Blake would be there on Turnover.

I pinched the skin between my eyes, trying to alleviate the pounding in my head. Blake thought Jared was hiding at The Rain. The idea was absurd. My parents would never allow that, the staff wouldn't allow it, and the entire idea of an Aged vampire *hiding* anywhere was ridiculous.

About as ridiculous as a powerful vampire marrying a naturally born werewolf.

"Ms. Rain."

My gaze jerked toward Sullens. He held out a thick folder. "Your signature."

"On what?" I asked.

"On everything."

Frowning, I stood and took the folder. It was filled with invoices and bills for electricity, gas, and sewer as well as a number of unopened envelopes that looked like junk mail. My parents wrote checks more often than they paid for things online. Otherwise, most of this would have been autopaid. Since Mom and Dad never delegated administrative duties to the staff, they'd added me as an authorized signatory when I'd turned sixteen. I was the only one there who could pay the bills, accept deliveries, sign checks for payroll, and a number of other menial tasks, like meeting with the inspector yesterday.

"Fine." I closed the folder and unplugged my now fully charged phone. "I'll look at them in the office."

The downstairs office was tucked behind Garion's bar. It

was a discreet location, allowing my parents to keep watch on most of the lobby through the wide window. I'd pointed out that it allowed most of the lobby to keep a watch on them too. Dad had always laughed that off and ruffled my hair. He must have finally listened though, because a curtain blocked the view now. It had that going-deer-hunting camo my mom hated.

After shutting the door behind me, I walked around the desk and pulled out the rolling chair. The formerly black seat was almost completely covered with a mismatch of camo and bright pink duct tape. Last I'd seen it, just a few rips had been covered in pink. My parents shared this office, and it looked like they'd entered a battle of who owns the chair. Mom was currently winning.

I rummaged through the desk for a pen and checkbook, then opened the folder Sullens had given me.

It didn't take long. Ten minutes and I'd taken care of all the obvious bills. I thumbed through the rest of the envelopes. They looked like generic credit card offers and junk mail, but one caught my attention. It might be another bill. I opened it and skimmed the letter.

My headache must have been impairing my brain because I had to read it again.

Then a third time.

I checked the name on the letter and envelope, confirmed it was to Sarah Rain, then read the letter a fourth time just to be sure I wasn't misreading anything.

I wasn't. It said my parents had missed the past three payments of an outstanding $367,000 home equity loan. It threatened legal action against The Rain if it wasn't paid in full.

It had to be a scam. We'd owned The Rain outright for three centuries. It didn't make sense to take out a loan.

*You should check the hotel's financial records.* That's what Nora had said after she'd demanded a wedding and plopped the cash-filled briefcase down on the desk. I hadn't checked into it because I'd rushed off to work.

A knot formed in my gut. I opened the next envelope.

It wasn't the same supposed debt. This one was a small business loan with $50,000 outstanding and one missed payment.

This had to be a hoax. Nora was messing with me. She was fabricating a crisis to manipulate me into signing her wedding contract.

Except... the second my parents returned, that deception would fall apart.

The office air went stale. I breathed it in, trying to untangle the jumbled thoughts running through my mind. My parents were careful with finances. There was an explanation for these bills. I just had to figure out what it was.

I looked at my phone. Then I dialed Mom's number.

Straight to voice mail. Ugh.

I hung up and texted: *Did you take loans out against The Rain?*

My left leg bounced while I waited for a response. A whole two minutes passed before I couldn't stand it anymore. I stuffed the loan notices into the desk drawer, then took the rest of the bills with me to the lobby. Sullens scowled when he saw me.

*Feeling's mutual, pal.*

I crossed the lobby to give him the bills to mail. We wouldn't have to put up with each other for much longer. My parents were due back—

The Rain's front doors flew open.

Wind whooshed inside.

My hair whipped into my face, and goose bumps prickled across my skin. I swept my bangs out of my eyes just in time to see something sail across the tile floor.

Not some*thing*. Some*one*. The man turned the end of his slide into a roll to his feet, then faced the open doors, his stance wide, his hands held ready to fight.

Sullens made a sound of disgust. A few other staff members glanced toward the doors too. As soon as they saw the newcomer, their expressions darkened. But no one made a move toward him. They returned to what they were doing, apparently content to ignore him.

Well, *I* wasn't content to ignore him, especially when I saw movement outside. But when I stepped forward to get a better view, the only thing on the other side of the threshold was the glow from a lamppost lighting the empty porch and stone walkway.

I scowled at the man who'd barreled inside. "Who the hell are you?"

His head whipped my way, and bright blue eyes hitched on me. Slowly, he lowered his fists. His chest rose and fell rapidly until he drew in a few deliberate, deep breaths.

"Kennedy Rain."

I didn't like the quiet way he said my name or the fact that he knew me when I didn't know him. I crossed my arms and put on my best answer-the-damn-question glower.

He glanced toward the office I'd just left. "Where are your parents?"

"They're out. Do you have permission to be here?"

Lehr and Arcuro decided which wolves and vampires could stay at The Rain, and if neither one had approved this guy, it would explain his wild entrance. But no one stood in the doorway, demanding he be sent outside. That likely meant he wasn't a vampire or werewolf. Elementals, fey, witches—all the other paranorms—were allowed to stop by The Rain. They usually chose not to though. Paranormal species didn't mix well.

The stranger's mouth tightened. After a quick look at the still-open front doors, he said, "I won't stay long."

"That's not what I asked."

He headed toward the restaurant. He was tall, his strides long and purposeful.

Typical paranorm dismissal.

Gritting my teeth, I walked to the check-in desk and dropped the bills on the counter. "Who is that?"

Sullens's mouth thinned. "He's Christian."

"And he normally barrels in here like hell is on his tail?"

"Not always." He turned his attention to the computer on the desk.

God, he needed to get that stick out of his ass.

Christian took a seat at the bar. Garion had a drink waiting for him, but they didn't exchange a word. No one else in the restaurant said anything either. They didn't even look at him.

My muscles were tense. I wanted to stride up to the bar and demand answers. It took a ridiculous amount of mental effort to remain where I was.

*Don't interrogate the paranorms, Kennedy. They bite when they answer.* That was Mom's way of saying paranorms wouldn't appreciate me sticking my nose into their business. I'd ignored that advice in the past. I wouldn't ignore it again. I would leave Christian alone.

I left the hotel, climbed into my Camry, and started the drive home.

---

ALMOST A FULL HOUR LATER, I turned in to my apartment complex. My phone rang as I pulled into a parking spot. Miracle of miracles, it was Mom.

"I missed your call," she said when I answered. "Is everything okay?"

*No.* That muscle in my throat that had locked up in Blake's truck locked up again. If I told her what had happened, she would have said I did the right thing, we had to let the paranorms take care of their own problems, I could not get involved.

But the right thing was wrong.

I swallowed to loosen my throat.

"Did you get my text?" I asked, avoiding a conversation that would only frustrate me.

"Your text?" There was a pause, probably her checking her messages. It sounded like they were in the car and I was on speaker.

"Mom?" I said when she took too long.

"Oh, the loan. Don't worry about that. Our accountant is taking care of it."

"Your accountant must suck."

"Kennedy," she said, using her mom voice.

"Why do you have a loan? We own The Rain."

"Yes, we do. That's why there isn't anything to worry about. Our accountant is shuffling things around for efficiency. Is that all you needed?"

Scowling, I turned off the engine. "Are you guys on the way home?"

"Actually, we wanted to talk to you about that."

My hand froze on the door handle. "You said you'd be back tomorrow."

"We decided to extend our vacation for a few more days. It will be a good opportunity for you to supervise Turnover."

"You're kidding me."

"You can handle it, sprite," Dad said.

"Have you guys read all my texts? Things aren't going well."

"You sound like you're handling them okay," he said.

"I'm not," I protested. "Nora isn't taking no for an answer. She had me go with her to shop for wedding dresses."

Dad's guffaw nearly drowned out Mom's laugh.

"It's not funny!"

"It kind of is," Mom said. "You should do more with your girlfriends."

"Nora isn't a friend."

"Nora is sweet. She's not the same person she was in high school. Neither are you."

"*I* was never the problem."

Mom laughed again.

"Did you guys know about this?"

"The wedding? No—"

"Did you know Jared is missing?"

"Missing?" That was Dad. Finally, someone sounded concerned.

"Blake thinks he's at The Rain."

"You didn't say anything about Blake." Now, he sounded more than concerned.

"Because I thought the Nora and Jared thing would be enough to get you to call."

"We don't have good cell service."

"Where are you? Don't tell me you're on vacation. What are you doing?"

One of them—Dad, I think—sighed.

"We're taking care of some business while we're away," he said.

"What kind of business?"

"We have to go, honey," Mom said. "Don't worry about the loan or Nora. We'll talk to her when we get home. If Blake bothers you again, tell him to call us."

"You don't answer your phone," I said. "And he—"

"Tell him to leave a message and we'll get back to him. We'll be back on Wednesday. All you need to do is be there for Turnover."

"Mom—"

"Bye, Kennedy," Mom said.

"But Blake—"

The line went dead.

I glared at my phone. That wasn't how the conversation should have gone. My parents were supposed to say they were on the way home, that they would be there for Turnover, and I could go back to my real life and forget about The Rain and all things paranormal.

What the hell were they up to? My parents didn't do this cloak-and-dagger shit. They were model citizens. Well, except for the we-play-host-to-paranorms thing. And The Rain's lack of inspections. And the overdue bills.

Maybe I'd been onto something the night before when my brain hadn't shut off to let me sleep. Maybe Nora wasn't orchestrating all my problems. Maybe it was them.

No. That didn't feel right either. My parents understood when I demanded to finish my senior year at a boarding school. Then they were happy when I went to college. They wanted me to live my life before I returned to The Rain. Something else was going on.

Shoving aside my worries, I opened my car door. Three more days until I could get some answers. I could wait, and maybe I'd get lucky and Turnover would run smoothly tomorrow.

My snort echoed in the night.

I locked my car, then climbed the stairs to the third floor.

"You owe me your firstborn child," Carrie, my roommate, said when I reached the landing. She sat in one of the four camp chairs arranged in front of our apartment. Alex and John, the neighbors who lived across from us, occupied two of the other chairs. Both had expressions that said they didn't envy me.

I stopped, my brow wrinkling, trying to remember what I might have forgotten.

Carrie crossed her arms. "I covered for you, but if you miss another meetup, they'll tell Dr. Durham."

Crap. Carrie and I were paired up with three others for an urban design project. We were supposed to meet today to practice our presentation. Our midsemester crit was a significant portion of our final grade. If I failed, it was going to be tough to keep my scholarship next semester. My grades were already borderline because I'd been working extra hours in an attempt to keep my student loans under control. I needed to study more, not less.

I dropped into the empty chair beside her. "I'm late on rent too, aren't I?"

"Yep," she said.

"I'll transfer the money to you right now." I took my phone out of my purse. "Thanks for covering for me. I'm really sorry."

The ice chest between Alex and John squeaked open. John reached inside, then leaned forward and handed me a beer. I popped open the top, took a sip, and for the first time in almost two days, relaxed.

This was good. This was normal. This almost made me forget about the two deaths I'd witnessed that afternoon.

Almost.

I took another sip of beer and focused on our pseudo campsite. We'd completely taken over our end of the landing. Only one of the other two apartments on our level was occupied, and the man who lived there was hardly ever home. More importantly, he didn't complain about the clutter we left out here or the noise. The chairs, the cooler, and the dilapidated side table we'd found on a curb were all permanent fixtures on the landing. We kept an old five-gallon bucket for a trash can and target practice, and Carrie made sure the railing was decorated with lights and whatever was seasonal. March Madness was in full swing, so she'd overloaded it with orange and white ribbons interspersed with wooden circles she'd painted to look like basketballs. And because the guys had complained it looked too girly, she'd added extra bows and glitter.

The guys only complained to mess with her. They were both laid-back and easy to get along with. They'd moved in across from us six months ago, and we came home to almost nightly country music until me or Carrie hijacked the Bluetooth speaker and started one of our playlists. The fact that Carrie hadn't done that yet meant they hadn't been out here long.

"How are your parents?" Carrie asked.

"They're fine." I took a sip of beer to make sure I didn't make a face. Carrie loved my parents, especially Dad. He usually took us to lunch when he was in town, and Carrie laughed at his bad jokes and ridiculous advice, which, of course, only encouraged him. She knew I'd gone home to help out at the hotel, but she thought The Rain was more of a bed-and-breakfast than a midsize hotel with an eclectic clientele.

Carrie propped her legs up on the ice chest. "We should go visit sometime."

"It's pretty boring out there."

"But it's in the mountains. It has to have a great view."

"It's okay," I lied.

Carrie gave me a doubtful look. Fortunately, before she asked any more questions, her gaze went to the parking lot below. She waved.

I followed her line of sight, knowing instinctively who she was waving to before I spotted him—Eli, one of the apartment complex's security guards.

Before we'd moved in, I'd tried to convince Carrie that this apartment wasn't for us. She'd said it was perfect, a good price and location, and most importantly, safe. The reason for the latter was the man—the elemental—walking below. The leasing consultant had pointed him out and highlighted the property's security when she'd shown us the apartment. Even from a distance, I'd known what he was. It was in the way he walked, the way he held himself, and in the *awareness* that prickled across my skin.

I was almost certain Eli didn't know I was Kennedy Rain though. It was a big apartment complex, and it was unlikely he knew every occupant. As long as I didn't do anything to draw attention to myself, my anonymity should be safe.

Still, he was a reminder I couldn't completely escape the paranormal world.

Mood souring, I took another sip of my beer.

## 7

My alarm woke me up at eight on Sunday morning. I needed more sleep. I'd tossed and turned and tried not to think about Keisha and Charles, so of course when I had finally faded off, I'd dreamed of them. Sometimes the scene played out exactly as it had in real life, with her feral gaze locking on me seconds before they all shifted to their wolf forms. Other times, I told her to get into the truck and we drove to The Rain. For a moment, I thought the latter was true, that I had saved her life and sanity. Then the fuzziness of sleep wore off, and I remembered the blood.

My boss at Parlay still needed me to work the early shift, so I grabbed a quick breakfast, showered and dressed, then I trotted down the steps. A few paces from my car, I beeped it unlocked. I was almost to the driver's side door when I noticed the man breaking into it.

He looked at me, metal bar lodged between the window and frame of my car. Then he shrugged and opened the door.

"Hey!"

"You the owner?"

"Yes." I put a few more steps between us and rummaged in my purse for my phone.

He reached inside, fiddled with something, then closed the door and held out a business card.

I stared at it. "Repo?"

"Yes, ma'am."

"But… this is my car."

He shrugged and placed his card on the car parked next to mine. "I just do the towing."

"It's paid off."

"Not my business."

"Wait, can you just…?" I fumbled for an excuse. "I just need to get to work. I can't be late again."

"Talk to your bank." He turned away from me, then hit a button on the back of the tow truck. The Camry's rear end lifted off the ground.

What god had I pissed off? I'd been working my ass off to pay for college and rent and a life that had nothing to do with The Rain. I'd had smooth sailing for almost five years, and now when my parents were out of town, all this crap happened?

Fuming, I watched the repo man get into his tow truck. This had something to do with The Rain. The Camry was registered under my dad's name. I was listed as an occasional driver for insurance purposes. Mom had said not to worry about the bills, that their accountant was handling everything, but she was obviously wrong. Either that or I was right and their accountant sucked. Who were they trusting with their finances anyway? We'd never contracted administrative help outside The Rain. Our finances weren't completely normal and…

Our finances weren't normal. Who did I know who had an inexplicable knowledge that The Rain might be struggling with money? Someone who had also claimed to be an accountant for her father.

I swiped my phone on, googled Nora's name, and found it in the small print on the website of one of the businesses Lehr owned.

The phone rang twice before Nora answered.

"Are you my parents' accountant?" I demanded.

"Good morning, Kennedy," she replied.

"Are you?"

"No. I am not."

"Then why did you tell me to check the finances?"

"I recognize the signs of a struggling business. Why?"

I thought I heard a male voice in the background. I hesitated, listening for it again.

"Kennedy?" she said.

"My car was just towed."

"Towed?" Something rattled in the background. "Have you received notices from creditors?"

"No." Technically, that was true. The notices were addressed to my parents.

"You called me for a reason. I can't help if you don't talk. Where are you?"

I snorted. Nora didn't help anyone unless someone helped her first.

"It doesn't matter," I said. "Forget I called." I hung up before she could say anything else.

This day was turning out to be just as bad as yesterday, and I'd only been awake for an hour.

Frustrated, I called a coworker and begged them to cover my shift at Parlay, then I opened a car service app and asked for a pickup.

"THIS IS YOUR STOP, RIGHT?" the driver asked twenty minutes later.

I stared out the window at Gamecraft and Witchery, which sat in the middle of a remodeled shopping center. A trendy bar and grill sat to its right, and on its left was a gelato shop. I hadn't stepped inside the store in ages, but I remembered the aisles of games and collectibles and the walls stacked with display upon display of plastic-sheathed comic books.

What the hell was I doing here?

"Hey," the driver said again, looking over her shoulder.

"Yes. Thanks. This is it."

*This* was a bad idea.

I climbed out of the car and waited for it to drive off.

Maybe it was the lack of sleep. Maybe it was the frustration with my parents and the paranorms. Or maybe it was the fact that I couldn't get the images of Keisha and Charles out of my head. Whatever the reason, when I'd opened the car service app, I hadn't typed in my work address. I'd typed in this one with the intent of striding inside and demanding information from the witch who had stabbed me in the back five years ago.

Gamecraft and Witchery sold all things pop culture with an emphasis on the games that were more often than not boxed works of art. I'd played quite a few during my senior year, sitting in the store's back corner at one of the white plastic tables. The soft buzz of the vending machines provided a soundtrack while I thumbed through rule books, waiting to meet with paranorms who weren't on Lehr or Arcuro's approval lists. I was an idiot back then, thinking I was in control of the situation. Thinking that I could trust the witch who owned the store. I hadn't been naive enough to think Owen was helping me for altruistic reasons, but I had thought he'd give me a heads-up if the wrong people learned I was smuggling unsanctioned vampires and werewolves into The

Rain. Instead, he'd greeted me with a smile and let me walk into an ambush.

I had no preconceived notions anymore. If I walked in there, Owen would give me information, but he'd sell me out the second he saw profit.

And if I walked in there, I'd be breaking my promise to never again get involved in the affairs of paranorms.

Jaw clenched, I stared at the glass door. My anger had subsided on the way there. My brain was kicking back into gear. Instead of returning tomorrow, my parents would be back on Wednesday. Then I could return to my routine of pretending The Rain and the paranormal world didn't exist.

At least, I hoped I could. I hoped these past few days were a test or a misunderstanding or some other problem that could be easily solved. But what if it wasn't any of those? What if my parents or The Rain were in some kind of trouble?

I wavered a few more seconds, then I started for the store. I was almost to the line of cars parked in front of it when the door swung open. Nora strode out.

I froze, but she didn't so much as glance in my direction. She tapped on her cell phone, put it to her ear, then opened the door to her convertible.

What was she doing there?

My feet restarted. I reached the back of her car. Then the passenger door. I could have kept walking straight to the store, and I don't think she would have noticed. Instead, I jerked open the passenger door and dropped into the seat.

She swung toward me, phone clenched like she was about to punch me with it. She stopped herself when she recognized me, and her snarl flattened out. She returned the phone to her ear and said, "I'll call you back."

"Why are you here?" I demanded.

"Why are you here?" she countered coolly.

"Someone is messing with me and The Rain. They need to back off."

She snorted at my accusation, then started the car. The sky was overcast and the wind chilly, so Nora left the top up, put the convertible into gear, and sped out of the parking lot.

I grabbed the armrest. Then, when it was clear she wasn't slowing down, I yanked on my seat belt.

"You can drop me off at Parlay."

"I'm not your chauffeur."

"It's on your way home."

"I'm not going home."

"Then where—" I snapped my mouth shut. It didn't matter. "Just pull over here."

She gave me an overly sweet smile. "I have an appointment, and your presence is perfect."

"Um. No," I said. "I went to an appointment with you yesterday. It didn't end well."

She waved her hand, dismissing my concern. "This won't take long, and I'll drop you off wherever you want afterward."

"So you are my chauffeur."

She threw a glare my way, then swerved onto the highway.

"How bad is it?" she asked.

My fingers tightened around the armrest. "Your driving or my day?"

Another glare, this one saying I was not very funny.

"It's not bad enough to host your wedding."

"That's not what I asked, Kennedy."

I crossed my arms and stared out at the road. I didn't like the prying question or how serious she suddenly sounded. If she wasn't behind everything, she didn't need to know more than she already did.

"I can't help if I don't have details," she said.

"I didn't ask for your help."

"You called me."

"To accuse you."

"Of what?"

"Sabotage."

"You really think I'd have your car repossessed?"

"I think it was a huge coincidence for you to show up while my parents were gone and right after an inspection of The Rain. You accuse us of having financial problems, then a girl happens to stop by the hotel and tells a vampire to bite her—"

"Melissa Geary."

"You looked her up?"

"We tried. We didn't find anyone by that name. At least, no one who lives in state. Is that why you were going to Owen?"

"I already told you why."

She blew out a breath. "I'm not messing with The Rain. My wedding will be there. Why would I draw human attention to it?"

It was a very valid point, one I'd been trying to ignore because Nora had always been my nemesis. She was the easy explanation, and if she wasn't the paranorm messing with The Rain, somebody else was.

"Do you have a lawyer?" she asked.

"Do I need a lawyer?"

She slanted me a look that said *Isn't that obvious?*

"Let's set aside the issues of the inspector and Melissa Geary. Your car was repossessed. That means collection agencies are taking action on your debt. Have you tried to renegotiate payment amounts?"

"I don't know. I haven't gone through The Rain's finances. I've just seen bills."

"And collection notices," she said. "I can help if you let me look at the bank statements."

I snorted. "Not going to happen."

"You know," she said, exiting the highway, "you do have cash you can use to pay off debt."

"How very convenient." And she wondered why I was suspicious of her.

"I'm just saying it's there."

"And I'm just saying my parents will return it to you on Wednesday."

"Is that when they're coming back?"

I ignored her question and tried to guess at our location. We were close to the bridal shop. There was no way I was going to watch her try on more dresses or get measured for the Rosefeldt or whatever it was she needed to do.

"Where are we going?"

She turned in to a shopping area. Fortunately, it wasn't Tulip Avenue.

"You saw the contract and my guest list?"

"No. It's locked up with the money you're taking back." I'd put it into our otherwise empty safe-deposit box at the bank because we didn't need Nora's money mingling with ours.

"Most of the guests are from outside the pack," she said. "Some are friends from school. They're human."

"Do you need me to point out how bad that idea is?"

"It will require everyone to be careful with their words and their behavior."

"You mean your dad and Arcuro."

She stared out the windshield and nodded. There was a somberness to her silence that pulled at my conscience, and my annoyance poofed like a vampire stepping into sunlight.

"You aren't planning to tell him, are you?"

"I am. Just not anytime soon." She adjusted her grip on the steering wheel.

"What do you expect to happen if you go through with this? You think your dad is going to ignore it?"

"Once we have a wedding contract that's signed in front of witnesses and sealed by a coven, he can't do anything."

A chill ran down my spine. "You're inviting a full coven to The Rain?"

"Magical repercussions. That's the only thing that will protect us. You should understand that."

A full coven—thirteen witches—had witnessed the signing of the treaty that protected my family. Nora would need the same for her marriage to be magically sanctioned.

"Is that why you were meeting with Owen?" I asked. "He's not part of a coven."

"I am aware of that," she said.

She must be using him as a middle man. Individually, most witches weren't dangerous. They could create spells and work some magic but nothing much more significant than parlor tricks and herbal remedies. That made them one of the weakest paranormal species out there, a fact which they resented. To counter it, they were constantly on the search for a compatible coven. The more witches in a coven, the stronger they all became. Problem was, witches didn't tend to get along well with each other, so forming a cohesive coven was difficult. When it happened, though, it was extremely powerful.

And extremely dangerous.

"You shouldn't trust a full coven," I said. She was the daughter of North America's strongest alpha. The price for a coven had to be steep, and even if she paid it, what would stop them from slipping something else into their spell?

"It's the only way," she said quietly as she pulled into a parking spot directly in front of a large window filled with elaborate, special-occasion cakes.

Wedding cakes.

All thoughts of covens and magically sealed documents evaporated.

"Really? This is what you need help with?"

"I like the taste of raw meat, Kennedy."

"You eat real food. Just pick a flavor. They'll all be good."

She turned off the engine but didn't make a move to get out of the car. "I don't want to do this on my own. My mother is dead. My friends can't help."

Her friends couldn't help? It made sense that she couldn't rely on another werewolf, but surely there was someone else, a human who knew about paranorms or a paranorm crazy enough to support her decision. She had to have someone other than me. We were the opposite of friends.

"Why are you asking me to do this?"

She didn't answer immediately. I was starting to think that she wasn't going to when she let go of the steering wheel and looked at me.

"You've never told anyone about The Rain. You've never told them about us."

"That's because I was raised keeping the secret."

"That doesn't mean it's been easy," she said. "It doesn't mean you haven't sacrificed."

I opened my mouth to retort, but my words died on my lips. I didn't know what to say. Nora was never this sincere. She was never vulnerable.

"You don't have to come inside," she said. "You can call someone to pick you up, and I'll get your car out of repo. I'll have it delivered to The Rain."

She opened the car door, then walked into the shop alone.

I wanted to bang my head on the dashboard. It would be a huge mistake to help. Huge! But, damn it, I was starting to hate Nora a little less. She was starting to seem… human-ish.

Muttering every cuss word I knew, I got out of the car and followed her inside.

A sweet, sugary smell enveloped me. It was so potent I was surprised Nora could tolerate it. She stood in front of a glass counter. She didn't glance in my direction, but the tension in her shoulders eased.

"Oh, fantastic!" the woman behind the counter said. "You

brought a friend!" She hurried toward me, took my hands in hers, and gave them a shake. "I'm Alisa. It's so good to meet you…?"

"Kennedy," I said.

She smiled. "Kennedy. Wonderful!"

She was short and thin with blond hair dyed pink and purple and blue. For someone so small, her hands were strong, and I couldn't help but look wide-eyed at Nora when Alisa bounced with energy, then motioned us to follow.

The corner of Nora's mouth quirked up. She shrugged. "Alisa's the best."

I regretted my decision to come inside. Bouncy people and I did not mix well.

We followed Alisa to the sitting area tucked between the glass display counter and the cakes that filled the storefront window. The cakes were impressive. There was one that looked like it belonged to the Mad Hatter and another that had so much detail I wasn't sure if the swirls and flowers were made out of icing or real.

The one I liked the most, though, was a silver cake with gold and bronze gears that circled up the three layers before spiraling around the top tier. A steampunk bride and groom stood on a raised gear in the spiral's center. The male robot wore a top hat and a long bronze coat that covered a body created from small pipes and mechanical parts. The bride's wedding dress was unique, too, with rivets circling the bottom and a bouquet of tiny gears in her robot hands.

"That's awesome," I said.

Alisa beamed. "Thank you! Maybe we can talk about it for your wedding."

An unexpected twinge of regret struck through me, but I forced a polite smile. A wedding implied that I could trust someone with The Rain's secret, with the knowledge that the paranormal world existed. Anyone who accepted that had to be at least partially crazy, and if I really liked someone, why the hell would I want to introduce them to this world? I didn't.

Nora glanced at me, her brow wrinkled. After a small, almost imperceptible sniff, she turned her attention back to Alisa. I don't know what emotion I was radiating, but she smelled it despite the sugar-filled air.

Alisa placed two thick binders on the coffee table. She opened the one with the white cover. "These are the more traditional cakes I've created. You can look through them and point out what aspects you like. And you will absolutely love this one, Kennedy." She pushed the black binder toward me.

A rumble from outside reflected my mood. I didn't consider myself a gloomy person, but Alisa was too much, and wedding planning wasn't my thing. The bakery's sugary aroma, all the flowers and the lace and the white icing, made me want to crawl out of my skin.

Alisa opened Nora's book. "This section lists our most popular flavors."

A second rumble came from outside. This time, it sounded more like a clatter. My weather app hadn't mentioned storms in the forecast, but the gray clouds looked darker.

"How many guests are you estimating?" Alisa asked.

Zero, I wanted to answer.

"Seventy," Nora said.

"Perfect number for a bloodbath," I muttered.

Alisa's overly happy expression hiccupped. She recovered quickly. "Will you want to save the top tier for your anniversary?"

Nora looked at me like I knew the answer. I had no idea. I'd never even been to a wedding.

"Sure," I told her.

Nora nodded.

"Fantastic! You'll want four tiers then. Have you thought about the shape?"

Again, Nora looked at me. What? Did she expect me to make all the decisions? She had eyes. She could answer the question.

"Square?" I said. The faster Alisa got her answers, the faster I could get out of there.

Alisa beamed. "That will be fun! Is this going to be a tradi-tional wedding?"

I laughed.

Alisa's eyebrows went up, and Nora threw a glare my way. My shrug said I was just being honest.

"Yes," Nora said, still scowling. "It will be traditional and—"

She went still. A second later, the bell on the door rang.

Alisa's gaze went behind us. Her eyes widened, and dread punched the bottom of my stomach. Too late, I realized I hadn't been hearing thunder.

## 8

I DIDN'T GET A CHANCE TO TURN. BLAKE HOPPED OVER THE back of the couch and landed in between me and Nora. He placed one arm around each of our shoulders, then smiled at Alisa. "What have I missed?"

I wasn't prepared for his touch. My brain stuttered, and I was pretty sure my face matched Alisa's flush. Or maybe mine was worse because the heat of Blake's body eased into me. I couldn't ignore his strength and the impact his presence made in the air.

Nora shoved his arm away. I tried to as well, but he didn't budge.

"You're the groom?" Alisa asked. She was still flushed. I'm sure she'd seen many hot grooms in her life, but she'd never encountered Blake. Even without his supernatural juju, he was swoon-worthy. Alisa had zero practice keeping her thoughts in order around someone like him.

"I'm a lucky man," Blake said, hugging me closer. I braced a hand on his thigh so I didn't fall into his lap. "I hope I didn't miss the tasting."

His eyes locked on me when he said that last word. My

cheeks heated further. To say my mind wasn't wandering would be a lie. The muscle under my palm was hard, and he smelled good. Wild.

Damn him and his I-know-what-I-do-to-you grin.

I shifted, trying to get away, but my hand slipped over his thigh and closer to… er, him.

"Kennedy," he admonished, his tone warm and amused. "This isn't the time or place for that, love." He met Alisa's eyes. "We have an untraditional relationship. On occasion, they get jealous and try more direct ways to get my attention."

If Nora didn't kill him, I would. I'd do it the second he stepped into the Null.

"We need a moment," Nora snapped. The sharpness in her tone broke the spell Alisa was under.

"Of… of course. Why don't I bring samples of our top three?"

"That sounds wonderful. Thank you."

As soon as Alisa was out of sight, Nora hissed, "How did you find me?"

"I didn't find you. I found Kennedy." He took my hand, brought it to his mouth, and kissed it. My hormones ricocheted through my body.

*Focus, Kennedy.*

I jerked my hand away. "You've been following me?"

He gave an easy shrug. "I'm a wolf. I enjoy tracking interesting things." He leaned toward me, his breath teasing my hair.

"Don't smell me!" I elbowed him in the ribs. I didn't get an *oomph*. I got a chuckle.

"Leave her alone, Blake," Nora said.

"I would, but my curiosity is aroused. I'd love to know why Kennedy is still helping with a wedding that she promises won't happen." He turned toward me and propped his arm on the back of the couch. He looked one hundred percent delectable. I wanted to satisfy him, which was wrong, wrong, wrong.

Nora stood with a suddenness that yanked my attention from him.

"Let's go," she said.

Blake clamped his hand on my shoulder, keeping me seated.

"Look," I said after she walked away. "I'm trying to convince her to cancel it. You showing up and acting like an asshole isn't helping."

His expression turned serious. "Neither is shopping for dresses and cakes."

The door chimed when Nora exited. If she ditched me again, I'd make sure she *never* asked me for another favor.

"It's not what you think—"

"Here we are," Alisa said, returning with a platter of small slivers of cake. She'd recovered her cheerfulness, but her gaze shifted between us and the door Nora had exited. "Should we wait for Ms. Lehr?"

"That's not necessary," Blake said smoothly. "Kennedy has excellent taste. She can decide."

I tried to stand again. No luck.

Alisa's smile wavered like a ripple across water.

Blake threaded his fingers through mine, then placed our clasped hands on his thigh. I tried to pull free without looking like I was trying to.

Alisa cleared her throat, then angled the platter and pointed. "You could start with this one, a chocolate cake with raspberry curd. The next one is a white cake with blackberry reduction, and this one is strawberry with a berry puree."

"They sound delicious." There was a dare in his eyes when he met my gaze. "Choose one."

"I'm diabetic," I said, my voice flat.

"I'll choose then." He plucked the strawberry cake off the platter. When he brought it toward my lips, I shrank back.

"It's just a taste, Kennedy." My name rolled off his tongue. The way he was looking at me, that rumble in his tone. An unaware human would be taking off her clothes. Despite the wrinkle between her brow, Alisa's gaze was freely wandering over Blake's body.

He was such a jerk.

I didn't know if it was possible to get the upper hand with an alpha werewolf, but I sure as hell was going to try.

Leaning forward, I closed my mouth around the bite of cake. I caught Blake's finger as well and met his eyes. Slowly, I drew back and moaned. I didn't intend the sound to be genuine, but the cake was *good*. So was the feel of Blake's finger sliding free from my lips.

Blake focused on my mouth. I couldn't look away, couldn't hide my thoughts, couldn't discern his. My heart thumped against my chest so hard and heavy even Alisa had to hear it.

Blake's sudden laugh boomed through the bakery.

"We'll take that one," he said. Then he released my hand, tweaked my nose, and stood.

All hints of desire shattered. Furious, I turned, grabbed the robot topper from the steampunk wedding cake, then chunked it at Blake's head.

He caught it. Then the cocky bastard raised the robot in a mini-salute and walked out the door.

Alisa made a noise. "Are you sure you want to marry him?"

———

NORA DIDN'T ABANDON me this time. She stood outside the bakery, facing off with Blake, her shoulders back, her chin lifted. A light wind swirled leaves around their feet, and pedestrians gave them a wide berth as they passed.

*I* wanted to give them a wide berth. They were both dominant wolves, and the air around them seemed to crackle and buck with their power.

"End it," Blake ordered, his tone cold. He had discarded the easy, haphazard illusion he'd worn inside the bakery and stepped into a skin that was strong and steady and sovereign.

Nora's feet shifted. It wasn't a retreat or submission, and her gaze didn't waver, but it was a small sign that Blake outranked her.

"You're signing his death warrant," he said. "I'll be the one ordered to kill him. As much as I'd like to drive a stake through his heart, I don't want to hurt you."

"Then leave us alone."

"I looked the other way when you were running off to screw, but that's all you can have. A short-term fling. No emotions. No attachments."

"You are cruel. Go dig up a conscience."

He stepped toward her. "You need to stay away from him. You *will* stay away."

Nora looked ready to go for Blake's throat. If we weren't on a public sidewalk, she might have done it. Werewolves didn't have the best tempers, and she and Blake were both upper tier. She could challenge him for dominance. They would fight and bleed, and Nora would lose. What would Lehr do then? Kill his second? Or ignore his daughter's death because it was Blake's right to take out challengers?

I needed to pull them back from the precipice, but how?

"Jared's not at The Rain," I said loudly, grabbing onto the one thing I knew would draw Blake's attention.

Nora looked my way. I thought I caught a flicker of relief in her eyes, but I was more concerned with Blake's reaction. His focus shifted to me too. There was nothing soft or sympathetic in his expression, and my fight-or-flight instinct slammed into me so hard I almost flinched.

"You've looked?" he asked.

I didn't answer. He would have smelled the lie.

He faced me completely now. My heart thumped quick and brutal against my ribs. I preferred the other version of Blake, the infuriating asshole who tweaked my nose and fed me cake. *This* Blake was terrifying.

He stalked toward me. I stood my ground. *Never run from a paranorm, Kennedy. They love a good chase.*

His eyes flickered yellow. I breathed in and breathed out. I didn't deserve this aggression. I wasn't a toy he could play with or one of his submissive wolves. I was a human who had done my damn best to stay out of their fucking world.

A dangerous anger simmered through me.

"Stop stalking me." My words were quiet and harsh. That's what he was doing, treating me like I was easy prey. He looked ready to bite.

"He can't hurt you, Kennedy," Nora said from somewhere behind him. "Feel free to knee him in the nuts."

Annoyance twitched over his too-close mouth. He didn't move away, but the air between us transformed. It stirred with a different emotion, one that was hot and daring. I didn't move because if I did, it would be to retreat a step, and there was no way in hell I was backing down from this wolf.

His mouth tightened. He gave me some breathing room, then looked at Nora.

"End it today," he said, "or I'll end it tomorrow."

---

NORA PULLED into The Rain's parking lot and stopped in front of the flagstone walkway. We'd spent the drive listening to the sounds of the road and our own unspoken thoughts. I'd almost broken the silence a dozen times, but I didn't want to get into an argument too far away from The Rain.

That's what I told myself, at least. I ignored the niggling thought that I'd been silent because I was starting to care. I shouldn't. It didn't matter how much she loved Jared. The rules of their world were against them. I'd tried to defy them years ago when I'd stumbled upon a vampire who'd been on the brink of losing her mind. She'd been one of the unsanctioned —someone not on the lists of Arcuro or Lehr—and it had seemed like such a simple thing to do to help her. That's why The Rain existed, I'd thought.

But apparently, I was the only one who'd felt that way. When my parents and the staff learned what I'd done, they'd looked at me in disbelief and horror, and they were all completely okay when Arcuro and Lehr sent their people to find and correct my "mistakes."

I stared at the etched surface of The Rain's front door. I didn't want to go inside. The vampires would be leaving tonight. The wolves would come tomorrow. If Nora didn't break things off with Jared, or Jared didn't show up somewhere other than The Rain, Blake would come with those wolves.

"If Blake searches The Rain, will he find Jared?" I asked.

Nora kept her hands on the wheel and her gaze straight ahead.

No response, not even the slightest flicker of emotion.

"Nora," I said, my voice firm. "Is Jared at The Rain?"

"You haven't seen him," she said.

"I haven't been here much, and he could have avoided me."

"Could he have avoided the staff?" Her tone was as flat as her expression.

"You're not answering the question."

She adjusted her grip on the steering wheel but didn't look my way.

I made my sigh extraloud and pulled on the door handle.

"You've met Jared before."

I paused, torn between leaving since she wasn't answering my questions and staying because maybe I could pry Jared's location from her. Maybe I could talk sense into her.

Sinking back into my seat, I nodded. "A long time ago. I was eight, maybe nine. A vampire refused to leave The Rain. My parents tried to reason with her, but she was scared, more scared of the person she was hiding from than of the wolves who wanted to slaughter her. This was just after Arcuro had killed members of a trespassing pack." I waited to see if she'd give any indication she remembered that near crisis. All I got was the movement of her slender throat when she swallowed.

"The tension between the vampires and wolves was intense," I continued. "But my dad asked the wolves to wait until nightfall so he could talk to Arcuro." A corner of my mouth quirked into a smile. "My dad can convince a tree to grow leaves in the winter. The wolves agreed to wait, and the moment the sun went down, Jared was there."

Nora's jaw turned to granite.

"I was supposed to be sleeping, but my parents weren't paying attention. I watched from the library window. Jared dragged the woman out the door. Another vampire was waiting, maybe the one she was running from. I don't know what was said, but that vampire left the woman with Jared. I thought he was going to let her go. She wasn't begging or fighting anymore. She was just…" I searched for the word. "Just sitting there. Then Jared knelt beside her."

That had been the first time I'd seen a vampire feed. He'd gently tilted her head to the side, exposing her neck. I'd overheard our guests boasting about what their bite did to their victims. With humans and weaker paranorms, they claimed they could spark an orgasm without any other touch involved. I'd thought the woman would be okay, that she'd been lucky and Jared had saved her. I'd been very, very wrong.

"He drained her."

Nora's hands tightened on the steering wheel. "He had to enforce the treaty."

That's what Garion had said when he caught me backing away from the window.

Nora finally looked at me. "If she'd been allowed to break the rules, another vampire would have broken them. Then another. Your parents should have let the wolves kill her."

"They were maintaining the status quo," I said. "Better for her to be killed by her own kind than by wolves." That wasn't exactly how my parents had put it, but that was the gist, and because I'd been young and stupid and had still believed in the promise of The Rain, I'd blocked out the episode, refusing to see that the paranormal world was not the harmless and fascinating pseudo fairy tale of my youth.

"If there is no order in the paranormal world, there is chaos." Nora sounded like she was quoting scripture.

"Your *order* is wrong."

She let go of the steering wheel, then grabbed it again. She was breathing harder. Her amber eyes were a shade closer to gold.

"Is that why you helped the unsanctioned?" she asked.

"I helped the unsanctioned because it was the right thing to do." Right and futile.

It was almost a decade later when I stumbled upon the vampire who needed help. After I'd successfully smuggled her in and out of The Rain, I'd smuggled in another and then another. I met the unsanctioned at Gamecraft and Witchery. Owen had been okay with it. He'd even connected me with a moonsick werewolf, and over a three-month period, I'd driven twelve paranorms to The Rain. I'd taken them to the family mausoleum on the edge of our property, then after a few days, I'd driven them out of the foothills and far past Lehr's and Arcuro's territories.

Then Owen called again, saying another werewolf needed

help. I'd driven to Gamecraft and Witchery, and the second I entered the store, Lehr had confronted me.

"That's why they sent you to boarding school," Nora said.

"I sent myself." I shoved open my door. "You can maintain your laws and traditions. I want no part of them."

"Kennedy—"

I slammed the door shut. Before I reached The Rain's front door, tires squealed and she was gone.

## 9

"ROUGH DAY?" GARION ASKED WHEN I PERCHED ON A barstool in front of him.

"You could say that." I scanned the restaurant, making sure no one was close enough to overhear us or take too much interest in me.

I lowered my voice. "Has Nora been around here often lately?"

"She was Friday. Saturday morning, too, I think. Why?"

Friday was the day I met with the inspector. Saturday, Nora woke me up and dragged me to the bridal boutique.

"Did you know she's dating someone?"

"Makes sense," he said. "She's pretty."

"Gorgeous, you mean."

He grinned. "Still don't get along with her, do you?"

"She made my life hell."

"I know," he said. He did. He'd been there my senior year. Things had started to go to hell long before I helped any unsanctioned. Nora had deliberately drawn the attention of any guy I'd ever liked. She'd even lured my friends away. I'd withdrawn from most social activities, choosing instead to hang out with The Rain's staff.

Until they'd abandoned me when I needed their support.

Those paranorms were gone now. Only Garion remained, and he couldn't have much time left in his five-year contract.

My mood soured further. "When is your time up?"

He gave me a tight-lipped smile. "I have a few more months. Drink?"

"Coffee."

"This late in the afternoon?"

"It's Turnover."

He frowned. "I thought Sarah and Derrick were due back today?"

"They're extending their vacation."

"Their vacation." His tone was completely deadpan. Apparently, I wasn't the only one who didn't buy that reason for their absence.

"Do you know what they're doing?" I asked.

He wiped down the counter.

"Garion."

"I don't know. But it's unlike them to be away on Turnover. I can't remember them being gone before. I'll get you that coffee."

He turned away. I stared at his back. Did he know more than he was telling me? He and my parents were fairly close. I think he'd been in some sort of trouble when he came here, and my parents helped him out. They'd agreed to keep his species secret.

He set a steaming mug on the bar. I pinched the handle between two fingers and slid it closer.

"Have things been normal around here?" I asked.

"As normal as an abnormal place can be."

I scowled. I hated it when paranorms gave me nonanswers.

"Has anyone been around who shouldn't?" I pressed.

"Are you talking about the inspector? Or the woman from the other night?"

"Anyone other than them," I said, bitterness slipping into my tone.

"Who, exactly, are you asking about?"

I looked over my shoulder, checking again to make sure no one was close enough to hear.

"Is there any chance Jared is here?" I asked.

"Jared who?"

"*The* Jared. Arcuro's scion. The vampire Nora wants to marry."

I'd never seen Garion's jaw drop before, but it hinged a good half inch open.

"Nora wants to—" He cut himself off, and his expression returned to its usual inscrutable state. "That won't go over well."

"Maybe you'll have better luck convincing her of that. But, apparently, Jared is missing. Blake thinks he might be hiding here."

Blake's name made Garion's eyes tighten.

"If Jared were here, we would know," he said.

I let out a breath. Thank God.

"Unless…"

My lungs froze again. "What?"

He shook his head. "Nothing. It wouldn't hurt to check though. If there's a stray vampire when the wolves show tomorrow—"

"It would be bad. I know." I lifted the mug to my lips, took a careful sip…

…and had to fight not to spit it out.

"This is terrible."

He smiled. "You'll have to take that up with the owners."

"Ha ha." I stood. "I'll walk around. If I'm not back by midnight, send a search party."

I meant that as a joke, but Garion froze in midreach for my mug. "Do you need someone to go with you? I can—"

"No, no. I'm fine. I'll be back." Although, if I did run into Jared, I had no idea what I would do. Politely ask him to leave? Call Arcuro? Call Lehr or…

Damn it, Blake had gotten into my head. I was entertaining the idea that Jared was here. He wasn't. I'd prove it.

The Rain didn't have security cameras or card-entry systems. I had to go about the search the old-fashioned way. I went to my parents' office and found the master key tucked into the seam between the top of the desk and the cabinets on the right. I'd search the wolves' rooms first, then the public and staff-only areas. After the vampires left at midnight, I'd go through their floors and…

My stomach dropped.

The mausoleum. I'd hidden paranorms there for three months.

My fist tightened around the key. I forced it to relax. I couldn't storm out of the office. Someone would notice, and I didn't need anyone to get curious and follow me. So I slipped the key in my pocket, wiggled my shoulders to loosen them, then stepped back into the lobby. I let the large room be my distraction as I headed toward the connecting hallway on its west side. The lobby formed the southernmost point of a pentagon, and it was the most eclectic structure inside and out. Great-grandma Mae had been a fan of the architect, Gaudi, and she'd been theatrical. She'd renovated the building into a modernist style and right up to the edge of the property line. According to Mom, she'd wanted to wow the paranorms when they stepped inside the hotel. With the tall, sloping ceiling, the curved columns, and slanted hallways, she'd done that and achieved an almost otherworldly look.

I loved The Rain's mismatched styles. I was intrigued by how a building could influence a person's emotions. While the lobby was whimsical, the bar and restaurant were rustic, the Silver Ballroom stunning and grandiose, and the barn-converted-into-employee-residence on the outside of the pentagon managed to be both quaint and modern. Every building wrapped you in different sensations, and if the place hadn't been filled with "approved" paranorms and a responsibility I couldn't shake, The Rain would have been my favorite place in the world.

I entered the west wing's long corridor. The lounge on the bottom level was empty. The next two floors would be as well. They were reserved for the werewolves while the upper two floors housed the vampires. Half the building was always empty. We couldn't book wolves in the vampires' rooms or vampires in the wolves' rooms. They claimed they could detect the stench of the other group. It was complete paranoia. More than once when I was a kid, I'd switched the bedding. No one ever noticed.

Shooting a look over my shoulder, I confirmed no one was watching, then I slipped out the door on the opposite end. I'd search those rooms later if needed.

Sun-warmed air fought the cool wind swirling down from the mountains. My hair whipped into my face. I pulled it into a messy ponytail and headed for the path I used to jog when I'd lived here. The trail was gone, the grass no longer flattened beneath the trees. I had no interest in wearing it away again. I had no interest in being here at all, but I was trapped. The Rains were connected to this land. Unless I could dig up some long-lost relative, I had to one day take over. If I didn't, the Null would disappear.

Some days, I didn't care.

I shoved away thoughts of the future and let my hand pass over the boulder that jutted up from the ground just before the path dipped. A few steps beyond that, and I was out of sight of the hotel.

Immediately, I veered left and strode toward the cemetery and mausoleum that marked the northern edge of the Null. Green moss crawled up the walls of the cement structure, and a crack zigzagged across its back wall. I walked around to its front, passing my grandmother's grave. She'd raised my mom on her own and had died before I was born. I knew less about her than Great-grandma Mae, who'd lived until I was six.

I passed the other scattered tombstones, one of which had tiny shards of dark glass on top of it. I scowled as I brushed it clean, then turned to stare at the mausoleum's door. Or rather, I stared at the chains keeping it shut. I hadn't been out here since Lehr and Arcuro found out about the unsanctioned. Guess they didn't want to chance some other paranorm hiding inside.

My nervous stomach settled when I stepped to the door and rattled the chains. They were secure, and a quick look through the metal latticework showed me what I expected to see: two huge stone coffins in an otherwise empty space.

Jared wasn't there.

Annoyance chased my relief. I pivoted away from the mausoleum and walked back to The Rain, shaking my head. Of course Jared wasn't there. He was a freaking old vampire who enforced Arcuro's edicts. Maybe he wasn't even missing. I mean, Nora definitely knew where he was. Maybe Blake couldn't find him because he made a piss-poor hunting dog.

I stalked up the hill, taking the direct route this time instead of my old jogging trail, and soon reached a gravel path that led into The Rain's gardens. We employed an earth elemental to tend to the grounds, and it seemed like he was immune to the suppression of his magic. Manicured hedges and the brightest blooming flowers created a wild tapestry over the hillside. This was where the vampires tended to gather at sunset. It was where Nora wanted to have her wedding.

It would have been the perfect location.

I pushed away that thought—it was *not* going to happen— and finished the walk up to the colonnade that connected the west wing to a smaller building at the northeastern edge of The Rain's roughly shaped pentagon. I intended to cut across the terrace, but a thump to my left made me pause.

I looked over my shoulder at the smaller building. It should have been empty.

I turned toward it and walked slowly. We called it the Catalan. The uneven, sloped roof and multicolored stone walls gave it a cottage-like look. Aside from our residence, the Catalan contained the only other multiroom suites on the property. They were only occupied if a vampire or werewolf had special permission from Arcuro or Lehr to stay there or if a paranorm from another species arrived. As far as I knew, neither of those applied now.

The staff still maintained the Catalan though. Most likely, it was one of them who'd gone inside.

Or it could have been the wind.

Or my imagination.

I pulled open the door. The bottom floor held a small recreation area with a pool table, couches, and the only big, flat-screen TVs on our property. It was empty, but the light was on.

Quietly, I shut the door behind me and tried to ignore my steadily increasing heart rate. I'd never been afraid of The Rain's old, creaky buildings when I was a kid. It had been home. The guests had been fascinating, their stories engaging. But the past five years had worn away my trust and my blindness to realities of their world.

My gaze swept the room. The Catalan contained five suites, one on this floor and two on the second and third. I moved toward the door on my left. Reached for the knob.

The door's edge slammed into my face.

I staggered backward and turned to see who'd darted out of the suite.

Before my blurry vision could focus, someone shoved me to the floor.

I yelled and threw back an elbow. It hit, but a knee dug into my spine and fingers twisted in my hair.

My attacker wrenched my head up, then slammed it back down.

I didn't lose consciousness, but shadows spotted my vision. They grew bigger, joining together until all I could see was a swirling blackness. It swirled and swirled until color shaded the dark. Not much. Just light smears of red and white that began to look like shapes. It took too long to realize they *were* shapes: the bed with its mattress torn off; a dresser overturned on its front face; an empty duffel bag. I'd fallen halfway inside the suite.

A cough wracked through me. I rolled to my back, wheezing air into my lungs. All I could think was *What the hell?* That hadn't been Jared. This person was shorter.

The sound of running footsteps came from outside the room. I rolled to my side and pushed into a sitting position just as Christian appeared.

He saw me on the floor and…

And I couldn't read his expression. It was more like a series of emotions colliding together into one startled look of dread. He erased it quickly, then took in the rest of the room. It was supposed to be unoccupied, but it was wrecked—ransacked—and someone's belongings were scattered across the floor.

He walked past me.

"I'm great. Thanks for asking." I braced a hand on the wall and slowly rose to my feet. When I turned, Christian held a blue rectangle that he squeezed and broke.

"For your face." He handed it to me.

I pressed the cold pack to my cheek. He didn't look away when I met his eyes.

"Hold on. This is your room?"

He blinked, then muttered a quiet, "Yeah."

"This building is supposed to be unoccupied."

"I stay here sometimes." He grabbed a duffel bag off the floor, then filled it with bandages, gauze, a bottle of hydrogen peroxide, and a myriad of other first aid items that had been thrown across the floor.

I took the cold pack away from my numb face. "You have a habit of traveling with disaster kits?"

He didn't respond; he just kept cleaning up the room. I took in the mess, looking for some sign of what he was, why he was here, or better yet, why someone had ransacked his room.

"Who did this?" I asked, facing him squarely because I needed answers.

"I don't know." He zipped the duffel.

"Was it the same person you were running from yesterday?"

"I said I don't know."

I was beginning to understand why no one liked him.

I blocked his path to the door.

"Why would someone ransack your room and attack me?"

He slung his duffel over his shoulder and stared at me like I was in his way, which I totally was.

"I was right before. You're bringing trouble to my hotel."

"Your parents' hotel."

"What?"

"This is your parents' hotel. Where are they?"

"They're out. I'm managing The Rain. Tell me who you were running from."

He looked behind me like he was considering shoving his way out.

I widened my stance, and his focus shifted back to me.

"Was it a man or a woman?" he asked.

"It was a…" I'd assumed man, but I hadn't actually seen the person. They'd made sure I hadn't seen them.

"Tell your parents to call me," Christian said.

I sidestepped when he tried to walk past me. He stopped and gave me a dark, dangerous look.

My nerves fluttered up. I was alone with an unknown paranorm. I'd been talking to him like he was human; I hadn't been thinking about how he would interpret my questions, my accusations. He could be a witch, a fey, a strong elemental, or something more rare and lethal.

I moved out of his way.

He held my gaze for several more seconds, then said, "I'm sorry about your face."

When he left, I released the breath I'd been holding.

Two damn days. That's how long it had been since I got the call to talk with the inspector. Then I had Nora throw a briefcase of cash into my lap. Add the threats from Blake, his killing of two wolves, and my car being towed away, and I was done with this shit. I needed to get back to my real life.

I took out my phone, texted my mom *Who is Christian?* then shut the door to the room. After Turnover, I was out of there.

## 10

I ICED MY CHEEK IN MY PARENTS' OFFICE WHILE I TRIED TO break into their computer. Miracle of miracles, Dad had actually taken my advice and purchased a password manager. Problem was, he hadn't given me the master password. I couldn't access anything important: not their finances, not their email, not even their end of our hotel management software, which was barely one step above a spreadsheet.

I couldn't figure out the combination to the safe either. They must have changed it. Another good security measure, but they could have told me the combination. It was starting to feel like they were deliberately keeping something from me.

Which they were.

Maybe they were just hiding their financial troubles? That was something they wouldn't want to leak out. Heaven forbid we do anything to shake the stability of the paranormal world.

Someone knocked on the door.

"Come in," I said.

It was Sullens. I wished I'd pretended I wasn't there.

"Ms. Rain," he said. "The list."

He walked to the desk and set down a piece of paper.

Lehr's embossed letterhead topped the page. Below it was the standard paragraph stating that only the listed werewolves should be allowed to enter The Rain.

I didn't want to sign it. Signing meant I approved of Lehr and Arcuro determining who could and couldn't stay at our hotel. As I expected, Keisha's name was nowhere on the list. For whatever reason, Lehr hadn't allowed her to come here. She'd probably been asking permission for months. If Lehr had approved her, Blake wouldn't have had to kill her.

Sullens hovered and scowled. I didn't know if the latter was because I was taking too long or if it was because my cheek was bruised and swollen. He hadn't asked what happened when I walked past him earlier, and I hadn't volunteered the info.

Gritting my teeth, I grabbed a pen and scribbled my name at the bottom of the page. I felt dirty.

He took the list back without a word, then exited the office.

I needed to exit the office. It was almost midnight. I had to supervise Turnover, which normally meant Dad shaking hands and chatting with our guests as they left. He was good at talking to people, and he thought paranorms were *interesting*.

I thought they were a pain in the ass.

Sighing, I rose from the desk, walked into the lobby, then found a spot near the front door so I could be seen, but not so near that it looked like I was open to a conversation.

The vampires *trickled* out. After an hour of standing there with my arms crossed, only five had left. Technically, they had until dawn to depart. The staff would then have until noon to turn over the rooms, and the wolves could arrive anytime after that. If I were lucky, they'd show up quickly and I could haul ass back to campus in time for Dr. Campbell's class. I'd miss my other two, but Campbell was the only one who would count my absence against my grade.

Another hour passed. Half our guests had departed.

Maybe Dad chatted with the paranorms out of utter boredom. Turnovers almost always went smoothly. Sometimes a vampire would ask for a job or beg to stay, but those instances rarely ended in a significant disruption. Not that I was hoping something would go wrong. Smooth and boring was good.

Not good enough for Sullens, though. He'd thrown more than a dozen glares my way, each one saying I was doing everything wrong.

I wasn't doing anything *wrong*; I was doing it different.

An hour before dawn, another vampire reluctantly walked out the door. I yawned for the hundredth time. There were only a few guests left. It was so awesome that they were waiting until the last second to leave.

The door to the terrace opened. I stood, ready to crawl into bed the second the vampires left. When I recognized one of the faces, though, my glower turned into a grin.

"Marco!"

"Kennedy." He beamed back at me and approached. "I haven't seen you in ages, princess." He took my hand and raised it to his lips in a kiss, just like he had when I was a kid.

I punched him playfully in the shoulder. "I'm not ten anymore."

He released my hand, took a small step back, then scanned me from head to toe. "No, you certainly aren't."

I punched him again. "That's creepy."

He chuckled but bowed his head in concession.

"What are you doing here?" I asked, walking with him toward the door.

"Supervising," he said. "Most of your guests are from clans Arcuro does not have strong relationships with."

"Ah. You're spying."

"*Mingling*," he said. "If I'd known you were here, *we* could have mingled."

"I've been busy."

I didn't mean that to come out bitter, but his eyebrows rose.

"Everything going well?" Something was off in the way he said that, like he was pressing for information.

"Of course." I put cheer into my voice that I didn't feel. "Why?"

"Oh, just the usual rumors."

"The usual rumors?" I waited for him to elaborate. Those rumors could be anything: The Rain's financial issues, Jared's whereabouts, Nora's wedding. God. When had things become this complicated?

He lifted a shoulder. "It is nothing for you to worry about."

"Should my parents worry?"

He smiled. "Let them have their vacation."

"That sounds ominous."

"That's because you've been away too long. Everything in our world is ominous."

There was a touch of humor in his eyes, but the words sat heavy on my shoulders.

We reached the door. He stepped across the threshold and paused, looking out over the nearly deserted parking lot. His expression darkened.

"They're early."

Frowning, I looked past him. Blake leaned against his truck. For me not to have heard that hunk of junk clanking into the parking lot, he had to have been there for a while. Two men were with him—Raj, the wolf who'd driven me home the other day, and another man I didn't recognize.

"Good night, Kennedy," Marco said.

I closed the door behind him. I really wanted some sleep before I dealt with Blake. Maybe I'd get lucky and Blake would get the message to stay out. I doubted it, though, so I crossed the lobby, heading toward the courtesy table for a glass of water. Sullens's eyes tracked me across the carpet. Annoyed, I stopped and turned toward him.

"Okay. What is your problem?"

Sullens sniffed. "You're uninvolved."

"What's that supposed to mean?" The question came out harsher than I intended, but I was tired, I wasn't used to being up all night long, and I had a very dominant werewolf outside, waiting for an opportunity to pounce.

"You're irresponsible," he said. "You're selfish. More than that, you're cruel."

*Cruel?*

"You don't know anything about me."

"Of course I don't," he said. "You don't visit. You don't call. Your parents have no idea what's going on in your life. You tell them nothing, and they spare you the details of anything that happens here. I'm shocked you've contributed a minute of your time to The Rain this week." He stepped toward me. "You want to know why no one here interacts with you? It's because *you* want nothing to do with *us*. And one day, you're supposed to run this hotel. Everyone expects you to run it into the ground because you can't be bothered to show the smallest amount of interest."

I clenched my teeth together until it felt like my jaw would crack. Of course I wanted nothing to do with them. Sullens and the others weren't here my senior year, but if they had been, they would have abandoned me when I needed them too. The paranorms didn't care about me or my family. They only cared about their laws and traditions and access to the Null. Sullens was angry because he wanted me to become a person who was okay with the rules of their world, a person who looked the other way when someone was rejected or killed just because they couldn't get on the right person's list.

"The vampires are gone now, Ms. Rain," Sullens said. "You are free until noon. Then you are *free.*"

He pivoted, then stalked away.

*I never asked for this life!* I wanted to scream the words at his retreating back. Instead, I closed my eyes and forced my clenched fists to relax. Maybe I was being selfish. Maybe I should—

"Problem with your employee?"

I grimaced. Blake.

Drawing in a breath, I turned around. "You're not supposed to be here until noon."

"I'm not a guest—" His expression went stony. "What happened to your face?"

The throb that had dropped to my chest with Sullens's accusation climbed back to my cheek.

"I ran into a door," I said. "I searched The Rain. He isn't here."

"You ran into a door?" Doubt soaked his words.

"Yes. It happens. Humans bruise. Now if you don't mind, I have things to do."

I started to move past him.

He caught my arm. "I don't believe you."

I looked at his hand, then slowly raised my gaze to meet his. "Do you want to step outside the Null to smell if I'm lying?"

"I don't mind stepping outside to smell you."

Ha ha.

"Let go of my arm, Blake."

He didn't. Not for a long time. He stared into my eyes. I didn't know what he was searching for. Maybe he thought I'd look away first, but it didn't seem like he was trying to intimidate me. It was more like he was assessing my mood, looking for what was really wrong.

He released me. I held his gaze a few more seconds, then walked past him. I was heading to the bar, but a noise drew my attention to the west wing hall.

Raj and the other werewolf were there. They started opening doors.

"I told you he isn't here."

"He's here, Kennedy," Blake said. "You searched for him. You must suspect it too."

"I searched out of spite."

A corner of his mouth looked like it wanted to smile.

Raj unlocked another door while the other wolf scanned the lounge area. What did he think? That Jared was ducked down hiding behind a couch? He was one of the Aged and…

Wait.

My gaze shot back to Raj. He had *unlocked* the door?

I stopped. Stared. "He has a *key*?"

He did. He finished his search of one room and unlocked the next.

I rounded on Blake. "How did he get a key?"

Blake's smile was infuriatingly smug. "I ask and I get."

"We're going to have to change the locks!"

He shrugged. "That's long past due."

My eyes narrowed. Yes, we still used metal keys, and yes, we should have converted to cards or phone apps years ago, but he had no right pointing that out. He had no right making copies of our master key.

"Do you know how much that will cost?"

"That's not my problem," he said. Then he added, "You're sweet."

If his last words hadn't confused me, I might have slugged him. "What?"

He stepped toward me. "Your suite. I want to search it. Will that be a problem?"

"You think I'm hiding Jared in my *home*?"

"I need to be thorough." He deliberately made that sound suggestive. He had that look in his eyes, the one that said he was alpha and the world—and the women in it—revolved around him.

"You're not going into my home."

"You can hardly call it your home when you've spent less than a week here this year."

What the hell? Was he keeping track of me?

"Get out," I said.

"Not until I'm satisfied."

"You're violating the treaty."

"By bothering you?" He chuckled. "You haven't read it, have you? If you were a paranorm, you would have it memorized. You would know exactly what we can and can't do. As long as I don't kill you, there are no magical repercussions."

He might have been right. I'd read the treaty when I was a kid. I didn't remember the details.

I looked back at the hallway. A staff member had either entered from the other door or stepped from a room. She was short and slender, but she stood in front of Raj like she could take him down. Outside the Null, it might have been a fair fight. Inside, her only advantage was being used to her nullified speed and strength. Raj wasn't. It might unbalance him, but it would still take an extreme amount of luck for her to win a fight against him.

I needed to do something before this turned violent.

"Tell them to wait outside," I said.

"That would make it difficult for them to search The Rain." He played with a leaf on a vase of flowers set on a small, circular table.

"I'll take you around."

"And let Jared scurry from building to building? No."

"Tell them to join the other wolves you have circling The Rain."

He looked at me. "What makes you think I have wolves surrounding the hotel?"

"You need more than three wolves to cover all the buildings," I said. "It makes sense to have more watching."

"Know us pretty well, do you?" He faced me fully again. I

was tired of this, tired of the way he studied me like I was something of interest. I was about to call him out on it, but his gaze shifted behind me.

"Is there a problem?" Sullens asked.

Blake would have seen me grimace, so I made sure my expression didn't flicker when I turned. Sullens stood with another staff member. Joash, I think. He worked in the kitchen.

"It's fine," I said. "His friends are leaving, and he's just about to admit that he's wrong."

Sullens's mouth dipped down, but Blake's inched up at the corners.

"Raj," he called out, his gaze remaining on me. Raj and the other wolf were still faced off with the woman in the hall-way, but the second Blake called his name, both men walked away. Blake gave the slightest nod toward the front door, and they exited, no hesitation, no weird looks or question in their expressions.

"Lead on, Ms. Rain," Blake said. "We will see who tastes satisfaction tonight."

## 11

FOR THE SECOND TIME IN LESS THAN A WEEK, I WAS IN OUR interminably slow elevator with an alpha werewolf. Blake didn't do the normal thing and face the doors when they closed behind us. No, he casually leaned back against the sidewall so he could keep me completely in his view.

Slowly, the ancient box continued to rise.

"It kills you, doesn't it," he said.

"What does?"

"The fact that you can't ignore me even when we're in the Null."

I snorted. "You need to get over yourself. You're attractive, sure, but so are a thousand other guys out there, and they're not paranorms."

He pushed away from the wall, moving in between me and the doors so that I had to see the grin that stretched across his face. "That's why I fascinate you, and they bore you."

God, his arrogance. It knew no bounds.

The elevator pinged. The doors slid open. I raised my eyebrows, a request for him to move the hell out of my way. He complied, but it felt like he was laughing.

Whatever. He would leave right after I proved Jared wasn't hiding in our residence.

Keeping my gait steady and unrushed, I walked down the hall, then stopped in front of the door to our living room.

"Allow me," he said, swiping my keys from my hand when I pulled them from my pocket.

He invaded my space. We would have been face-to-face if I'd been half a foot taller. Instead, I stared at his chest and inadvertently breathed him in. He reminded me of wild berries growing in the deep woods, a scent that most girls would want to wander around and become lost in.

He slid the key into the lock, then pushed open the door.

I made it half a step inside before Blake's arm hooked around my waist, wrenching me out of the doorway.

I yelped, reached for his arm to shove it away, but he'd already released me. He stood there blocking my view of the suite. Something in his posture, in the poised-to-spring alertness, made the hair on the back of my neck rise.

Jared *couldn't* be in there.

I pushed my way between Blake and the doorjamb, then froze.

The suite was wrecked. From the entryway, we had a view of the combined living, kitchen, and dining areas. All the cabinets in the kitchen were open, the drawers too with their contents dumped on the counters and floors. Our small pantry had been destroyed. Broken plates littered the ground.

I stepped over the split entry table.

The living room hadn't fared any better. The couch was overturned, the cushions thrown across the room. The ancient TV lay facedown on the floor, the bulky frame cracked and broken.

I turned to the right, toward the skinny hallway that led to my room and my parents' study.

Blake's hand clamped on my shoulder. He scanned the suite and sniffed.

Then he sniffed again.

After a third time, he cut me a look that could wither a cactus.

I didn't smell anything, and… oh. He didn't smell anything either.

I shrugged free from his hand. It wasn't my fault his nose didn't work in the Null.

"Stay here." He moved toward my parents' bedroom.

I went the opposite direction, toward my bedroom on the right. It was as destroyed as the rest of the place.

What the hell was going on? First Christian's room, now our residence? They had to be related. While I'd been watching the vampires depart, Mom had replied to my message asking who Christian was. All she'd said was that he bought my old dojo, the one I'd attended for almost seven years, and didn't come around The Rain often. So helpful.

"Did you not hear me tell you to stay?" Blake rumbled behind me.

"I heard you just fine." I moved farther into my room and bent down to lift my overturned dresser, ignoring the glare that was searing the back of my head.

"When did this happen?" he demanded.

"They didn't leave a note with the time of break-in." I picked up a picture frame from the floor and dusted off the broken glass. It was my parents and me in front of my apartment the first time they'd dropped me off at college. Our smiles were forced—my parents because I'd insisted on moving early in the summer. Mine because I'd just spent two weeks at The Rain and had despised every second of it.

"Kennedy." Blake growled my name.

I set the frame on my dresser. "It wasn't like this yesterday morning."

"Who did it? And do not sidestep my question."

I recognized that voice. It was the one he'd used yesterday when he talked to Keisha and Charles. If we'd been outside the Null, it would have had power behind it. The world would have pressed in, demanding I drop my gaze. Demanding I submit and do what he ordered. He expected compliance, even here in The Rain.

"I am not one of your wolves."

His nostrils flared. Tension hardened the muscles of his shoulders. It looked like his wolf wanted to burst from his chest.

I turned back to my room and picked up my comforter from the floor. "This is going to be a pain in the ass to clean up."

"Someone invades your territory and you're worried about cleaning?"

I looked over my shoulder and kept my tone light. "*You're* invading my territory."

Some of the anger left his face. Probably because I had a point.

I walked to my bookshelf. Fortunately, it was attached to the wall. I grabbed several books from the floor and placed them back on the shelf, one at a time to give Blake more time to cool off.

"Your room is more trashed than your parents'," he said. "Any idea why?"

I shook my head, surveying the mess. Someone had taken advantage of my parents being out of town. Could it have been Christian? Maybe our residence was ransacked before his room. Maybe he'd ransacked his own room as a cover. He could have done it right before I entered. He could have been the one who…

No. The person who'd attacked me was too short.

I righted a floor lamp and switched it on.

"Ms. Rain," Blake said. "Who have you pissed off recently?"

I looked at him. "Other than you?"

The lamplight was a bright gleam in his eyes. It made his smile threatening. "You haven't seen me angry."

"I've seen you kill." The words escaped, and I immediately wished I could claw them back. I didn't want to talk about Keisha and Charles or remember how easily Blake had ripped out their throats. I don't know why I brought it up, why I'd slung the words at him like an insult. He wouldn't care what I thought about his actions.

The light in his eyes dimmed. "I shouldn't have taken you there."

"I tried telling you that." I fidgeted with the lampshade.

"It was a mistake," he said. "She shouldn't have been that far gone."

My fingers stilled on a rip in the shade. Was that an apology? Wolves said they were sorry less often than they said please.

"Charles was her brother," he said.

I didn't know why he was telling me that. It made the killing worse.

"It's wolf business. I don't need details." I picked up a cute straw hat I hadn't seen in years. "You should go. Jared's not here."

"Are you returning to your apartment today?"

"I have to be here to check wolves off Lehr's list." He should know that.

"I mean tonight. Are you sleeping here?"

I tossed the hat onto my bed, then put my alarm clock back on my nightstand. "That's a personal question."

"Is it?"

Something in his voice made me turn. He stood less than

an arm's length away, mouth quirked and a pair of unicorn undies hanging from his finger.

I snatched them away.

"Don't you have anything better to do?" I shoved the undies into a drawer with the other clothes I hadn't taken to college.

"Plenty," he said. "But none of my other responsibilities are as fun as antagonizing you."

He'd slipped back into his devious persona, and his gaze lingered on me long enough to make my face flush. It was a struggle to maintain eye contact, to not let him know that his composed confidence resonated in me in a way that made my blood burn.

"You do know that your werewolf juju doesn't work here, right?"

He cocked his head. "Juju?"

"Your magic, your superpowers, whatever you want to call it."

"You call it juju," he said, his tone dubious.

"Yes."

He moved closer, and the left side of his mouth curved into a barely there smile. "So I'm not making you uncomfortable?"

"You're making me annoyed." Blake was more than attractive. He was charismatic and confident. The combination made it almost impossible not to think about slipping under the covers with him. Fortunately, paranorms and assholes weren't on my prospective dating list.

"I will assign a wolf to watch you," he said.

"Uh, no. This isn't about me."

"Then tell me how this really happened." He lifted his hand toward my bruised cheek.

I lurched out of the way. "For all I know, one of your wolves did this."

He dropped his hand. "So you *were* attacked."

"I was searching for Jared."

His gaze sharpened like a wolf finding his prey. "It was him."

"It *wasn't* him."

"Then who?" He looked like he wanted to kill. If I mentioned Christian's name, Blake would hunt him down. I'd already told him more than I should.

And I'd already spent far too much time alone with him.

"You really do need to go." I left the room, intending to show him out. We had another exit to the hallway, though. It was via the study. Usually, the door that connected it to our residence was open. Now, it was closed.

I stared at it too long. Blake walked past me and shoved it open. It took some effort because a filing cabinet was over-turned in front of it.

I followed him inside. Same story. More mess. More chaos.

"They were searching for something, not someone," Blake said.

"Something like the master key?" I quipped. This wasn't Blake's doing, though. I was almost certain of it.

Blake's chuckle drew my attention. "We've had a copy of that key for months."

My stomach flipped. He looked so *normal* when he laughed.

"You're psychotic, you know," I said, keeping my tone light.

"How so?" he asked, staring down at a stack of papers on the desk.

"You're"—I waved my hand at him—"relaxed right now. You're not the bastard alpha werewolf who intimidates people into doing what he wants."

He made a noncommittal *hmm* and rummaged through the paper.

"Whoever it was came here first," he said. "He or she took their time. The rest of the suite was destroyed because they were pissed."

"How do you know?"

"Neat stacks." He gestured to the desk. "They went through the paperwork methodically."

"Are you a private investigator now?"

"Investigations are one of my duties."

Of course. He was Lehr's second. His henchman and enforcer and apparently on-call detective.

But he was right. The papers weren't strewn across the floor like the dishes and ripped couch cushions and everything else had been. Despite the overturned filing cabinet, they were all semiorganized.

"Do you think it might have something to do with this?" He pushed one of the stacks over.

I tried not to grimace when I saw the overdue bills peeking out. My parents had been collecting late notices for months.

"That's nothing." I grabbed the papers off the desk.

"Is this why you agreed to host Nora's wedding?"

"We're not hosting the wedding." I shoved the papers into a desk drawer.

"Not without a groom, you aren't."

"You agree he isn't here then?"

He met my gaze. "No. Could your financial troubles be the reason for the break-in?"

"We don't have financial troubles." I said that with a completely straight face.

He leaned against the desk. Crossed his arms. "You're not telling me something."

"I barely know you. I'm not telling you a lot of things." I focused on a stack of papers, thumbing through it as an excuse to avoid eye contact with Blake. He was dissecting me again. Figuring me out. I didn't like it. Blake wasn't on the fringe of the pack. He was one step away from its head. I didn't want his attention. I wanted to…

I wanted to go back to school and avoid all this.

I pressed my lips together. That's what I would have done if my parents had been here. I would have taken off, letting them handle everything without asking questions I didn't want to know the answers to.

Damn it. I would not let Sullens get to me.

The floor in the hallway creaked. Blake darted to my side as I spun toward the doorway.

"Is there a problem here?" Garion asked. His gaze locked onto Blake. He was broader than the werewolf and just as tall. I might not know what kind of paranorm he was, but I knew he was a hand grenade—completely safe until you pulled the pin.

"Everything's fine," I said. "Blake is leaving."

Garion's focus shifted to me, then to the ransacked office.

"Well, maybe not completely fine, but—"

"Someone's invaded The Rain," Blake said.

"I see that." Garion's gaze had locked on Blake again. It was an outright challenge.

Shit.

I grabbed Blake's arm. "He really is leaving."

He didn't budge when I tried to pull him toward the other door.

Garion took a step forward. Blake moved to meet him.

"Don't." I slipped between them, my back to Garion because I trusted him. That put me too close to Blake, though. His scent swept over me again, and my body thrummed as if we were outside the Null and he had his abilities back, that magical something that toyed with a person's good sense.

Blake smirked and looked down. My hand was on his chest.

I dropped it and sidestepped out from between them. Garion took up position on my right.

"*Blake*," I said. That was the closest I would come to saying please. This was my family's hotel. I wouldn't beg. If he didn't leave, I'd help Garion throw him out.

Blake studied me again, and for once, I was glad his attention was on me. I tried not to be transparent, not to let him see how much I didn't want to physically remove him from The Rain. I wasn't bluffing, but I really, really didn't want that altercation.

A century passed before Blake dipped his head.

I didn't breathe until he'd left the study.

"Did he do that?" Garion demanded.

I stepped toward the paper-strewn desk. "It was like this when we got here."

"No." He turned me toward him. Nodded toward my face. "That."

"Oh no. Not him. Someone else…" I grimaced. "Christian's room was ransacked like this. The person was still in there. They slammed the door into my face and ran off."

Garion stood very still. "Christian?"

"It wasn't him. I didn't get a good look at the person. Someone close to my height. Who is Christian?"

"A friend of your parents," Garion said. "You should call them. I'll notify the staff."

I straightened a stack of already straight papers. "What if it was one of them?"

He hesitated, then shook his head. "No. The newest hire has been here for six months. I know them, and they respect your family too much to violate your privacy."

"You mean they respect my parents."

Garion's mouth tightened. "They don't disrespect you. They don't know you."

*Wouldn't matter if they did.* I didn't voice that thought out loud.

"I don't suppose Dad has installed security cameras, has he?" I asked.

Garion laughed. "He's more behind the times than I am. I had to fix his computer once. With the Restart button."

I rolled my eyes. That was just sad.

"I'll tell the staff to watch for unsanctioned visitors," Garion said, moving toward the door. He stopped before he exited. "Are you okay?"

"Yeah. I'm fine. Thanks for coming up."

"You shouldn't be alone with Blake."

"I was trying to prevent a confrontation downstairs."

"By bringing him up here?"

I gave him a sheepish smile. "It made sense at the time."

He gave me the same *be more careful* look Dad would have given me if he'd been there.

## 12

Just after three p.m., our last guest parked my Camry in front of The Rain.

"Courtesy of Ms. Lehr," the werewolf said after giving me her name.

"Thanks," I mumbled, marking her off Lehr's list. I glanced at the time on my phone, then back at my car. I was itching to get out of there, to get back to my normal life. It would be tight, but I should be able to make it to campus in time for Campbell's class. Afterward, I could go home and crash. It had been over twenty-four hours since I'd slept, and I needed a good, uninterrupted night in my own bed.

Twenty minutes away from The Rain, though, I realized I would pass right by my old dojo. It was just off the highway. Mom had said Christian bought the place as if that was an explanation for his existence. He might be there now, and he might have answers.

I watched the exit approach. This would be the second time I missed Campbell's class. If I missed a third time, my grade would be docked ten percent. And did I want answers?

The Rain was my parents' business, not mine. Not yet. I shouldn't get more involved.

At the last second, I cursed and swung toward the exit. Two turns later, I pulled into the broken and potholed parking lot, then parked between two faded yellow lines. The strip mall was almost exactly how I remembered it except for the sign above my old dojo, which now, in an overabundance of creativity, said GYM. The words MIXED MARTIAL ARTS were painted onto a window, and it looked like Christian had knocked down the wall to the left, extending the dojo into the next retail space.

Tilting my rearview mirror toward me, I checked my face. I'd raided my mom's makeup cabinet after Blake left. Or rather, I'd raided the floor where everything had been thrown. She'd taken most of her makeup with her, so I had to make do with samples and an almost empty bottle of foundation that didn't quite match me. I thought I'd done a rather good job masking the bruise. My face was still swollen, but the discoloration was hardly noticeable. If this was an MMA gym, though, the people inside might not even take note of the bruise.

Pushing my door open, I climbed out of the Camry and crossed the lot. A bell fastened to the door rang when I pushed it open, and the smell of sweat and metal hit me. Hard rock music crackled over a speaker. It wasn't loud enough to cover the sound of fists hitting the punching bags lining the side wall or the clatter of free weights dropping to the ground. Close to twenty people were inside. A small group stood in the center of a mat, watching someone demonstrate a grappling move, and in a fenced octagon that took up most of the added retail space, two men faced off. I allowed myself a few seconds to absorb their bare, sweat-soaked torsos before I focused on their faces. Christian was there, dodging a double jab his opponent threw at his chin.

It wasn't fair. Paranorms shouldn't have their supernatural juju *and* bodies of a god.

I walked toward the octagon, watching Christian move in and out, testing his opponent, landing some hits. He was quick but not abnormally so. Either he was holding back so that he didn't come off as superhuman, or he was something that didn't have increased speed as an ability.

I stopped several feet away from the octagon, and he saw me. I knew it because his opponent landed a solid punch to his jaw.

Oops.

"Give me a minute," he said. He grabbed a towel when he exited and wiped his face and chest before he stopped in front of me.

"Are you okay?" he asked.

*Keep your eyes on his face, Kennedy. He asked you a question.* It was an unexpected question. I thought he'd greet me with a "What are you doing here?" or a "Get the hell out of my gym."

"My parents' rooms were ransacked," I said. "Funny how that happened the same day as yours."

The eyes that met mine were so blue they could barely pass as human. Had they been that bright in The Rain? Though his gaze didn't wander, I felt it across my skin, a brush of awareness that was almost electric.

"Are they back?" He bent to pick up a water jug off the floor.

"I wouldn't be here if they were."

He paused halfway to lifting the jug to his mouth, nodded once, then finished the action and took a drink.

"How do you know them?" Right after I asked the question, I realized it was a stupid one. Every paranorm knew who my parents were, at least by name. They knew who I was.

"They're friends," he said.

"They've never mentioned you."

"They've mentioned you." The skin around his eyes tightened briefly before his expression smoothed to blank again. "Have you talked to them?"

"A couple of times. Have you?"

"They aren't answering my calls." He took another long drink from the jug.

"How did you meet them? And why do they let you stay at The Rain? You didn't have a reservation. I checked."

He lowered the jug. "This isn't your world, Kennedy. You should go back to school."

His tone might have been kind, but the words scraped across my patience like a knife. "I was born into this world. I might escape for a few years, might get a job and have some semblance of a life for a while, but eventually I'll get pulled back to the hotel. I'll have to run it. I'll have to play nice with you people, keep the peace and keep your damn secrets. So don't tell me to walk away and ignore this. My parents have been gone a week, and your world has been nothing but a pain in the ass. I—"

My heart sped in my chest. I didn't know where that came from. I was too tired, my patience too fragile. My self-control had snapped, and too much had spilled out. And now, Christian stood in front of me with a scary kind of stillness.

The person he'd been fighting looped his fingers through the octagon's chain-link fence. "Hey, man, how long are you going to be?"

"A minute," Christian replied without turning.

I kept my lips pressed together. No apologies would come from me. Every word I'd said was true.

"Coffee." The word punched the air.

"What?" I stuttered.

"There's a donut shop on the corner. They have good coffee."

*Never eat pastries with a paranorm…*

"Will I get answers over coffee?" I asked.

"Tomorrow morning," he said. "Eight a.m."

He set the water jug down and started to turn.

"No."

He paused. "No?"

He obviously didn't hear that word enough. "No. Not tomorrow. I need answers today. Right now."

"Kennedy, I—"

My phone rang from the back pocket of my jeans. I kept my gaze locked on Christian.

"You going to answer that?"

I didn't want to. I wanted Christian to finish what he'd been about to say.

My phone rang again. My heart rate, which had been beating faster than the blaring music, had slowed to a hard, foreboding thump. Nothing good would come from this call.

But Christian was waiting—staring—and I was starting to draw attention from the man in the octagon and others.

I slipped it out of my pocket. Sullens's name lit the screen.

Gripping my phone too hard, I tapped it on and lifted it to my ear.

"What is it?" I asked.

"An unsanctioned is at The Rain."

---

THE RAIN's door opened before I reached it.

"They want him dead," Sullens said.

"Who is it?"

"An old vampire."

Goose bumps prickled down my arms when I stepped over the threshold. It wasn't Jared. Sullens would have used his name. It had to be someone else, someone the werewolves felt they had a right to kill.

Sullens led the way to the west wing.

"I crossed all the names off the list," I said.

"I know." He kept his gaze straight forward, his stride long, his mouth set into a firm, displeased line.

"Forty vampires left this morning. You watched them leave too. Marco was the last out the door." This wasn't my fault. I'd counted carefully. I'd asked every vampire their name, and every name had matched the list.

He pushed open the door to the colonnade. "Yes, Ms. Rain."

So much condescension in his words. How much trouble would I get into if I punched him?

I glared at the back of his head when he stepped into the garden that spilled down the hill to the northwest. Even in early spring, bright flowers dotted the landscape, thanks to our earth elemental. It was his skill, not his magic, that crafted the beauty in the Null. Ruhl's hands kept weeds from the flower beds, wrapped vines around trellises, and trimmed the hedges into tight formations.

My gaze shifted from our path to the sky. The sun hid behind a layer of gray clouds. They were thick and heavy, hovering over me and The Rain and the mountains to the east. It was worse than a clear blue sky though. All it would do was delay the inevitable. If I forced the vampire to leave now, he would burn and suffer before he went poof.

The path twisted, and there was the unsanctioned vampire. He teetered in the middle of one of Ruhl's formerly immaculate hedges. His long blue coat tangled in the thorny hawthorn, and his boots broke and crushed the greenery. Tiny rivulets of blood streaked his cheeks and hands. He plucked a thorn from his palm, scowled, then flicked it away.

My clenched jaw relaxed. At least half The Rain's guests were in the garden. The wolves had the vampire pinned between them and the edge of the Null, which was just on the other side of the hedge. The only thing holding them back was the presence of two staff members: Joash, the fire elemental who worked in the kitchen, and another employee whose name I didn't remember. This was going to be tricky.

The vampire's gaze lighted on me.

"You must be Ms. Rain," he said, a faint accent giving his words a genteel flair. "I would love to say it is a pleasure to meet you, but…"

He waved a hand toward the paranorms that cornered him, then winced when thorns stabbed and clung to his sleeve.

"Who are you?" I demanded.

"Deagan Dentremont, at your service." He didn't bow; the flourish was all in his voice.

I looked at Sullens. "He wasn't on the list."

"No," Sullens agreed.

He couldn't have been here with the vampires. We would have noticed him. His elaborate coat was blue, embroidered, and unbuttoned over tan pants tucked into black boots. The ruffle on the front of his shirt added to his out-of-time appearance. He looked like a Regency-era gentleman who'd signed on to be the Goblin King in a *Labyrinth* sequel.

"Why are you here?"

He gave me a sheepish smile. "Would you believe I confused Turnovers?"

The wolf standing at the front of the mob growled.

Deagan shifted, breaking more foliage and fisting the prickly hawthorn to keep his balance. "Perhaps we could discuss this outside the hedge?"

"I could arrange that," the head werewolf said.

"What clan do you belong to?" I asked quickly, an attempt to keep tempers from escalating. I wasn't good at this. Dad was. He always knew what to say. He'd interject a little joke, make the paranorms laugh, then *ta-da*, the crisis would be averted.

Deagan's gaze shifted from the wolf to me. He lifted a shoulder. "I am local."

If true, that meant either directly or indirectly, he was under Arcuro's jurisdiction.

I chewed on my bottom lip. Would Arcuro have sent him here to search for Jared? If he was Arcuro's emissary, he didn't need to be on a list. Like Nora and Blake, he could enter the Null to speak with me or my parents or to have a conversation with another guest.

But Marco had been here on behalf of Arcuro, and Deagan hadn't invoked Arcuro's name. In fact, it seemed like he'd deliberately *not* mentioned the master vampire.

The wolf who'd apparently made himself head honcho made another noise. "If he is local, he should be especially aware that it is our time. We awaited your arrival, Ms. Rain."

I expected him to say more—some explanation for why they should be allowed to deal with Deagan—but he stalked toward the vampire without another word.

It took my brain too many seconds to figure out his intent. He was three steps away from Deagan when I figured it out.

"Wait. No!"

At the last second, Joash stepped into the wolf's path.

"Move," the honcho wolf growled.

"No," I said again, moving to Joash's side. According to their rules and traditions, Honcho had every right to kill a vampire that trespassed on the wolves' time, and it wouldn't matter if I contacted Arcuro. I'd seen this before. Deagan was dead.

Unless I completely broke my personal vow and got involved.

"His life is forfeit," Honcho said.

My lungs felt like they'd turned into iron. A sick dread built in my stomach. I knew what I was supposed to do, knew I should step back and let the paranorms deal out their justice. I could turn my back and walk away. I didn't have to stand there and witness this murder.

But I'd be an accomplice. I'd *feel* like an accomplice.

"No." There should have been a lightning strike or a deep rumble of thunder that vibrated the air. There would be repercussions from this.

Honcho stepped toward me, a deliberate move to intimidate me.

I didn't lower my gaze.

Honcho's chin dipped like he was ready to charge. A muscle in his cheek twitched repetitively. It was possible he'd been as moonsick as Keisha before he stepped into The Rain. He might not be fully sane just yet. He might be violent. He might be reckless.

"I will remove him immediately from the property," I said.

Honcho's nostrils flared. "Lehr will hear about this."

"Yeah, well, Lehr's going to hear about a lot of things soon."

I thought that would be the end of it. Honcho broke eye contact, a sign that he was submitting. He started to turn, to walk away, but instead of angling back toward The Rain, he hooked a sharp right and lunged for Deagan.

I grabbed Honcho's sleeve, but he still made it past me. Deagan shifted, presumably to defend himself.

The hedge gave way.

He fell backward, then hissed in pain. His hand had gone past the edge of the Null. His exposed skin bubbled and steamed.

I yanked back hard on Honcho's sleeve.

He spun toward me, a knife in his hand.

I raised my arms to protect my body. The blade cut across my forearm.

Honcho's scream pierced the air.

It was so loud and sudden and *agonized* that I froze. The whole world seemed to freeze.

Joash pushed me back, and still, Honcho screamed. He dropped to his knees. He curled into a ball.

The paranorms stepped away from him too, all but Deagan, who remained trapped in the hedge's thorns.

The screams didn't stop, and my entire body went cold. He was in so much pain, and no one was helping him. No one was doing a damn thing.

I reached toward his shoulder, intending to provide some sort of comfort. That's when I noticed the blood running down my arm.

Wide-eyed, I looked back at Honcho. This was… Holy shit. This was the treaty, the magic that protected my family.

But we were in the Null. How did that magic work here?

I couldn't begin to think through the answer, not with him writhing on the ground.

"How do I stop it?" I backed away in case my proximity made it worse.

His screams didn't abate.

I looked at Sullens. "How do we stop it?"

My voice sounded desperate. I wanted to cover my ears. I wanted to close my eyes. I wanted to run.

Sullens glanced at me, then returned his attention to Honcho. Another millennium passed. Sullens's expression tightened. He moved forward, dipped toward the ground near Honcho, then picked up the knife.

"Sullens!"

He stabbed the blade into Honcho's heart.

The screams stopped.

The silence bashed against me like a storm against a cliff. I couldn't look away. Couldn't move. Couldn't even think.

Deagan cleared his throat.

"Well," he said from the hedge. "That answers some questions."

I stared at the vampire. I couldn't wrap my mind around any of it, not until the wolves unfroze themselves. They turned almost as one to look at Sullens. I swear to God I heard one of them snarl.

When a wolf made a move toward Sullens, I unglued my feet from the ground and stepped into his path.

"Go to your rooms."

"He killed—"

"Go."

His eyes narrowed. If we were outside the Null, he would hear my heart thudding. I had to break up this pseudo pack. They needed time to cool off away from each other and away from the staff.

"One of ours was murdered. We demand a life in return."

"Do you need an escort?" I don't think I'd ever heard my voice so cold, but I kept my shoulders back. My chin up.

It took forever for him to back down, for them all to begin to retreat. I watched them walk toward the west wing.

"Sullens, go to the Barn. Joash and"—I looked at the third employee whose name I didn't know—"you. Make sure they make it to their rooms. You…" I turned to Deagan. "Come with me."

I didn't wait to see if he followed. I retraced the steps Sullens and I had taken from the colonnade. The past few minutes replayed in my head with Honcho's screams as the soundtrack. Where had I gone wrong? I'd tried to defuse the situation. I was removing Deagan from the scene. Aside from letting the wolves kill him, was there something else I could have done differently?

"I greatly appreciate your intervention, Ms. Rain," Deagan said.

"Shut up."

"Certainly." He said it like he was doing me a favor. A favor would have been not invading The Rain during the wolves' occupancy and being honest about his reason for being there at all.

We crossed the terrace and entered the lobby. I took him directly to the staff corridor that lay between the office and the restaurant. Boxes were stacked high on one side, making it uncomfortably narrow. This was one of the violations the inspector had listed—a fire hazard. We needed to find another place to store deliveries.

What a stupid thing to be worried about.

The low purr and tumble of a dryer filled the corridor. The laundry room was small and stuffy. Fortunately, it was empty, so I didn't have to explain myself when I grabbed an armload of folded blankets off a wire rack.

I shoved them into Deagan's arms.

"*This* is your plan?" he said.

"I'll pull my car up outside." I stared at the bright red streak on the white blankets. It was from my arm, not Deagan's hand, though the latter was leaving its own disgusting stain.

My arm began to sting, then throb, then hurt. I didn't want to look at the wound, so I wrapped a towel around it and scanned the laundry alcove. I found a first aid kit stuffed between the washer and the wall.

"I can help you with that," Deagan said.

I slapped his hand away.

"Really," he said. "I am used to the sight of blood."

"The only thing I need you to do is wrap yourself in those blankets. Do it before I shove you out of the Null uncovered."

His eyes didn't stray from my arm.

"Deagan," I snapped. "We're going to my car. You're getting in the trunk. I will drive you to... Where can I take you?"

He looked up. "I have a place I stay during the day, but I do not share the location with others. For obvious reasons."

"You're going to share it with me."

"I have a policy—"

"I don't care about your policy, Deagan. If you don't want me to know where you live, move afterward."

His face screwed up. "I dislike moving."

Oh my god. I should have let Honcho kill him.

"Do you want to die?" It was so wrong that I asked that question without any kind of sarcasm. It was a serious concern. Older vampires sometimes grew bored. They greeted the sun or found other ways to end their existences. Maybe this had been Deagan's chosen form of suicide.

"Of course not," Deagan said. "I merely have rules that I have followed for two hundred years. They have kept me alive. I do not intend to break them."

"But today, you decided to break The Rain's rules?"

He frowned. "I see your point. Very well then. Like a hot dog?"

"What?"

"Shall I wrap myself like a hot dog? Like this." He made a swirly motion with his finger.

"As long as you can walk and don't go poof, I don't care."

"For the record, I believe you are overreacting."

I gave him a look that would have made a human wither in fear. It was lost on him, though, the Master of Obliviousness.

Gritting my teeth, I opened the first aid kit, grabbed a stick-to-itself bandage, and wrapped my arm.

I changed my mind about pulling my car up. I didn't want to leave him alone. He'd wander into a staff member, another one of the guests, or he'd do something else stupid and deranged. I wasn't parked that far away. He could shuffle his way there.

I waited for Deagan. He'd wrapped himself hot dog style

but only up to his shoulders. He looked down, toward the blanket on the floor he could no longer reach.

I grabbed it and threw it over his head.

"Perhaps another one for safety?" he said. "I doubt these have UV protection."

I threw another one over him, then put my hand on his back and guided him to the door.

He shuffled forward. "I'm not sure this is a good idea."

"You don't have a choice."

"I have never done this before." The words were muffled beneath the blanket.

"It will be fine."

We reached the door. I opened it, and light spilled over his blanket-covered boots.

"If you have a spare closet—"

"Door's open and you're not smoking." I took his arm and pulled him forward.

"I dislike this very much."

I led him down the paved drive we used for deliveries. It curved to the east side of the parking lot. It took forever to shuffle down it, one tiny inch at a time. I was sweating by the time we reached my car, but not from the weather or any exertion. It was catching up with me, what I had done. I'd gotten involved. Good things wouldn't come from this.

No going back now.

I opened the Camry's trunk. "Climb in."

Deagan bumped against the car's back fender once, twice. After the third attempt, he turned toward me. "I am not sure how to—"

"Roll." I pushed his shoulder hard, causing him to fall inside the trunk.

"This is demeaning," he protested.

"Not any more than standing butt-deep in a hawthorn bush." I shoved his legs inside, then slammed the trunk shut.

## 13

Deagan shouted directions from the trunk. I intended to follow them, but when I should have merged onto the highway, I kept to the feeder.

Three deaths in three days. Keisha and Charles had been bad enough. Seeing someone in human form die, seeing Honcho in so much pain…

I'd always known the treaty protected my family; I just hadn't known how. The werewolf had intended to hurt me, to kill me. Logically, I knew I was lucky. If the treaty hadn't intervened, I would be the one dead.

But this shouldn't have happened. Deagan shouldn't have been there, and I hadn't saved a life; I'd only changed the life that was lost.

"I feel like you have missed your turn, Ms. Rain."

I glanced in the rearview mirror like I could see Deagan in the trunk. This was his fault.

I turned onto a rough, gravel lane and put the Camry into park.

"It is impossible for us to be there already," Deagan said, his voice clearer now that we weren't driving.

"It's time to talk. What were you doing at The Rain?"

"I told you. It was a mistake."

"You have no idea how much trouble you've caused."

"I think I have an understanding—"

I pulled the trunk latch.

Deagan yelped. "Good God, woman!"

A thump followed his words—him pulling the trunk shut again.

"If you're not going to talk, you're getting out here."

"You don't mean that, Ms. Rain."

I popped the trunk again.

He cursed. "Stop that!"

I glared into the empty rearview mirror. "A wolf is dead because of you. Why did you crawl into The Rain?"

He sniffed. "I did not crawl."

I popped the trunk a third time.

"Okay! Okay, Ms. Rain. You win. I was searching for my master."

"Who is your master?" I didn't want to hear the answer. I really didn't.

Deagan's sigh was loud even through the seat blocking the trunk. "Jared. He disappeared last week. I cannot feel him at all. The Rain makes sense."

"The Rain doesn't make sense. He could be dead. Turned-to-ashes dead."

Deagan snorted. "He is one of the Aged."

"The Aged can die. Maybe he…"

A car turned onto our road. I noticed the thin bar of lights on its roof a moment before they began to flash blue and red.

"No," I breathed.

"What was that?" Deagan asked.

The patrol car pulled behind me.

"Shit!"

"Kennedy?"

In my rearview mirror, the cop exited his vehicle and started to walk my way.

"It's a cop," I said. "Don't move. Don't say a word."

Was I parked on a private road? Did I have a taillight out? I hadn't done anything wrong.

"What strange timing," Deagan commented.

I wanted to pop the trunk again except that would be bad. Really bad.

I needed to get it together. Panicking wouldn't do anything except raise the cop's suspicions.

As discreetly as possible, I slipped on the cardigan I kept in my car, covering the bandage that wrapped my left arm.

The officer stopped outside my door.

I lowered the window down and gave him a bright smile. "Hi. I think I made a wrong turn. My cell isn't getting good reception. Can you tell me how to get to Gatlinburg?"

He studied me behind his aviator glasses, then bent down to look inside the car.

"License and registration," he said when he straightened.

I didn't breathe. I just handed him what he'd asked for and waited for him to tell me all was good.

"Ma'am. I need you to step out of the vehicle."

"Excuse me?" I said in the politest voice I could manage.

"Out of the vehicle now, ma'am." He stepped back to give me room to open my door.

His hand rested on the grip of his gun. He was serious. He was asking me to exit my car.

"Did I do something wrong?"

"I won't ask again."

What the hell? I hadn't done anything. At least, I hadn't done anything he could possibly know about. There was no reason for this.

Arguing with a cop would get me nowhere, though, so I opened my door and stepped outside.

"Pop the trunk."

"The trunk?" My voice was too high, but what was going on here? He was too aggressive, too specifically inquisitive. "What are you looking for"—I peered at his badge—"Officer Tanner?"

His face was chiseled from stone. "We received a call that a vehicle matching this description has a corpse wrapped in blankets."

My body temperature dropped ten degrees. Who the fuck called that in?

"I…" I cleared my throat. "You think I have a body back there?"

"Open the trunk, ma'am."

"There's nothing back there. Just some old blankets. For emergencies. It gets cold in the mountains."

"Open it, or I'll do it for you."

I was so screwed. What was I going to do? If he saw Deagan…

If he saw Deagan, the vampire would scream and burn and go poof. How the hell would I explain that?

"Hands on the vehicle," Officer Tanner said.

"What?" I squeaked.

He took out his handcuffs.

"Okay! Okay. I'll open it."

He kept the cuffs in hand. Waited.

I reached inside the car and pulled the lever.

Tanner stepped toward the trunk and lifted it up.

No screams split the air.

I walked to the back, stared down at the blankets.

"See," I said. "Nothing. Just blankets—"

"There is someone back here, Officer Tanner," Deagan said, "but as you can hear, I am quite alive."

Tanner wrapped his hand around his gun, one impulse away from pulling it out. "Get out of the vehicle."

*Oh God. Oh God. Oh God.*

I scanned the woods on either side of the gravel road, searching for something. I didn't know what.

"I would love to, Officer," Deagan said. "However, I have a rather severe sun allergy. For health reasons, I must decline."

"Get out, now." Tanner raised his voice, making it even more authoritative, more threatening. This was out of control.

Deagan sighed. "Very well."

The blankets moved. Deagan sitting up.

A corner lifted.

Two hands darted out.

It happened so fast I couldn't shout a warning. The cop couldn't draw his weapon.

One second, Tanner stood there. The next he was beneath the blankets, yelling and fighting.

"Deagan, no! Stop!"

I grabbed fistfuls of blanket and tried to pull it off.

Deagan or the cop or both grunted. There was a shout of pain, and the blankets went still.

Or mostly still. Someone was on top of the other person. There was a soft moan, then a sound that had to be Deagan sucking at the other man's neck.

"Deagan, stop! What are you doing?"

"I am subduing him, Ms. Rain," came his even reply. "Shut the trunk, please."

Panic gripped my chest. I pulled as hard as I could on the blanket.

This time, it slipped free, uncovering half of Deagan's body. The back of his neck smoked and turned red.

He snarled and yanked the blanket back, but what I'd seen was plastered in my memory. Blood gushed from the wound on the cop's neck, and he'd gone limp. Not dead—not yet at least —but I recognized the glazed look in his eyes. He'd looked entranced. Sated.

"Get into the vehicle, Ms. Rain," Deagan said. "I have him under control for now."

I closed the trunk, then covered my face with my hands and began pacing behind the car.

What had I done?

I'd saved a vampire. Now a werewolf was dead and a human life was at risk.

"Ms. Rain," Deagan said. "The sun exposure has weak-ened me. If Officer Tanner comes out of his daze, I will have to kill him. I trust that is not the outcome you want."

No. It wasn't. But how the hell was I going to fix this?

I fisted my hair in my hands, pulled hard as I walked back to the driver's side door. I needed to breathe. Just breathe and think. This… this probably wasn't as bad as I was making it out to be. There was a solution. I just had to remain calm and see it.

I climbed behind the wheel.

"You can erase his memory, right?" I asked. "You can do your thing, and I can drag him back to his car?"

"If this were a casual and consensual encounter, yes."

I grimaced. "But it was an attack."

"Self-defense." He sounded offended. "In these situations, it is best to turn him. We will have to wait for nightfall—"

"No! You're not turning him. He's a cop. He was doing his job. He didn't—doesn't—deserve this."

"If you have another suggestion, I am open to it, but these things happen."

"These *things* happen!" I wanted to pop the trunk and rip the blankets completely off him. Tanner probably had a wife. He probably had kids. He would definitely have friends on the police force who would notice his disappearance. If he vanished, they would look for him. They would investigate. They would trace everything back to me. They'd search The Rain and…

And everything would end badly. The stability of the paranormal world would be upended.

What were my options? Turning Tanner was out. Maybe I could talk to him? Explain things?

*Hey, Officer. I'm saving you from becoming a vampire, and oh yeah, they do exist. Would you mind keeping that a secret? Your life depends on it.*

No. I needed help. I needed…

I closed my eyes. Arcuro could do it. He could erase Tanner's memory. He was one of the oldest vampires on the planet, and while I might despise him, he would take care of this.

"We'll go to Arcuro," I whispered.

"Ah, I would not suggest that," Deagan said, his vampiric hearing picking up my words. "He will not like my involvement in this."

"*I* don't like your involvement in this."

"Arcuro is as likely to turn the human as he is to erase his memory," Deagan said. "And would it not be a shame to go through all this effort to save me only to have him kill me so soon?"

At this point, I wasn't so sure about the latter. The former? Arcuro would make sure there were no repercussions on the paranormal world. How he would go about doing that, though, I didn't know. If he found a way to turn or kill Tanner without adverse consequences, he would do it out of animosity for my helping the unsanctioned years ago.

I gripped the steering wheel and stared out at the gravel road. There might be an alternative.

"Could Jared erase his memory?"

"Of course," Deagan said. "However, I do not know where he is."

"I know someone who does."

I turned on the engine and put the car into gear.

I PULLED to a stop behind Nora's car and took in the two-story, white farmhouse.

It was in impeccable condition just like it had been five years ago when I'd been cursed with a group assignment with Nora and two of her friends. It hadn't gone well. Nora had ended up making out with the star of the basketball team, and the fourth member of our group rarely showed. After a week of attempting to get everyone to focus on our project, I'd given up and finished the thing myself.

It had been a relief to walk away from the house that last time. It wasn't just because Nora had smirked and offered to invite one of her boyfriend's teammates over for me to play with. It was a relief because Lehr was often there.

The boyfriend had been too busy grinding against Nora to notice her father pass by. But *I* had noticed. Twice, he had stopped at the edge of the living room. He'd watched his daughter for a moment, then his gaze had shifted to me. It had taken all my self-control not to squirm, to not show any sign that I had smuggled an unsanctioned to The Rain the night before. But Lehr's mouth had only quirked. He'd given me a polite nod, then without one word to his daughter, he'd continued on his way.

Werewolves were sexual creatures, but it was screwed up that Lehr wasn't worried about his daughter toying around with a human, that he hadn't even blinked when he caught her making out with a guy.

But he would become unhinged when he learned she was toying around with a vampire.

I didn't know what he would do when he learned a wolf had been killed at The Rain. Kill Sullens? It hadn't been his fault, but Lehr wouldn't see it that way. If the alpha was inside, I was screwed, but I'd heard he'd given this house to Nora and had moved farther into the mountains with the pack. I hoped that was true.

"Stay here," I said to Deagan.

"Where have you brought me, Ms. Rain?" There was a warning in his voice. Maybe a little trepidation as well.

He likely sensed Nora inside. As a naturally born werewolf, she was special, and I'd been told by other paranorms that she felt different. Unique. They were drawn to her. Fortunately for her, she happened to have the dominance gene, and she could more than take care of herself if things turned physical.

"I'll be back." I exited the Camry and walked up the stone steps to the wraparound front porch.

I stared at the door, willing myself to raise my hand and knock. Was there anything else I could do? Somewhere else I could go besides Arcuro's? I'd called my parents on the way over here. It had gone straight to voice mail every time.

My thoughts and emotions were too twisted, and I didn't have time to slow down, to think this through more. When Officer Tanner didn't respond to dispatch checking in on him, they'd send other cops. There would be a search. An investigation.

I needed help.

I finally raised my hand.

The door opened before I knocked.

The words I was going to say tangled on my tongue. Blake stood in front of me, wearing nothing but a smug expression and athletic pants. I'd known he had a hard, muscled body under his clothes, but I'd forgotten about the impact he'd have on the atmosphere outside the Null. The air heated and vibrated around him, around *us*, making me extremely aware that he was male and I was female, that he was dominant and I was… not submissive. But I could be, wanted to be, would be with him. His broad, bare chest blocked the doorway, and when he folded his arms and leaned against the doorjamb in that confident, sexy I-control-the-world way some men could pull off, the muscles in his arms bulged.

My brain stuttered, then restarted. The bedraggled hair, the naked torso, that cocky, satisfied look on his face…

Fury rocked through me. If Nora was sleeping with Blake, I would kill her. She'd convinced me she *loved* Jared.

"I knew you would come crawling to me eventually," Blake purred.

God. Why had I come here? This was a mistake.

I didn't know what he saw in my expression, what he might have sensed, but the arrogance left his face. With a bare foot, he nudged the door open farther. Nora rose from the couch in the living area.

She was fully clothed, thank God, and her hair was perfectly styled into an updo that looked purposefully messy and wild.

"Are you two sl…" Wait. What had Blake said? I'd crawled to *his* doorstep.

Nora reached the front door.

"This is your house," I said.

"I sold it to Blake a few weeks ago. That's where the money for the wedding came from." A small vee formed between her eyebrows. She scanned me head to toe.

I realized what she was searching for one second before Blake grabbed the cardigan I'd thrown on. He yanked it off my shoulder, ripping a seam and revealing the bandage wrapped around my arm.

I tried to pull free, but he was angry. The only thing he let go of was the thin shell that contained his power. Like in the forest with Keisha, the cloud-covered sky, the boards of the farmhouse, all the world bowed to his authority. Instinct screamed *run*, but if I did, he would chase me. I widened my stance instead, painted defiance on my face, then glared insolently into his eyes.

He stepped closer, glaring down. The atmosphere wrapped around me and squeezed, insisting I lower my gaze. I didn't.

"You've been in charge of The Rain for less than a week," Blake said, his voice a low rumble, "and you are injured twice. Your parents have been in charge over thirty years and neither has received so much as a scratch. What are you doing wrong?"

Everything, it seemed. Including coming to Nora for help.

"Nothing," I said. "Just forget I was here."

I turned my back on him and trotted down the steps.

"Why is there a vampire in your trunk?" Nora called out.

I froze.

"Who else is in there?" Blake asked. His voice wasn't soft, but it wasn't as bone-breaking hard as it had been.

I stared at my car. Where else could I go? Deagan's solution was to turn the officer into a vampire. Not only could my conscience not handle that, it wouldn't keep the police department from investigating his disappearance.

I was so fucked.

"Pull your car around back," Blake ordered. "I'll open the garage."

The door shut. Him going inside? Had Nora left too?

I looked over my shoulder. No, she was still there, staring at me with something that might have been concern on her face. She erased it quickly.

"Pull around," she said. "Drive off and we'll come after you."

Jaw clenched, I nodded and climbed into my car. I didn't have a choice.

Blake was waiting with the garage door open and his arms folded across his chest. He didn't move when I pulled inside, less than an inch separating him from my side mirror. I turned off the engine.

With a rumble, the garage door lowered, eclipsing the afternoon sunlight an inch at a time until it was too dark to see.

Too dark for *me* to see. Blake and Nora wouldn't have a problem adjusting. Neither would Deagan.

My car's interior lights came on when I opened my door. At the same time, someone opened the trunk.

"Finally," Deagan said. There was a rustle of blankets and a soft squeak of the car's shocks as he climbed out of the back.

Blake grabbed Deagan by the throat. "Who the fuck are you?"

Deagan snarled, kicked.

Blake launched him across the garage. He smashed into a workbench. Tools clattered to the floor.

Deagan rolled to his feet and crouched, ready to attack.

"Watch out!" Nora yelled.

A bang shattered the air, and the car lights clicked off.

Another gunshot. Then a third.

I dropped to the ground. The cop. Deagan hadn't removed his weapon, and the hypnosis or trance or whatever the hell Deagan had done to keep him compliant had worn off.

Curses and a scuffle. Other sounds I couldn't identify. I needed light, so I shut the car door, triggering the interior lights again. They were just bright enough to see the officer flat-faced on the floor. Blake knelt on his back and bound his hands.

Tanner turned his head my direction. Blood ran from his nose and crusted over the bite on his neck. He was pissed and scared, and he was staring straight at me.

The light went off again. Damn it!

I opened the car. This time, I looked for the light switch, spotted it on the wall, then hurried over to flick it on.

Nora stood over Blake and the cop, Deagan still waited, ready to pounce, and Blake... Blake had put a black hood over the cop's head.

Every other threatening look, every other glare he'd given me paled in comparison to the way he looked at me then.

"What the hell have you done?" he demanded. Blood leaked from a hole in his upper arm.

I stayed near the light switch, which also happened to be near the door. "Someone called the police. They told them I had a body in the trunk."

"You had a *vampire* in the trunk," he snarled.

The cop struggled beneath him, trying to shake Blake's hand off the back of his head. Or shake off the hood. Where had that come from anyway? Did paranorms keep a supply of black hoods stashed around their homes just in case?

"Why was Deagan in your trunk?" Nora asked. There was something in the way she said his name that made it sound like she knew him well. Interesting because Deagan seemed not to know her at all.

"Have we met, Ms. Lehr?" Deagan's words weren't quite a question, not quite a statement either. His brow wrinkled as he tried to work it out. "He erased you from my memory."

Deagan's brow smoothed. His whole face did. There was no way to judge what he thought of that, if he was offended his master hadn't trusted him or if it was par for the course.

Slowly, he straightened from his crouch.

Nora's accusing eyes shifted to me. "You went to Deagan."

"What? No. He was at The Rain. The wolves were going to kill him." Instead, a wolf had been killed.

I glanced at Blake. He didn't know yet.

"It's the week of the full moon," he said. "They had a right to kill him. If I'd been allowed to do a complete search of The Rain, he would have already been dead."

"Actually," Deagan said, "you are the reason I was still there. I fully intended to leave, but wolves surrounded The Rain. In a way, this whole mess is your—"

"Deagan," I snapped. "Shut up." I turned back to Blake. Braced myself. "There's something else you need to know."

"Oh." That single syllable came out as a slow threat, like a sword sliding free of its scabbard.

"My arm." I lifted it. "A werewolf attacked me. He… screamed." I could still hear him, still see him writhing on the ground. "He didn't stop. He was in pain, and he kept scream-ing. I couldn't stop it, and it went on forever, and the only reason it ended was because he died."

The words came out too fast, too breathless.

Blake stood so fucking still. "He died, Ms. Rain? Or he was killed?"

I swallowed. "Killed."

Slowly, he looked at Deagan. At some point, the vampire had drifted closer to me.

"It wasn't Deagan," I said.

"Was it you then?"

"No, and no one else is going to die today."

"I can't guarantee that," Blake said.

Chill bumps prickled down my arms. Blake kept his eyes on me as he took off the shirt he'd thrown on. He ripped it down its center, then wrapped it around the bleeding gunshot wound in his arm. It would heal quicker than my knife wound.

I concentrated on my breathing. With each exhale, I pushed away a little of my guilt, my fear, my frustration.

"Vampires?"

The whispered word came from Tanner. The officer had sat up. He faced Blake, his head still covered in the black sack and his breaths coming quick and shallow.

"Yeah." I walked away from the door to crouch beside Tanner. He stiffened when I put my hand on his shoulder.

"Not me, though. I'm human. This was a…" I grimaced. "A mistake. It shouldn't have happened, but you're going to be fine."

"It's daytime," he said.

"That's why he was in the trunk and covered in blankets."

"Where are we?" he asked.

"Enough." Blake's voice boomed through the garage. "Where were you pulled over?"

I straightened. "A little road near Cherish. I don't think it has a name."

"How long ago?"

"I came straight here. Fifteen, maybe twenty minutes."

He slipped his cell phone out of his pocket and tapped in a call. "Cherish Lane. There's a patrol car pulled off on a side road near there. Find it. Move it. Clean it. Take care of the electronics."

He lowered the phone, his eyes still on me.

"I should thank you," he said, his tone cold. "I have a meeting with Lehr tonight. Now I don't have to go."

Nora's gaze shot to Blake. "What?"

He held out his phone. "Call Jared."

Nausea tinged with regret churned in my stomach. This was why I'd come there. She knew where Jared was, and to protect the paranormal world, she would have to take us to him.

Her hands tightened into fists. "I told you. I don't know where he is."

"I told you, it ends tonight." He faced her. The garage suddenly seemed too small. "You will call him. He will erase the cop's memories."

"I won't." Those words were a struggle. Nora might be a dominant wolf, but Blake's power eclipsed hers to a barely there glow. A gentle puff of wind, and even that light would vanish like a smothered candle. "This is Kennedy's fuckup. Let her solve it."

"She came to us. This is her solving it. Call him."

Nora was using all her willpower to resist Blake's order. She loved Jared that much. I didn't like seeing the fear in her eyes. I didn't like the way she shook her head no, more in disbelief than challenge. I didn't like the pain this was causing her.

Blake advanced, and the three-car garage felt like a closet. Nora's eyes widened. She maintained eye contact but retreated, and I had to consciously tell myself to breathe. Even Deagan shifted his weight from foot to foot, sensing Blake's dominance, his power.

"Blake, please." The way her voice broke sounded like a heart cracking.

"The relationship is over," he said. "If Jared doesn't erase his memory, Tanner will lead the police to Kennedy. To The Rain."

"Kill him," she whispered.

"They will investigate his death."

"Then change him." Her eyes glistened. I bit my lower lip and looked away.

"It's two days until the full moon," Blake said.

Two days until a werewolf's bite would have a chance to change a human. Even if I could allow that, the police would look for Tanner before then. They might have already sent a car to his last location.

I closed my eyes. This wasn't how I wanted Nora and Jared to end. I wanted them to fall out of love, cancel the wedding, then go their separate ways. But Nora looked like her future, her whole world, was crashing in on her. She looked like she was *hurting*.

She was hurting, and I wanted to fix it. I wanted to fix the whole paranormal world, but every time I tried, it blew up in my face. That's why I'd stayed away from The Rain. That's why I didn't want to have anything to do with it now. Some things couldn't be fixed.

## 14

The Rain peeked over the top of the hill ahead, its small parking lot lit by a pair of streetlights that created dim circles on the dark pavement. It looked more foreign tonight, more like it was the home of somebody else and I would be nothing but an unwelcome visitor. It was partly true. Jared had taken up residence there. Nora wouldn't say why or how he was hiding; she'd only said things hadn't gone according to plan.

She sat seething in the back seat. She was pissed, blaming me, and I was okay with that. I could deal with her anger. I couldn't deal with her other emotions.

"There's a dirt road that runs to the left of the property," I said to Blake. "It leads to a back gate."

"Don't feel like dragging a cop through the lobby tonight?" he asked.

I didn't respond. He'd been in nonstop asshole mode since I'd knocked on his door.

Blake slowed, found the road despite it being overgrown, and we bounced over the uneven terrain. We were in Blake's Jaguar. It was a fiery orange and must have had every upgrade available. Such a stark contrast to his beat-up Ford truck. They were as different as his personalities, one hot and untouchable, the other banged up around the edges, broken in and hazardous.

Weeds slapped at the sides of the car, and it bottomed out more than once. Had I not been so miserable, so sick to my stomach, I might have found some satisfaction in the damage being done.

Blake pulled to a stop in front of a gate. It was wide enough for the car to go through, but vines and vegetation had wrapped around the metal in a suffocating hold that would be difficult to break. Blake could have managed it, but he killed the engine and walked to the trunk. By the time I got out of the car, he had Tanner hoisted over his shoulder.

Tanner struggled, but his efforts were weak, uncoordinated. He'd worn himself out, struggling to escape, and Deagan had taken a significant amount of blood. He'd wanted to come with us, but Blake threatened to kill him if he saw him again. I believed him. Deagan, apparently, did as well. He vanished as soon as the sun set.

Blake flung Tanner over the gate, vaulted over it himself, then wrenched Tanner back to his feet and yanked his hood off.

"This is almost over," Blake said. "You run or fight or resist in any way, it will be over permanently. Do you understand?"

Tanner didn't reply, but he stopped struggling.

"Walk," Blake ordered.

Nora jumped over the gate with grace and ease. I clambered up it, the foliage pricking my palms while the metal rocked and swayed beneath me. It wasn't half as sturdy as I thought it would be, but I managed to land on my feet on the other side. I jogged to catch up with the others.

We weren't in the Null yet, just on our property and out of

sight of the hotel and garden. We headed for the family cemetery. The Null wasn't a perfect circle. It was an irregular, oblong
swath of land that curved around a secluded gazebo, then
reached for the graves and mausoleum at the northern part of
our property. The headstones marked the edge of the magical
dead zone, and standing just behind the invisible line was Jared.

Even from a distance, he towered over the world. His
powers were stripped away in the Null, but he still projected
strength. He still had a presence that demanded attention. He
was dressed in black and stood unmoving. He could have been
a statue, carved from stone and placed to guard the souls of the
dead.

Tanner froze. Cursed.

Blake shoved him forward. Tanner took two steps, then
looked to the tree line.

"It's okay," I told him. He probably thought we were going
to put him in the ground with the other bodies. "We're erasing
your memory. We won't hurt you."

I hoped that was what would happen. What if Jared wasn't
strong enough to erase it? Usually, vampires only used that
power when they took blood from a human in a brief
encounter. There was nothing brief about our time with
Tanner, and he was hurt and bound. We couldn't erase the
physical signs of his abuse. How would he explain them away
in the morning?

Tanner looked at me with an expression that clearly said *Go
to hell.*

We kept walking. I felt sicker with each step. A nearly full
moon glowed behind thin clouds. I didn't want to witness this,
but I would. I needed to make sure Tanner made it through
this okay.

Halfway to the cemetery, my phone vibrated.

I slipped it out of my pocket, glanced at the screen.

It was Mom. She'd said she would call to check in after Turnover.

Now wasn't the right time to answer. I shoved the phone back into my pocket. I would call when this was finished.

We reached the cemetery. Jared's gaze slid past Tanner and Blake and locked on Nora. The world around us shifted. His expression softened, filling with love and longing and sorrow. It was the expression I'd seen on the faces of vampires who were witnessing the sun rise for the first time in decades.

My chest hurt. His connection with Nora was almost tangible. I hadn't believed that depth of love existed outside fairy tales. But they'd scraped the words from the page and wrapped themselves in the letters. They were the star-crossed lovers, and I was…

I was the villain tearing them apart.

That was how Nora had been treating me since we left Blake's.

Blake shoved Tanner to the ground at Jared's feet. "Do your thing."

The vampire looked at Blake, and his expression turned bored. Then, as if Blake wasn't significant enough for more than a moment's pause, he looked at me.

I didn't know who scared me more, the werewolf seething beside me or the vampire piercing me with a cold, measured gaze. Authority and intelligence shone in the eyes of the latter. Jared was one of the Aged, a vampire who had lived more than a quarter of a millennium. Blake was strong and lethal, but he hadn't earned his position as Lehr's second by living the longest; he'd earned it by outwitting, maiming, and killing all other challengers.

"Don't do this," Nora whispered. "Don't step out of the Null."

Jared looked at Nora as if he'd already lost her. "The Rains must be protected."

If I hadn't felt so sick and brittle, I would have snorted. The paranorms didn't truly care about us. They cared about the Null and keeping the secret of their existence. We were nothing to them.

"We'll find another way," Nora said.

"I am open to suggestions."

Nora's mouth thinned. Her brow wrinkled, trying to think of a better plan.

"Are you the only one besides Arcuro who is strong enough to do this?" I asked. That bruising gaze came back to me.

"I am the only one you can trust," he said.

Trust. I held back a laugh that would have come out deranged. The only thing I knew about Jared was that he belonged to Arcuro, he was one of the Aged, a killer, and impossibly, he'd been hiding out in The Rain. He was one of the last people I should trust.

"Then we str—"

"No." Jared cut her off. "It is too soon."

Blake's head angled slightly. Mine probably did too. Too soon for what?

"Then you won't answer his call," Nora said.

She didn't mean a phone call. She was talking about a mental one, an almost telepathic connection a master vampire had with his scions. Once Jared left the Null, Arcuro would feel him. He'd know Jared was here.

"He is my master," Jared said. "I cannot defy—"

"You love me."

"I do, but I cannot—"

"You *love* me, Jared." She held his gaze, and her determination and strength permeated the night air.

"Nora."

"You can resist his call," she growled.

He closed his eyes, and his jaw worked, clenching and unclenching. When he looked at her again, he pulled her close, then lowered his forehead to hers. He said something else, but his words were too quiet to hear. He pressed a kiss to her temple, then he stepped out of the Null.

Fear dug its fingernails into my heart. I stumbled backward as every blade of grass shuddered with awareness of the vampire. I'd thought him strong and commanding inside the Null, but he split the darkness like no other man could. He was *other*, a violent shadow on the world.

Tanner made a run for the woods. Blake caught him and slung him back to the ground.

"Do it," he snarled. He was tense, agitated. Yellow gleamed in his eyes.

Jared crouched in front of Tanner and locked his hand on the officer's shoulder. Tanner's eyes refocused, his expression relaxed, and he nodded as if he was remembering something that made sense. When he smiled, then chuckled, goose bumps prickled across my skin. It was like watching a movie where a child becomes possessed by a demon: the mannerisms were wrong. This was some caricature of the police officer, and all the details were filled in by a stranger's whims.

"Sleep," Jared said.

Tanner's eyes closed. Jared gently laid him on the ground. "He will awaken in a few hours."

I filled my lungs with air that tasted sour and watched Tanner's chest, assuring myself that it rose and fell in a healthy pattern.

"Thank you," I whispered.

Jared rose. Nora took his hand.

"Come back to the Null." She tugged.

He was facing away from her, so she didn't see his eyes close. I did and wished I hadn't. He wore the expression of a broken man. The power that had radiated from him in nuclear waves had cooled, diminishing into something tolerable.

He drew in a breath, turned to Nora, and kissed her.

I should have looked away, given them privacy, but I hadn't expected the kiss or the impact their fused auras would have on the atmosphere. Their bond defied the laws of physics. Their longing upended the night.

Blake snarled something under his breath and paced like a wolf on the edge of a cliff, eyeing his prey a deadly distance below.

Jared and Nora parted.

"He is calling, Snowflake."

She paled, realizing the kiss had been a goodbye.

"No."

She pulled on his hand again.

"It's one step, Jared. I can resist my father's call. You can resist Arcuro's."

"I love you, Nora." He took a step, but it was in the wrong direction.

"Jared." Desperation slipped into her voice.

He took another step away.

Nora's face hardened. "This is a choice. You are *choosing* Arcuro over me."

"I chose you over everything."

Without thinking, I grabbed Blake's arm. "Help her. Get him into the Null."

Blake's nostrils flared, the muscle beneath my hand flexed, but he didn't move.

"Blake—"

Golden eyes locked on me. My breath caught in my throat. Blake was a dominant wolf, second only to Lehr. He had the instinct to protect pack members, and Nora was hurting. He wasn't thinking like a human anymore.

I let go of his arm.

Jared looked at me. "Thank you for saving Deagan."

"You're giving up," Nora hissed.

Jared shook his head, still backing away. A vein stood out on his forehead, a sign of his struggle.

He started to turn, but his gaze caught on Blake.

Apprehension crawled up my spine. The night slowed, quieted. It was the stillness before a world-ending cataclysm.

Jared stared straight into Blake's eyes, a challenge no dominant wolf could ignore.

Blake lost his mind the same instant I did. I threw myself in front of him, knowing a fight between him and Jared would end in bloodshed and death.

Blake slammed into me. I hit the ground, him on top of me, my hands gripping his shirt.

He snarled in my face. Pushed up.

I rose with him. "Don't!"

I tried to cut off my fear, tried to stop my hands from shaking. He could crush me. He *wanted* to crush me.

I should have released his shirt and ran. Instead, inexplicably, I moved my hands to his face.

His jaw tensed beneath my fingers.

"I don't want you to fight," I said. "I don't want you to kill."

Rage burned in his eyes. They gleamed with threat, with the power and strength of a dominant paranorm. The wolf was in control, the man caged and absent. I was dead, dead, dead. Only...

A new horror clawed at my heart. If he hurt me, the treaty would kick in. He would scream like Honcho.

"Please," I whispered.

His growl rumbled through me. Then his hands gripped mine and removed them from his face.

The air chilled. The sound of crickets broke through the silent night. For a long time, he held my hands, his fingers digging hard into my palms. The storms in his eyes calmed. Not gone, just seething beneath the surface.

He released me and rose. I stayed where I was, giving him time, waiting until his breaths evened out, paralleling my own. My fear quieted one heartbeat at a time.

"You can get up," he said finally.

I wasn't sure I could. My legs felt weak, like I'd been swimming for hours and hours and had to finally climb out of the pool.

I managed it though, locked my knees, then scanned the area. Jared was gone. Nora was, too. I didn't know where she would go. She couldn't follow Jared. She wouldn't want to return to the pack. Not yet.

I looked down to where Tanner lay unconscious on the ground.

"I need to get him to his car," I said.

Something passed through Blake's gaze. He turned away before I could make out what it was.

I looked toward The Rain. It was a sanctuary, protection from Blake's influence. It was also the last place I wanted to be. I wanted to escape this nightmare, but it was something permanently woven into my reality now. None of this could be undone.

"I'll do it," Blake said, his back still to me.

"What?" I asked softly, returning my attention to the werewolf.

"I'll take Tanner to his car," he said.

I swallowed. Nodded.

Without looking back, he grabbed the officer, threw him over his shoulder, and walked into the night.

## 15

Raj dropped my car off. He also took away Honcho's body. I stood on The Rain's porch and watched him load it into the back of a truck.

The world pressed down on my shoulders. Usually, the Null only extinguished the paranorms' magic. Tonight, it felt like it crushed spirits as well. My chest ached. I was fatigued and hurting and hollowed out. For the hundredth time, I questioned every decision I'd made in the past twenty-four hours. If I hadn't saved Deagan's life... If I hadn't stopped on that side road... If I hadn't gone to Nora for help...

And what had I been thinking, anyway, reaching for Blake's arm like that?

What had I been thinking when I leaped between him and Jared? When I'd touched his face?

Shivering, I pulled my cardigan tighter around me. It wasn't enough to protect against the chill of the night. It wasn't enough to erase the feeling that I was being watched.

Well, of course I was being watched. The entire staff had to know about Honcho now.

And someone had called the cops to tell them I had a body in my trunk. Who the hell would do that? One of our guests? One of the staff? But why would any paranorm put me and The Rain at risk of scrutiny?

There was something in that line of thought, some clue my fingers were brushing against, that would connect the pieces together, but with Turnover during the early morning hours and everything that had happened since, I hadn't been able to find time for so much as a nap. My mind needed a reset, a good night's sleep so that I could think things through.

Instead of going inside, I walked to my car, dropped into the driver's seat, and turned on the engine. The wound on my arm throbbed, and my muscles were sore from being tense for so long. The drive to my apartment was going to take forever, but I'd never be able to sleep in a ransacked room and surrounded by paranorms, especially when one or more of them might have betrayed me.

Forty-five minutes later and half-asleep, I pulled into the parking lot. It was just after ten p.m. Carrie would still be awake. I had to pull myself together and pretend I hadn't seen someone killed or kidnapped a cop.

A resident in the building across from ours was having a party again. I had to park on the other side of the complex. I glared at a group of people heading into the apartment. They shouldn't be allowed to…

I slowed. Stopped. Squinted. Was that *Melissa*?

Before I could get a good look at her face, the dark-haired girl disappeared inside the apartment.

I stood frozen on the sidewalk. It was Monday, the day she said she wanted money transferred to her account or she would sue. But Nora hadn't been able to find her—she'd given a fake name—so why would she show up here?

That apartment frequently had late-night parties. People

went in and out constantly. I could probably walk in without a problem and…

The dark-haired girl moved past the window and turned to talk to someone behind her.

I blew out a breath. God, I was paranoid. It wasn't Melissa, just some other pretty girl with long, shiny hair.

Shaking my head at myself, I turned toward my building and climbed the stairs. Halfway up, whoops and hollers from above broke through the night. A game was on. Carrie and the guys would be outside on the landing, their chairs lined up against the wall of our apartment and facing the boys' open window. The guys would have turned their flat-screen around so they could watch the playoffs from the breezeway.

At least that part of my life made sense. That part was normal.

I climbed the last few stairs and managed to plaster a smile on my face.

"Kennedy, you're alive!" Carrie said when she spotted me, pouring way too much drama into her voice.

"I'm sorry," I said. "I was busy. And…"

Carrie's eyebrows went up, waiting for my excuse. My mind was mush. I couldn't come up with even a weak lie.

"Your parents needed your help?" she finished for me.

"Yeah. Sorry. I'm exhausted. I'm going to go crash."

"No," Carrie said. "Permission denied. We've barely seen you this week. It's seven minutes until game over, and we're up by three. Sit."

She patted the top of the ice chest that was pressed up against the decorated handrail.

John opened it and reached inside. "Last beer?"

Carrie plucked it from his hands before I could answer. "Nope. This one's mine. She can go grab that six-pack you've been hiding in the fridge."

She meant the boys' fridge. We never had beer in ours.

Alex threw an empty can at her. She swatted it away with a laugh.

Maybe this was what I needed, a few minutes with my friends, a few minutes to remember that not every part of my life was screwed up.

I opened their door and went inside.

The boys' place was bare except for a few pieces of furniture that looked like the discards from a Goodwill store: a broken-in leather couch, their semistable TV stand, and a coffee table that had so many stains on it the original color was a mystery. Their two-bedroom apartment was the exact same size and floor plan as ours, but ours was comfortable, mostly due to Carrie. She was focusing her degree on interior design; the boys and I were not.

What their apartment looked like didn't matter though. The important thing was that they had food. Their fridge was filled with it. And it wasn't just pizza pockets and ramen. John liked to cook. He made biweekly trips to the grocery store for fresh produce, and bright-colored fruits and veggies filled the drawers. He'd recently bought a slab of salmon that would undoubtedly be delicious when he cooked it. Plastic wrap covered a half-eaten quiche, and I was pretty sure another container held the lasagna he'd made Thursday night.

My stomach growled. When was the last time I ate? And where was the six-pack Carrie had mentioned?

"It's behind the orange juice," John said. "We were trying to hide it from her."

I looked over my shoulder. He had sounded annoyed, but he was smiling. He loved people digging through his fridge.

"Ah," I said. I took out the juice, and he reached in to grab the beer.

"Have you eaten?" he asked.

"Not recently." I gave him a smile that was actually genuine.

He nudged my shoulder with his. "Food is the way to a man's heart."

"The saying is the stomach is the way to a man's heart, and I'm pretty sure I'm supposed to be the one cooking."

"Oh, of course. I always forget about proper gender roles. Here." He reached into the fridge and took out the container I'd been eyeing. "This reheats well."

It was enchiladas, not lasagna.

"I'll take it," I said.

He grabbed a plate, added two enchiladas, then put it in the microwave before he turned his back to the counter to lean against it. "Everything okay with your parents?"

My emotions were torn between enjoying the sight of a normal, human man in the kitchen and closing myself off from the question he'd asked. I avoided talking about my parents and the hotel as much as I could. Anytime someone other than Carrie brought them up, I became suspicious.

I looked into his eyes, searching for some sign that he might not be human. His pupils weren't too big, there wasn't an unusual glint in his eyes. He was also smart, funny, and built exactly how I liked a guy to be built: tall, wide shouldered, and just muscular enough not to be intimidating. He was built a lot like Blake, actually.

I shut down that train of thought. I didn't want to think about him or Nora or Jared. I didn't want to think about anything related to paranorms or The Rain.

"Yeah. They're fine. You do anything fun over the weekend?" I asked, deliberately changing the subject.

"I was at my sister's wedding," John said.

*Of course* he was.

"Was it nice?" I forced myself to ask. I wanted to undo it,

the damage I'd done to Nora and Jared's relationship, to the chance, however slight, they might have had to be together.

"There was alcohol," John said, "so it was tolerable."

He had the cutest smile. I tried to concentrate on it, on his dark brown eyes and his words, but my mind wandered back to what I could have done to avoid the disaster of today. Let Deagan die? I tried to picture it, tried to see me standing there and watching the wolves shove him out of the Null. He was old enough that it would have taken a while. He would have burned for fifteen, maybe twenty seconds before he turned to ash.

The injury on his hand had been horrible. To see the skin on his face and neck and the rest of his body bubble up, to hear him scream... No. I wouldn't undo that decision.

The microwave beeped. John turned to take the dish out.

"It was at a hotel near Gatlinburg," he said. "Do you guys host weddings?"

My heart gave an uncomfortable kick. Was he fishing for information on The Rain? Or was he just making polite conversation?

"Not really," I said.

Paranorms didn't usually bother me here, but I'd been burned once. I hadn't recognized the supernatural allure of a guy I was dating. We'd made out, lost most of our clothes. Then I'd seen the flash in his eyes. When I called him out on it, he'd said he wanted a job. He needed the five-year reprieve from whatever he was running from, and he'd heard about me helping the unsanctioned. He thought I might help him. If he accepted a job with us, he would be untouchable for the duration of the agreement as long as he remained...

He'd be *untouchable.*

"Are you sure you're okay?" John asked, his brow furrowed.

"I have to go."

"What?"

I backed toward the door. "I'm sorry. I just… I forgot something."

Outside, I murmured another quick apology and a good-bye. Carrie said something, but I scrambled down the stairs, my mind focused on what I was about to do because there was a way I could get some answers tonight and mend a broken heart. All I had to do was give a vamp a job.

## 16

Arcuro's compound was located in an abandoned missile silo halfway between Gatlinburg and Knoxville. Arcuro had bought it sometime in the '60s and built a home aboveground and a deep, multilevel safe house in the colossal cavity beneath it. It took an hour to drive there, and if the moon hadn't been almost full, I never would have found it in the dark. Vampires weren't fans of landscape lights, and the tall trees and privacy hedges camouflaged the curved driveway to the house.

The white, two-story home had tall, thin columns evocative of Greek Revival architecture. Smooth stucco walls and decorative railing along the front porch and the perimeter of the flat roof made it look virtuous and dignified, like the home of a well-respected judge. But the verdicts passed by its master didn't follow the laws of the human world. This was a place where an old man's whims took precedence over the well-being and wishes of the people who stepped inside his door.

A wave of apprehension went through me when I parked in front of the walkway that slithered up to the front steps. It wasn't just because I was about to walk into the den of one of the Aged; I was fully breaking my vow. I was involving myself in the affairs of paranorms and interfering with their world order.

I turned off the engine. A part of me knew that I should leave, that I should forget about Jared and let Arcuro deliver whatever punishment he saw fit, but I'd been standing back for the past five years. I'd walked away from this life because I couldn't not care, and now some asshole had decided it was a good time to screw with me and The Rain.

I stuffed my phone and keys into my pocket and walked to the front door.

My knock disturbed the too-quiet night, and goose bumps leaped to my skin. Where were the chirping crickets, the croaks of frogs, the scurry and calls of the area's wildlife? Even the wind had fallen silent.

*Only the dead live here.*

That wasn't my thought; that was the compound's supernatural security system urging passersby away.

I knocked again. This time the door opened.

A tall, slender woman in a chic black jumpsuit locked a dark-eyed gaze on me. Her halter top revealed envy-worthy shoulders and perfectly smooth skin. She was gorgeous and classical, and I was suddenly conscious of my clothing. I still wore jeans, a T-shirt, and my ripped cardigan over the clean bandage I'd wrapped around my arm.

"Come in," she said.

Her voice compelled me forward, but I stood my ground and said, "I'm Kennedy Rain. I need to speak to Arcuro."

Her head tilted. "Rain?"

"Yes. Please tell him I'm here."

That unnerving stillness all vampires possessed took over the woman, making her look more like a model in a wax museum than a real, conscious, and animated person.

"You may leave," she said. It was a suggestion, a gift, a choice I was fortunate to be given.

"I need to speak with him and with Jared."

Her sculpted eyebrows rose. Another moment passed before she said, "Kennedy Rain." It sounded like she was tasting my name. "You are brazen, aren't you? Come in."

The door opened wider, and she stepped aside to let me enter.

I followed her farther into the house. If a human who didn't know paranorms existed entered this place, it would seem like an ordinary home. We passed through an empty sitting room and entered a living area toward the back of the house. A dining room lay to the left and, beyond that, a granite-counter-topped kitchen.

But people who were like me—people who had experience with the supernatural world—would note the accents of crimson that decorated the home, the pillows and rugs and throw blankets that would make it easy to hide bloodstains.

The vampire led me through a short hall and to the study set across from a small restroom. A man sat in a chair behind a giant desk. Another sat in a corner of the room, his quiet presence framed by shelves of hardback books.

"A new toy, Gloria?" the vampire behind the desk asked.

Irritation sparked through me. I had a thing against being treated as insignificant.

Gloria's smile showed her fangs. "She has requested to speak to Arcuro."

The vampire stood, walked around his desk, and looked down at me. "He is, unfortunately, busy."

"He is, unfortunately, in violation of the treaty." That might have been a technicality. Jared had been outside the Null when Arcuro called him, but he'd still been on our land. As a Rain, I had a right to finish my conversation with him.

The vampire's expression turned threatening. He stepped too close.

"Humans do not get to request an audience with Arcuro. If he wishes to speak to you, he will send for you."

Yeah. This guy was totally dismissing me, the puny human. The vampire in the corner looked bored. Gloria looked entertained.

"You must be daft, coming here as you are." His focus shifted to my left arm. His hand darted out before I could retreat, and he yanked my cardigan off my shoulder, revealing the bandage.

His nostrils flared, and his eyes became rimmed with a hunger that made my entire body go cold. He had a compound full of vampires to keep him sated. He didn't need human blood.

When his gaze shifted to my neck, I jerked free. "Should I look for Arcuro myself, or would you like to tell him Kennedy Rain is here?"

He went still. "Kennedy Rain?"

I smoothed down my cardigan, trying to hide the fact that my hands were shaking. "Yes."

He looked at Gloria. "You neglected to mention her name."

She smiled in a way that said the slip was deliberate.

"Take her down," the vampire growled.

The vampire in the corner stood, then pushed aside a section of the floor-to-ceiling bookshelves. He made it look easy, but the scrape and groan of the secret panel sliding open said it would be far too heavy for a human to manage.

"Lead on," I said, keeping my voice steady.

Gloria led the way down, down, down into the depths of Arcuro's compound. I kept one hand on the smooth, central column as we spiraled underground. Artwork added a beauty and sophistication that contrasted with the jagged rock closing us into the staircase. Sometimes, the path widened, revealing narrow crawlways or stalactites and stalagmites that were undamaged by the explosives used to expand the silo. Other times it narrowed enough to make me claustrophobic.

I'd been caving before. It was with Carrie and a few other friends. I recognized the wet-rock smell and the cool dampness in the air, but there was an undertone to the atmosphere, a menace that swirled through the air and caused a feeling of doom to cling to my skin.

*Like descending into a catacomb.*

I smelled something else. Something metallic—blood. God, it permeated the air.

We passed four tunnels, each a dim, rock-cut corridor with floors smooth enough to indicate they were worn down by years of foot traffic. Rumor had it the compound contained an underground pool and grotto, a recreation room, even a gym though the latter seemed unlikely due to the vampires' natural fitness and strength. Maybe they used it as a diversion during the day, or maybe they'd installed it for the few humans who served them. Either way, the place was supposed to be as self-sustaining as a fallout shelter.

We had to be fifteen to twenty stories underground when we spiraled into a large, open chamber. Three separate sitting areas hosted wooden furniture topped by white cushions. Given the vampires' eating habits, white seemed like a bad choice. Somehow though, the furniture and color scheme gave the area a sophisticated feel. It helped that thousands of books completely filled one long wall. The shelves were cut into the rock, creating short and unevenly spaced alcoves. It was strange and intriguing and it should have been listed as one of the most unique libraries in the world, especially with the way it was framed by two glass-enclosed wine rooms.

A rock formation rose up in the center of the room. In another setting, the formation might have been beautiful. Here it looked like thousands of knobby fingers were reaching toward the world above.

My heart thudded against my chest. My gaze swept across the vampires who lounged on the furniture. They emitted satiety and strength, and they would have had my full attention if another vampire hadn't stepped through a door to my left.

"Kennedy." Marco gave Gloria a vicious glare as he pulled me away. "What are you doing here?"

His voice matched his expression, incredulous and angry. I breathed easier, seeing a familiar face.

"I need to meet with Arcuro."

"Are you mad? Only claimed humans come down here!"

I pulled my arm free. "My parents have been here a dozen times."

"Not *here*," he said. "Only above."

He ran a hand over his face. He'd always been kind and composed, like when we'd crossed paths on Turnover. Now he was *worried*.

"Why are you here?" he asked again.

"Arcuro summoned Jared from The Rain. I need to speak to him."

"Jared is—" His mouth snapped shut. His spine straightened, and I felt his withdrawal in the way his expression flattened. He was no longer my old friend. He was all vampire.

"Good evening, Ms. Rain," a voice purred behind me.

Some people had the ability to command the world's attention when they walked into a room. Arcuro had that times one thousand. You couldn't *not* notice him. He was intensity and charisma and a promise of unending life, and if I moved even an inch, I wasn't sure whether I'd be rushing toward him or away. I'd never been near someone giving off this amount of pure, blatant power. I wasn't prepared for it. I didn't know if it was possible to be prepared.

He circled until he stood in front of me. Black shirt. Black pants. His body language was cool and casual with one hand tucked into a pocket. His dirty-blond hair was swept back in a way that made it seem like he was channeling a young Leonardo DiCaprio. His style, his presence, and the depths of knowledge and experience in his eyes almost hid the fact that he'd been changed two or three years before he turned twenty. Despite that, no one who encountered him would make the mistake of thinking him a true teenager.

"Master," Gloria said. "Kennedy Rain."

I concentrated on breathing in and out, in and out. It wasn't my fight-or-flight instinct I was resisting; it was a fall-at-his-feet-or-flee impulse. The push and pull made me uncertain. It made me forget why I was there.

Why *was* I there?

A frown creased my forehead. I was there to right a wrong, to claim a vampire—to claim Jared—and to discover what exactly was happening at—

I slammed a door on my thoughts.

Son of a bitch.

"Stay out of my head," I said, doing my best to control my tone. The treaty kept me safe, but I didn't want to anger one of the most powerful vampires in the world before I had a chance to speak to Jared.

At least, I didn't want to anger him again.

"My apologies." Arcuro's voice brushed across my skin. "It is a deeply ingrained habit to leaf through the minds of unusual individuals."

Leaf through, like I was a book to read. An object.

"I need to speak to Jared."

"Whatsoever for?" he asked.

I hated everything about Arcuro. I hadn't met him before now—Lehr had been the one to confront me in person about the unsanctioned—but Arcuro had sent messages to my parents, clearly expressing his displeasure. I'd built up an idea of who he was, what he was like, and a not so little part of me wanted revenge for hunting down the vampires I'd helped.

"I need to ask him some questions," I said.

Arcuro smiled as if I were a child. "Jared is one of the Aged. We do not tolerate questions from humans. Gloria, you may have your turn."

Gloria made a sound, something that was half astonishment, half anticipation.

"Thank you, Arcuro," she breathed. The raw lust in her eyes creeped me out.

I watched her stroll through the door Marco had entered. "Her turn for what?"

"Dinner," Arcuro said pleasantly.

My stomach took an inopportune moment to growl. The sound was loud enough to make Arcuro chuckle. With their sensitive hearing, every vampire in the room must have heard it. I should have eaten something earlier. The last thing I wanted was for Arcuro to get hit with a sick epiphany and invite me to a meal.

I swallowed, made myself focus. "Jared was on Rain property without permission. I need to know who helped him stay hidden."

It was important to establish that fact, that my parents and I had nothing to do with his presence.

"He will be questioned," Arcuro said. "I will send a messenger if anything of note is discovered."

"I need to speak with him directly. I would have already had my answers if you hadn't called him." I let suspicion slide into my voice, an implication that the timing of his call might have been deliberate.

"He left on his own accord," Arcuro said.

"He left because you summoned him, and he can't defy his master."

"Oh." The smile slipped from his face. "I believe he has been defying me. Repeatedly."

Undoubtedly, that was a reference to Nora.

Arcuro strolled to a small table near the rock formation. He picked up a bottle and poured a crimson liquid into one of two stemmed glasses. "Thirsty?"

It was *probably* wine, but still, my stomach churned.

"No, thank you."

Watching me, he raised the glass to his lips. Sipped.

"Nora is your friend," he said.

"No. We just attended high school at the same time."

"You have been seen with her, however. More than once. You are her bridesmaid."

"What?" I choked. "Uh. No. I am definitely not. I've had a few conversations with her, mostly to say that we aren't hosting her wedding."

"Because it would violate the treaty." He stared like he was waiting for an answer, but any response felt like a trap. Besides, it wasn't Nora and Jared who would be breaking the treaty by marrying; it was Arcuro and Lehr who would spill blood across our land.

"The treaty has served us well for almost three centuries," he continued. "If a vampire under my roof were to threaten the peace, I would be obligated to mete out punishment. It has served you well too. Without it, my vampires would rip you apart. So many want to. You are forbidden fruit, Kennedy Rain. Sweet and tantalizing. Do you agree, Marco?"

"Yes, my lord." He stood right behind me.

Arcuro was trying to spook me. It was working, but not in the way he expected. Marco was a vampire, a paranorm. He would do whatever his master wanted, and if Arcuro wanted him to hurt me, he would. My worry was that the treaty would kick in. I couldn't handle any more screams tonight, especially when those screams belonged to someone who was... not a friend but an acquaintance from the past.

Arcuro took another sip of wine, then placed the glass on the table. "Fetch him."

Marco bowed, then turned and exited.

Arcuro motioned to the nearest cluster of furniture. "Sit."

"I'm good standing," I said.

"Sit." The word came out harsher this time, an order.

Biting my lower lip, I walked to the nearest couch and sank onto the white cushion. Arcuro followed and sat in the chair on the other side of a low, glass-topped table.

He examined me. I emptied my mind and focused on the air I drew into my lungs, then the air I pushed out.

"My vampires tracked an unsanctioned to The Rain's doorsteps two nights ago."

My breath caught in my throat. It took all my willpower not to cough, not to blink, not to react at all. Was he toying with me? Testing me?

"And?" I delivered the single syllable with zero emotion.

His eyes narrowed just perceptibly. "You were there Saturday night."

Saturday night. That was after Blake killed Keisha and Charles. Raj had dropped me off at The Rain. I'd gone through the hotel's bills. Then I'd left…

No. Then *Christian* had barreled into the lobby.

But Christian wasn't a vampire.

"You must be mistaken," I said. "If an unsanctioned came to The Rain, I'm sure your vampires would have let me know."

"Perhaps they were aware of your past indiscretions."

I was so damn glad I was there. I was about to whip that pristine white carpet out from under his feet.

"Where are your parents, Ms. Rain?"

"They're on vacation." I was getting better at delivering that lie.

"They check in with you, I presume. Do they know you are here?"

"I haven't spoken to them since you summoned Jared."

Arcuro leaned forward. "You knew Jared was at The Rain."

"I—"

"You knew *why* he was there. You have communicated with Nora every one of the past four days."

"Yes, but we aren't friends, and I'm not—"

"And here you are, asking to speak with my enforcer." He sat back and crossed an ankle over his knee.

"I'm here because you summoned him." A bead of sweat carved a path down my spine. I needed Jared to show up quick.

"It is my right to do so," Arcuro said. "Again, you are interfering in vampire matters. You are interfering with the pack as well. How will Lehr react when he learns his daughter has been fucking my vampire?"

The crude word made me flinch.

"How will he react when he learns you have been helping her plan that farce of a wedding?"

"I wasn't planning her wedding!"

His eyebrows rose.

Damn. My composure was fraying. I had to hold it together.

"I was trying to talk her out of it," I said.

Arcuro gave a thoughtful hum before he focused over my shoulder and smiled.

Dread crawled between my ribs. I turned.

Marco approached with an almost unrecognizable Jared. He was a shell of the vampire who'd loomed at the edge of the Null. Dark circles swooped beneath his eyes, his lips were dry and cracked, and an ugly purple bruise extended from under the right side of his jaw all the way down his shoulder. His shirt was in tatters. Claw marks raked down his chest, and bite marks pierced his torso, looking like a macabre work of art.

He walked toward us. Sort of. His legs moved, but the only thing keeping him upright was Marco's grip on his arm.

*You may have your turn.* That's what Arcuro had said to Gloria. Jared had been served up, not just to her but to the other vampires in this room. That's why they looked full and sated. Vampires received more power from drinking from each other than from humans. Humans were empty calories. Dessert. Playthings. But older vampires? They were strong and seductive, and younger vampires craved their blood.

I met Marco's gaze, and I knew. He'd tasted Jared too, and there was no regret in his frigid, gray eyes.

I was going to be sick, right there on Arcuro's pretty white carpet.

"Leave him," Arcuro ordered.

Marco dragged him forward.

I wanted to steady Jared when he swayed, but it's hard to save someone when you're paralyzed by horror. Jared had been Arcuro's enforcer for eons. He'd killed and threatened and intimidated for his master. He was Arcuro's representative and one of the Aged—that almost untouchable group of upper-tiered vampires. They were old and powerful and cunning, and the only mistake Jared had made was to fall in love with Nora.

"Sit, Jared," Arcuro said, motioning to a chair.

"No." The word was a whisper. He didn't move. He stood there staring at nothing.

My heart tripped into a quick, stuttering panic. Jared wasn't supposed to be like this. He was supposed to be strong. He was supposed to be firm. He was supposed to help me return to the surface and move aside that heavy bookshelf.

Arcuro's smile was sinister. "But you have a visitor."

Jared's blinks were slow, the shifting of his gaze to me even slower. Recognition didn't come for several seconds. He licked his cracked lips but didn't otherwise move.

"Ms. Rain has questions for you." Arcuro steepled his fingers.

When Jared turned his head to look back at his master, his body followed, lurching left.

I sprang from my seat and caught his arm. He was too heavy and too off-balance. I couldn't keep him upright; I could only guide his fall into the chair he'd refused to sit in.

Gracelessly, I fell over his lap. His hand tangled in my hair, and he grabbed the arm that wasn't trapped underneath me.

I thought the way he held me was an accident, but when I tried to rise, he pulled on my hair, wrenching my head to the side.

"*Stop!*" Arcuro's order snapped through the air.

Jared's hand loosened, and I was able to look up. He was looking down at me, his eyes hungry and his lips parted, showing a glimpse of fangs.

He was cold and depleted, and I was warm and alive.

The side of my neck throbbed. It wasn't an unpleasant feeling.

Arcuro yanked me away.

"Bleed a Rain and there will be war," he snarled. "That bitch you bedded will join her pack in retribution. They will hunt us all."

Life sparked back into Jared's eyes. He met his creator's gaze, then slowly, carefully he rose from the chair.

He might as well have said fuck you. Arcuro saw it in his eyes too. This was going to turn into a repeat of Keisha's killing, but instead of Blake slaughtering someone in his wolf form, Arcuro would rip Jared's throat out with his hand. Rumor had it he'd done it in the past to more than one vampire.

It was time to get out of there. If Jared was going to come with me, we had this one chance. He might not be cognizant or quick enough. He might not understand at all.

"Jared." I waited until his eyes settled on me. "I offer you employment at The Rain."

Silence for one second. Then for two. Then—

"I accept."

"No!" Arcuro roared. He snarled, showing his elongated fangs, and grabbed Jared. He shook him, and Jared's head bobbed and lolled. "No. Take it back."

Jared managed to keep his head straight long enough to growl out, "No."

Arcuro threw him across the room. *All* the way across it. He slammed against the glass enclosing one of the wine alcoves. It shattered. So did an uncountable number of bottles.

If he'd been human, he'd be dead.

I stared at him, willing him to get up, to move, because if we didn't get aboveground before sunrise, he was toast.

*Come on, Jared.*

Arcuro spun toward me.

"You," he hissed. "You have made a terrible mistake. It should be a *fatal* one, manipulating your way into my compound for *this*. For *him*."

He stalked toward me.

I almost took a step backward, almost let him see my fear, but I'd committed to this course of action before I arrived. There was no undoing this.

"What position?"

I blinked, unsure if I heard Arcuro's question correctly.

"What?" My stomach felt more empty, more hollow, like I might cave in on myself.

"What. Position."

"He's… a chef," I said.

"A chef." The two words were a mocking snarl.

"Yes," I said, doubling down. "We're expanding our menu."

Among the broken glass and splash and puddles of wine, Jared found the energy to lift his head and look at me as if I'd lost my mind. Maybe I had. The only thing vampires hungered for was blood and sex.

"Morning will be here soon. We should go."

Arcuro studied me, and every cell in my body screamed to run. He sensed it, my fear. He seemed to drink it in. He swirled it like the first taste of a highly rated wine and came to a decision.

"You are an interesting thing," he said finally. "Very well. Five years is a blink of time. I will be waiting. If he lasts that long. And when your parents return, child, we will have words."

# 17

I WAS ESCORTING A CORPSE UP THE STAIRS.

Sweat saturated my shirt. My back ached, and my knees and shins were bruised and scraped from hitting the steps so many times. Even my hands hurt, raw and sore from bracing against the rock.

Jared slipped. His chin clipped an edge of stone.

He pushed himself up, climbed another step, his face tilted upward toward the life—the woman—he'd left behind.

I needed information from him, but that wasn't the only reason I'd come to Arcuro's compound. I came for the moment Jared and Nora had shared, that connection that had snapped between them under the cloud-obscured moon. It had been discolored by anguish and fear, but their love had been tangible. So had the heartbreak that followed.

It shouldn't be that way. They should be allowed to be together.

I placed Jared's arm over my shoulder.

We swayed up the steps, crawling more than climbing. At this rate, we might not make it to the surface by morning.

Arcuro must have used some unheard-of vampiric magic to double the depth of his compound.

My knee buckled and slammed into the rock. Again.

Wincing, I tried to rearrange Jared's arm. He didn't move. His gaze had locked onto my leg.

I looked down to the rip in my jeans. Blood welled from the cut on my knee. It wasn't much, but Jared was completely fixated on the wound.

A predator shone in his eyes.

I tightened my grip on his arm, this time to hold him away instead of to help him climb. The treaty protected me, but he was depleted and starved. How long would Arcuro's words stay in his mind? How long would he remember I was untouchable?

A sharp clap reverberated through the air when I slapped him, knocking him to his ass four steps below.

"I've made it twenty-two years without being bitten by a vampire," I said. "I plan to make it at least twenty-two more."

He blinked in shock. I doubted he'd been knocked on his ass once in the past century.

His expressions smoothed. "Foolish then, to come to the compound."

The words cost him. He slanted left.

I grabbed his arm, then pushed him against the central spiral. I shook him until his eyes refocused.

"We're almost there," I said. "You can make it a little farther."

"We're not halfway."

I wanted to slap him again. We had to be halfway. We'd been climbing for half an hour. Yes, we were slow, but it hadn't taken more than ten minutes to descend. If he was right, though...

I looked up at the endless spiral.

"Can you call for help?"

"I have been declared livestock. No vampire will acknowl-
edge me." His eyelids fought gravity. Closed.

Freaking fantastic.

He had to be wrong. We had to be close to the surface. We
just had to keep going, one step at a time. He could do it. I
could do it.

"Come on." I hooked his arm over my shoulder again.

My legs burned. My lower back felt ready to crack, but I
kept my focus on the steps. Kept going. Kept counting. Jared
hadn't given up. As long as he didn't lie down defeated on the
stairs, I wouldn't either.

I didn't know how much time passed before we reached the
door. I would have kissed it if I hadn't remembered the heavy
grating noise it had made when the vampire slid it aside.

I lowered Jared down, then grabbed the metal bar that
looked like a handle. It took me putting all my weight behind it
to get it to move. I heard something slide, a bolt maybe, but the
door didn't budge.

I drew in two deep breaths, then *pushed*.

Still nothing.

I kept trying. Each attempt was weaker than the last. There
had to be vampires on the other side. They were probably
laughing at my pitiful efforts.

I looked at the vampire wasting away at my feet. He was on
all fours, trying to rise even though he no longer had enough
strength. He was our only hope of getting out of there before
dawn.

Pushing myself away from the door, I scooted down until I
was level with Jared. I needed him to be stronger. Gripping
both his shoulders, I squeezed until he focused on me.

"Jared, listen. *Listen!* We're at the surface. We just need to
open this door. It's too heavy for me to do alone. I need your
help. Do you understand? If we get this door open, you can see
Nora again."

His eyes dilated when I said her name. A moment passed, then his head lowered in what I took to be a nod.

I helped him to his feet, then up the steps to the door.

He put his hands on the bar. Looked at me.

I'm not sure what passed through his gaze then. Confusion and despair tinted with hope? It was a jumble of emotions he snuffed out when he leaned into the handle.

I leaned too, my hands just below his, pushing with all my human strength. It had to be enough. We had to move the damn door.

The screech that filled the stairwell stabbed into my brain.

It moved! Just an inch but we could get our fingers in the crack. It gave us more leverage. I braced against the wall and pushed again.

Two more inches.

From the desk in the study, a vampire watched. It was the same one who had been there when I went down.

*Screw you, asshole*, I thought, and the door moved again.

That glimpse of escape, of freedom, must have reinvigorated Jared. He shoved the door open the rest of the way.

The vampire at the desk watched warily. I bit the inside of my cheek and concentrated on getting out of the room, then to the front door, then off the porch and onto the dew-covered ground.

Either the fresh air or the threat of morning spurred Jared on. He carried me to my car more than I carried him. We both opened the doors, collapsed into our seats, then we just sat there breathing.

A minute passed. Then another and another. I wanted to close my eyes and let the time tick by, but I couldn't rest yet. Sunrise was less than an hour away. I had to get Jared into the Null.

I started the engine and drove away from Arcuro's compound.

Halfway to The Rain, Jared mumbled, "Deagan."

I intended to ignore him, thinking he was talking in his sleep, but then he placed a hand on my leg.

"Stop," he said.

"What—"

Someone stepped into the middle of the road.

I slammed on the brake. The Camry swerved, fishtailing left then right before it skated off the road, lurching over rough ground until it came to a stop.

The headlights blazed on a tree a few inches in front of the bumper. I stared at it, my exhaustion too great to fully realize how close I'd come to slamming into it.

The passenger door opened. Deagan leaned down to peer inside.

"Ms. Rain," he said. "You are pleasantly reckless."

My mind scraped up enough energy to grind out, "You stepped in front of my car."

His head tilted. "Would you have seen me if I'd remained on the roadside?"

"I would have hit you if Jared hadn't said something."

"I assure you my reflexes are far more speedy than that." He knelt, then redirected his attention to Jared. His mouth turned down like he tasted something sour. "He is vile, my lord. You should skewer him."

"He is my master," Jared said. I couldn't interpret the emotion behind those words.

Deagan *tsked*, took off his embroidered cloak, then rolled up the sleeve of his shirt.

Jared moved with more speed than I'd seen from him that night. His teeth pierced Deagan's skin, and power writhed through the air.

I *yearned*. There was no other word to describe it. I'd never been this close to a feeding vampire. I'd definitely never sat two feet away from one of the Aged who was doing nothing to control the pheromones he was emitting. Even Deagan seemed overtaken, a quiet, satisfied noise escaping his lips when he cupped the back of Jared's head, holding him to his arm.

I'd used all my willpower, carrying Jared upstairs. I had nothing left to resist the pull of the two vampires. Heat shot through my body, and my pulse throbbed in my neck.

I wanted Jared at my throat.

Shit!

I fumbled for the door handle. Escaped to the roadside.

On hands and knees, I dragged fresh air into my lungs, trying to erase the invigorating scent of pheromones. It took close to a minute to regain some semblance of control. I leaned my back against the Camry and looked up to the faint glow on the horizon.

Jared didn't have much time.

"You may return, Ms. Rain," Deagan said. His voice was a purr along my skin.

I gritted my teeth, then turned to glare at him over the roof of the car. "What the hell was that?"

"What do you mean?" He rolled down his sleeve.

"You did… *that*." I waved my hand in a gesture that was meant to encompass him and Jared.

"What did you expect? He was blood starved. Only his age and self-control kept his teeth from your neck."

My pulse throbbed again, and Deagan's gaze went to my throat. He seemed to be seeing me—or rather, my reaction—for the first time. "Oh. Well, perhaps I should have asked you to leave first."

"Perhaps!"

"He is old. Sometimes I forget—"

"Deagan," Jared called.

Deagan pressed his lips together, then knelt out of sight to speak to his master.

I jerked open my door.

"Gather the others and run," Jared said to Deagan.

"Jared—"

"Run. Arcuro may not be able to touch me at The Rain, but he will make me suffer. If he does not kill you, he will override our bond. He will hurt you and everyone connected to me."

"We will not run," Deagan said, anger eclipsing his usually jaunty tone.

*"You will."*

Deagan's nostrils flared. I felt the command in Jared's words as clearly as his scion must have. I tried to ignore the pull, tried to ignore *him*, but pheromones still filled the car, and the light from the radio highlighted all the reasons Nora was attracted to the vampire. His chest was smooth and toned and his shoulders powerful despite what had been done to him. I locked my eyes on his neck so my gaze wouldn't travel down. Blood had crusted over the scattered bite wounds, and the bruising looked lighter than it had before. That was either a trick of the light or Deagan's blood was already helping Jared heal.

Deagan's gaze shifted to me. "Ms. Rain, take care. He will not die, but he is not well. He did not take enough to fully restore himself."

"Go, Deagan," Jared ordered.

"My lord." The vampire bowed, then retreated to the woods where he must have had a car or a shack or some deep, dark hole to hide in. I didn't care where he ended up. I was done worrying about him turning to ash.

Jared closed his door.

"He's concerned about you," I said.

"Deagan likes to talk."

"Will Arcuro really send vampires to kill your people?"

"Drive."

"Could you kill him?"

Again, some unidentifiable emotion passed through his gaze.

"A scion does not kill his master," he said. *"Drive."*

I waited a few seconds before I put the car into gear. Then I pulled back onto the road. "But *could* you? When you erased Tanner's memories, you were powerful. Arcuro was too but… not always." I hadn't felt like dropping to my knees the entire time I was down there. At times, Arcuro had felt faded.

Jared stared out at the road. "For a human, you are sensitive to our power."

"I went to school with Nora," I said. "I also had a habit of standing outside the Null at Turnover. I liked to guess who outranked whom when our guests left. I was good at it."

"Arcuro dims his aura," Jared said. "If we flaunted our power, we would lure every human and vampire in the region to us."

"Are you dimming yours now?"

He snorted. "No. I am this weak at present. Why did you risk coming to the compound?"

I turned onto the road that led to the hotel. "I need to know who helped you hide at The Rain and if you had anything to do with the ransackings."

"I remained unseen," he said.

"That's not helpful."

He stared out the windshield.

"How did you hide?" I pressed. *"Where* did you hide? You are human at The Rain. You had to eat. Someone had to help you."

It was like I hadn't said a word.

I should pull over, let the pressure of the rising sun force answers from him.

"She will not come back to me," Jared said softly.

Was that an answer? I glanced his way. He was slouched in his seat, the elbow he'd propped on the armrest the only thing keeping him upright.

"If that's true," I said, "I wasted my time breaking you out of Arcuro's compound."

He stared blankly at the road.

"That was a joke," I said. "She'll come back."

"I stepped out of the Null, knowing what would happen. Nora will not forgive me."

"You didn't have a choice."

"I did not look hard enough. I saw only the end of us. The end of everything."

"You knew Arcuro would…" How had he put it? "… declare you livestock?"

"Yes."

"Deagan's right. He's vile."

"It is his right."

"Bullshit."

"It is his right," he repeated. His tone said to drop it, that Arcuro had done something acceptable, something Jared himself would have done if someone had defied him. Maybe Jared *had* done it before, declared a vampire livestock. He'd drained one as punishment. I'd be naive to believe that was the only time he'd killed someone.

"If I had looked past the inevitable," he said, "I might have created another option. You created one."

He grew quiet again, and my eyes grew heavy. Just a little farther. I would make it. I'd drag him inside The Rain, then I'd crawl into bed.

"You should not have gone to the compound," he said. "It has not benefited you, and without Nora…"

When you scraped off the weight of his hundreds of years of existence as a vampire, he was as human as any of us. He'd let emotion crack his cold facade, something I'd bet hadn't happened in decades. Nora was hurt and angry now, but he still wasn't looking past what he saw as inevitable. He didn't see the way to create a future with her.

"If you love her," I said, "you'll shatter for her. Then you can pick up the pieces together."

One day, when I had enough sleep and a big city between me and The Rain, I was going to look back on the past few days and figure out exactly when I'd stopped being Nora's enemy.

---

THE RAIN STRETCHED into the sky, blocking the view of the pinkening horizon. We'd cut it close. Jared was sweating. Another ten minutes and he'd burn.

I turned onto the narrow strip of cement that led to the entrance on the east side of the building. It was the same door Deagan and I had exited yesterday. It felt like decades had passed since I'd saved his ass. It felt even longer since I'd scoured the property, looking for Jared.

He opened his door. I hurried to get out, too, and beat him to the entrance. The back hallway didn't get much traffic, but I wasn't ready for the staff to see Jared. I needed to think about what I would tell them, and right then, all my brain could focus on was getting inside and into bed.

I cracked open the door.

"It's clear," I said and motioned for him to enter.

Jared stepped over the threshold...

...and dropped to the ground like a discarded rag doll.

His head slammed into the concrete floor.

"Jared!" I pulled him upright. He was even more pale than he had been outside. I should have thought about this—we both should have—but a half-drained vampire had never, to my knowledge, entered the Null. He was human now, with human strengths and human weaknesses.

"Jared?" I shook him.

"Outside," he rasped. His eyes weren't focusing. They rolled back in his head, jerked forward, then rolled back again.

I cursed, then dragged him back out the door, sharp spasms of pain shooting down my overworked back. I didn't have to move him far though. The second he exited the Null, he pulled himself into a crouch, carrying his own weight and holding himself steady.

Steady but unmoving.

I put my hand on his shoulder. "You okay?"

He lunged for my throat.

The attack came so fast I only had time for a short cry before my back hit the cement, knocking the air from my lungs. I brought my knee up to ram into his junk but didn't have enough room to make it hurt.

I went for his eyes. He knocked my hand aside and bit my neck.

My body jerked in pain then pleasure then both. The sensations wrapped around me, and I forgot to fight.

Jared's hand moved to my hair, smoothing it down in a gentle caress. He sucked and his cool skin heated. I needed to be closer, to give him more. Sustain him. Care for him. I wrapped my arms around him and would have murmured words of encouragement if a problematic corner of my mind hadn't been screaming *wrong, wrong, wrong*.

That warning wouldn't go away no matter how hard I pushed. It sparked into a memory: Jared holding a vampire in The Rain's parking lot, drinking from her until she faded off. Until she died.

I jerked out of the daze. "Stop!"

Jared's mouth lingered on my neck, but he no longer pulled at my blood. He remained frozen where he was. I did too. I couldn't fight him off, and I didn't know what to do, didn't know if I should stay still or struggle or scream for help.

And I didn't know why he wasn't writhing in pain.

He cursed, then rose off me.

I stayed flat on my back, looking up at him. His face went in and out of focus. I couldn't lock my gaze on him, and I was cold, almost cold enough to want his arms around me again.

A shiver wracked through my body, and he cursed a second time.

"I am sorry," he said. "I should not have… The Null. It made me weak. I… I am sorry."

I blinked, then my hand went to my neck. It was sore and wet and warm with blood.

Shock spread out from the center of my chest, snaking through my veins in frozen rivulets of ice.

Jared had bitten me.

I'd been bitten by a vampire.

"We must get inside," he said. "Sit up. Slowly."

He put a hand behind my back, helped me sit, then held me steady when I started to tilt over.

"I'm going to throw up." The world spun and spun and spun. I couldn't make it stop. I needed to lie back down.

"We must get you to your room. The staff must not see."

My stomach lurched, but nothing came up.

"I just need a minute," I slurred. I tried pushing him away so I could curl up on the ground.

His hand tightened on my arm. "My blood would help you recover, but you would smell like me."

"No one will smell me in The Rain." He really needed to let me go so I could sleep.

"You plan to stay in the Null?" he asked. "Kennedy?"

He shook me. I attempted to focus on his face.

He had spoken words. What words?

My vision blackened, then cleared.

He was still speaking but not to me. He had a phone to his ear. *My* phone.

I tried to grab it, but I had the coordination of a baby swatting at a mobile.

Jared turned his attention back to me. I couldn't look away from those eyes. They were a dark, deep brown ringed with a color I'd never seen before, a color that mesmerized me. A color that said *sleep*.

## 18

The two male voices were muffled by the weight of an ocean overhead. One man was cold and monotone, the other aggressive and angry.

"You violated the treaty," the angry man said. "You violated her."

"It was unintentional."

"What happened?"

"I was not prepared for the Null."

"You've been in the Null for a week."

"I left," the monotone voice said. "Then I returned."

A silence long enough to stretch across the ocean fell between them. I should wake up. I didn't have to get out of bed. I could stay cozy and just watch the men. They would have interesting expressions.

I managed to turn my head, tried to open my eyes. No luck.

"Don't touch her," Angry Man said.

"This is too slow. If she drinks—"

"Derrick will kill you."

Dad? He was too mellow to kill.

"Kennedy." I thought it was Angry Man again, but the voice had softened, and the touch that smoothed my hair back from my face was gentle. Tender even.

My arm itched. I tried to scratch it, but someone trapped my hand at my side.

"Shh," the man soothed. "Drink this."

He lifted my head, then pressed something to my lips. A sweet and tangy liquid splashed over my tongue, making my jaw ache. I choked and coughed and opened my eyes.

Christian wiped my chin with a cloth.

"You need to drink," he said, lifting the glass to my lips again.

"What are you…?"

Jared stood behind him, and my heart kicked my chest. I lurched up, memories of the past twenty-four hours slamming against my skull one after the other. Deagan. Tanner. Arcuro's compound.

The room spun. Christian held me upright. *Christian*, the paranorm who'd burst into the lobby the night Arcuro's vampires chased someone to The Rain. The paranorm Sullens and the rest of the staff loathed. The paranorm who was quiet and cryptic and a member of a species I hadn't yet identified.

"What are you doing here?" I rasped out.

He met my eyes and went still, his expression flattening so completely that I thought he must have been the monotone man. But the other voice, the angry one, didn't fit Jared. He hadn't been angry when he'd had to erase Tanner's memory. He hadn't been angry in Arcuro's compound. He hadn't even been angry when he talked about losing Nora. Jared didn't do angry.

Christian was still holding my shoulder, keeping me upright. I shoved at his hands, but I was uncoordinated and he was strong.

"Lie down," he ordered.

If I'd had the energy to do the opposite, I would have. But gravity pulled at me, and I sank back onto my pillow.

He straightened the IV tubing taped to my arm. That's why I had been itching. I was attached to a blood bag. It was taped to a hardback copy of *Where the Red Fern Grows* and propped against the wall on top of my headboard.

The sip of juice I'd taken turned sour in my stomach.

He set the glass of orange juice on my nightstand, then stood to adjust the book and nearly empty blood bag.

"Do this often?" I asked.

He looked down. "No."

He had definitely been Angry Man. He didn't want to be there. Not in that room. Not with me.

My gaze shifted to Jared. He looked at my neck, and I blushed. It was a strange sensation, starting at the place where he'd bitten and spreading quickly to my face, then to my core. I should be repulsed by what he had done. Instead, I ached in a not quite unpleasant way.

I touched my neck. My hand was ice cold.

"I'll get another blanket," Christian said. For someone who claimed not to do this much, he knew exactly what I needed.

"There should be a heated one in my parents' closet," I said.

He acknowledged my words with a nod, then left the room.

Jared moved closer, and it took a second for my vision to bring him into focus. That little effort made teacups spin in my head. I always hated those carnival rides, the way they made me feel off-balance when they ended, the nausea that clung to me the rest of the day, the headache that just wouldn't go away. I'd stop riding them when I was twelve.

"You are pale," he said. "I should have stopped sooner."

I rubbed my temple with my free hand. "You shouldn't have bitten me in the first place. You shouldn't have been able to."

He tilted his head.

"The treaty," I clarified. "When Honcho attacked me, he—"

"Honcho?"

"One of the wolves who wanted to kill Deagan. That's what happened to my arm."

We both looked down at it. Someone—Christian, I presumed—had changed the bandage again.

"Your blood is interesting."

I looked up. He didn't.

"Jared," I warned.

He blinked. "The wolf intended to kill you. I did not."

"You bit me. You drank enough for me to need this." I jabbed my thumb toward the blood bag.

"You would not have needed it if I gave you my blood," he said.

A foggy memory came back. He'd said I would have smelled like him. *That* wouldn't have gone over well with the wolves.

"My intention was to strengthen myself enough to slip inside undiscovered, a desire you shared, I believe."

"You could have killed me."

"I have more control than that."

"You had— So you're saying the treaty didn't kick in because you didn't *intend* harm?"

"Precisely."

"But it was harmful!"

He was unmoved by my objection. But, really, the intent thing felt like a giant loophole. A paranorm could reason something away as being good for me. And what had Blake said about it? As long as he didn't kill me or cause me permanent harm, there would be no magical repercussions.

I needed to read the treaty.

There was no sense in arguing with one of the Aged about

it though. Jared wasn't looking at me anyway. He focused on the window over my right shoulder, his gaze distant and troubled. Was he worried about his people? About Arcuro and what he would do for revenge?

Or was he thinking of Nora?

"You two don't match up," I said.

He blinked, then looked down at me. "I know."

"Was the wedding her idea?"

"It was ours both." He pulled up the chair from my desk and sat by my bed. "A coven-backed contract, executed before witnesses, was the only way to stay together."

"You sure about that? Because I'm not feeling very positive about magically enforced documents right now."

"Nora gave you the guest list. Many of the Aged were invited. Strong alphas. Leaders of courts and covens."

"I do remember thinking it would be a bloodbath."

A small quirk of the mouth. It was the closest I'd come to seeing him smile, but it was tinged with heartache.

"The more power present at a contract's signing, the more powerful the contract," Jared said. "We would have been inseparable."

His melancholy filled the room, and his gaze drifted back to the window.

"You can work it out with her," I said quietly. "She loves you. One moment of weakness won't change that."

His expression said it would.

"You're going to have to put effort into it though. If you don't want to do that, if you don't want to try, it's you who doesn't love her enough."

His gaze hardened. He might have denied my words if Christian hadn't returned with the heated blanket. Jared backed away so the other man could find an outlet close to the bed. He plugged it in, then pulled back my comforter to put the other blanket directly on top of me.

"Need anything else?" Christian asked, turning the blanket on.

"She needs sleep," Jared said.

"And Advil. My head is killing me."

Christian nodded. "Drink more of the orange juice. I'll check the medicine cabinet."

"You seem to know your way around our suite."

He hesitated, glanced at Jared. Something passed between them before he left the room.

"What was that about?" I asked.

"What?"

"That look. You aren't telling me something."

"He would prefer to keep it secret."

"I'd prefer you don't."

He returned to the chair. "You wanted to know how I remained hidden. There are passageways between many of The Rain's walls. They are narrow and dark, but they allow access to all buildings. It is how I brought you here unseen."

"No."

His head tilted. "Pardon?"

"No. There's no way The Rain is filled with hidden passageways," I said. "I grew up here. Believe me, I searched. This place is probably as old as you. I dreamed about finding hidden nooks and crannies, and I spent half my childhood knocking on floorboards and pulling out books in the library. There was no secret switch."

"They are not easy to find."

"Is there one here?" I asked.

"It is in your parents' room."

"They know about it?"

"It is their hotel. I would assume so."

He took the blood bag off the headboard. It was almost empty. Thinking about having someone else's blood in my veins made me queasy.

"With hydration and sleep, you will be okay," he said. "I will remove the IV."

"Have you done this before?"

"No. I take care of my…"

He met my gaze.

"If you call me food, I'll kick your ass."

"Prey," he said. At least he had the decency to grimace. "I do not usually drink from humans, and when I do, I refuel them."

He slid the needle out. A drop of blood welled from the hole in my arm. He wiped it away with his thumb then, after only a brief hesitation, wiped his thumb on the cloth by my bed.

"Sanitary," I muttered.

"Here's the Advil." Christian entered the room again and handed me the bottle. I shook two pills into my hand, then swallowed them with the orange juice, which didn't taste too tangy anymore.

"Thanks," I said.

"We'll leave you so you can rest."

I nodded as I looked in the direction of my parents' closet. My curiosity was kindled. I *needed* to verify that Jared was telling the truth. When he and Christian left, I could do that.

Christian followed my gaze. "Or I can stay until you fall asleep."

Heat returned to my face. Paranorms couldn't read minds in the Null, just expressions. Obviously, I needed to guard mine more.

---

MY PHONE RANG.

I put my hand to my head, trying to keep it from splitting open.

A long, blessedly silent pause followed, then the ringing picked up again.

I flailed for my nightstand. Found my phone.

"What?" I barked.

"Are you always this polite?" Sullens asked.

"Do you always call at"—I eyed the time—"three in the afternoon?"

His pause was long enough that I was hopeful he'd hung up.

"Your presence is required, Ms. Rain," he said finally.

His voice didn't drip with as much disdain as usual. I couldn't decipher his tone, whether he thought I should have handled Deagan better yesterday or at least handled him differently.

"How long will it take you to get here?"

"That depends," I said slowly, realizing he didn't know I was already at The Rain. "What is the size of the catastrophe today? On a scale of one to ten?"

"Lehr is here."

I needed a bigger scale.

I pushed up to sit on the edge of my bed, my body aching all over. When was I going to catch a break?

"Tell him I'm not taking visitors?" I asked.

"No. How long, Ms. Rain?"

I sighed.

"I'm on my way," I said, deliberately leaving out a time frame.

I hung up and tossed the phone back to my nightstand. An unopened Gatorade sat there, courtesy of Christian, I presumed.

My legs shook when I stood, and my back and neck hurt. It wasn't just from blood loss and Jared's bite. Those damn stone steps had kicked my ass last night. I never wanted to see another staircase again.

Twisting open the Gatorade, I headed to the living room.

The first thing that made me pause was Jared. He sat in my dad's recliner, ankle crossed over his knee, newspaper in hand. He'd found clothes. I hadn't noticed that when I'd awoken earlier—I wouldn't forget seeing a half-dressed Jared. The black slacks could have been my dad's, but I was fairly certain the black button-up wasn't. Dad was king of the Henley and, when he wanted to be embarrassing, the Hawaiian shirt. I'm pretty sure I'd never seen him in anything business casual.

The second thing I noticed was the living room. It wasn't exactly back returned to normal, but instead of books and electronics and knickknacks strewn across the floor, they were returned to their places or neatly arranged on the coffee table. Belatedly, I realized that my room hadn't been wrecked when I woke either.

"You cleaned?"

"No," Jared said. "Christian did." The downward twist to his mouth said cleaning was obviously beneath him.

He and Nora deserved each other.

"He left?" I took a swig of Gatorade.

"Yes."

"Will he be back?"

"Eventually."

"Do you always answer questions so succinctly?"

He lowered the newspaper. "You would like to speak at length about Christian?"

"No. I mean yes. I want to know how he knows about the secret passages." And I needed to see them for myself.

"I would assume your parents told him."

"That's insulting," I called over my shoulder as I stepped into my parents' bedroom. Christian had picked up in here too. That was just weird. Normal people—humans—would stay out of a person's bedroom.

"Insulting?" Jared stood behind me in the doorway, news-paper still in hand.

"If my parents told Christian about them and not me." I opened their closet door.

It was still a mess. My mom's shoes and purses were pushed against a wall. Her jewelry littered the floor, and my dad's ties were...

Huh. My dad owned ties.

It wasn't a big closet. Shelves filled the left wall, and half-empty clothing rods partially hid the back and right sides. I pulled on the shelves to make sure they were secure, then pushed aside the clothes and patted around on the back wall. It looked one hundred percent normal.

I knocked. Did it sound hollow? Didn't all walls sound hollow? Weren't there gaps for insulation and wiring?

Jared stepped to my side, then reached up and pushed at the top corner of the back wall. It moved half an inch, then clicked.

He made a *go ahead* motion.

Scowling, I put my hands flat on the wall, then slid it aside.

"Holy hell." The gap behind the wall was wide enough for a broad-shouldered man to walk in, and it stretched both ways as far as I could see in the dark.

The mini-me in my head did a happy dance. She'd always wanted to find a secret passage. She wanted to go exploring, be a pretend spy, hide gold and silver, and plan all sorts of mischief. Growing up among paranorms, I'd believed that anything was possible, that there was adventure and romance and magic everywhere, and that The Rain was a part of that world. It was a beacon of hope, a place that helped keep humans safe by keeping paranorms sane, and it was old and beautiful and laced with an enchanting mystery.

I stepped into the dark gap, eager to explore.

Jared's hand locked on my shoulder.

I whirled around, knocking it away.

"I have been instructed to keep you in bed," he said unfazed.

"Do you have a flashlight?" I looked at the closet shelves. My parents probably had one in here somewhere.

"I believe I spoke in English," Jared said.

I raised my eyebrows. "Is that sarcasm? I didn't think the Aged were capable of it."

He stared at me.

"I can't go back to bed." I slid the wall shut. I'd explore the passageways later.

"It is for your health."

"Sullens called. Lehr is downstairs. He wants to see me."

Jared went supernaturally still. That must have been ingrained in his muscle memory, carved into his identity so completely it wasn't vanquished by the Null.

"Want to go in my place?" I asked.

"It would cause difficulty with the staff," he said. Then, "Did Sullens say Lehr was alone?"

"He didn't say he was *not* alone."

We left my parents' closet and went back to the living room. I grabbed the Gatorade I'd set on the coffee table and took a good guzzle. Before I faced Lehr, I needed to get my head on straight. Get my thoughts together. I felt like I'd gone binge drinking and had somehow woken up still drunk and with a hangover.

Hamburger and fries. That's what I needed. My hangover meal. The kitchen should be open downstairs. Maybe I could take the secret passageway there, bypass Lehr, and get sobered up.

"I will go with you," Jared decided.

I snorted. "I was joking about going in my place."

"I am going with you, not in your place. Lehr will already know I am here."

"Then why didn't he ask for you?"

"You are easier to intimidate."

I crossed my arms. "Who pulled you out of Arcuro's dungeon?"

"Compound. He will want your permission to execute me. Arcuro will have already granted him his."

"You're employed here now. Killing you would violate the treaty."

"Not if you fire me," he said. "That is why he is here."

"He could be here to cancel the wedding."

Jared's expression darkened. "The wedding is already canceled."

"I haven't received written notification, and I still have the deposit."

He stared for several silent seconds. I refused to look away, refused to uncross my arms or shift my weight or give any other indication I was uncomfortable.

"You look grisly," he said finally. "Go restore your face."

Grisly? If I looked grisly, it was his fault. I'd dragged his ass out of Arcuro's compound, and he'd thanked me by sinking his fangs into my neck.

"If my day doesn't get better," I said, "you *are* fired."

I was joking. Mostly.

## 19

MY SHOWER TOOK LONGER THAN I INTENDED AND NOT JUST because I was procrastinating the confrontation with Lehr. The heat melted the ice in my body, and it took a good amount of scrubbing to feel anything close to clean. I'd sweated my way up more than a thousand steps and had been bitten by a vampire. I couldn't scrape the contaminated feeling from my skin. I wasn't sure I wanted to. If I didn't feel contaminated, I'd feel something else, and I was very purposefully *not* picturing Jared at my neck.

For the second time that week, I spread out the makeup I'd gathered from my mom's bathroom. It took twenty minutes, but I was able to give my face some color with the scrounged-up cosmetics and old samples, and I think I covered the bite mark.

I stared at my neck again, looking for a shadow. When I was sure I didn't see one, I arranged my hair so that it covered the area, then I stepped back into the living room.

Well over half an hour had passed. The timing should work though. That was about how long it took to drive here from campus.

"How do I look?" I asked Jared.

"You are not my type."

Huh. The Aged did joke.

"That's right," I said when he didn't look up from his news-paper. "You like your women spoiled, rich, and hairy."

The newspaper flattened to his lap. "Nora is not hairy."

"She is when she's a dog."

"Wolf."

"Does she shed on the furniture?"

Unamused, he set the paper aside and stood. "Are you ready?"

"How does *my neck* look, Jared?"

His eyes shifted from my face to the hopefully invisible bite mark. I'd considered wearing a turtleneck or scarf, but that had seemed too obvious. Lehr wasn't stupid, and if he knew Jared had been half-drained when he left Arcuro's compound, he might demand to see my neck. Makeup had seemed like a better bet. If it wasn't working, though, I'd have to grab a My Little Pony Band-Aid from the cupboard and lie my ass off.

Jared stepped forward. He moved my hair aside, then stared at my neck so intently my cheeks heated.

"Normally, I would feel kinship for someone I fed from," Jared said. "All I feel for you, however, is annoyance."

I scowled. "The feeling is mutual. But do you see anything?"

"No," he said. "It is sufficient. Follow me."

I glared at the back of his head when he led the way out of the suite like this was his home, not mine. Werewolves might be smug, but I'd rather spend ten minutes with one of them than two with an arrogant, Aged vampire.

Speaking of homes, where was Jared going to live? We never employed upper-tier paranorms. They never asked. They had power and people, and they wouldn't take orders from anyone who was younger than them.

The staff wouldn't want Jared in the Barn. Could he stay on the vampire floor in the west wing? He wasn't technically a guest, but the wolves would claim favoritism if we put him in a suite in the Catalan.

We reached the end of the hall and stepped onto the elevator. When we descended, my head spun, which was ridiculous since we were on the slowest elevator in the universe. It was a sign I wasn't one hundred percent yet. The other sign I wasn't fully recovered? I hadn't thought about the optics of stepping out of the elevator with Jared at my side. Not only that, our elevator was located in the back of the lobby between the check-in counter and the office. It wasn't anywhere close to the front door where I should be entering if I'd spent the night at my apartment.

The elevator eased to a stop.

I grabbed Jared's arm when he stepped toward the opening door. "Lehr's going to know I was here."

"Yes." He stared down at my hand.

"He'll think I deliberately delayed."

"It is likely."

"He'll interpret that as a dominance play."

His gaze slowly shifted from my hand to my face. His expression didn't change, but there was something menacing in that deliberate movement.

Of course. This *was* a play for dominance.

I let go of his arm. "I should have thought of it first."

He stared at me a few more seconds, then exited the elevator.

I strode out beside him until I took in the restaurant. My steps faltered. Half our guests must have been sitting at the tables or lined up alongside the bar. They weren't waiting for food or drinks. They were waiting to pay their respects to Octavian Lehr.

If I hadn't met Nora's dad before, I wouldn't have been

able to pick him out of a group. He dressed more like a high school basketball player than one of the most powerful were-wolves on the continent. Despite the athletic pants, fitted T-shirt, and running shoes, he exuded power and control. We were in the Null, but every wolf recognized his dominance and lowered their gazes when they greeted him.

They all owed something to Lehr. It was the only way to get on his approval list.

Lehr's gaze shifted from the wolf in front of him to Jared. Something banged to the floor.

The line of guests shifted away from the sound. Away from Blake. His chair was on the ground behind him. If Lehr had known Jared was at The Rain, he hadn't informed his second-in-command.

"Leave us." Lehr didn't raise his voice, but the wolves instantly cleared out. They passed Jared with looks of disgusted curiosity.

In less than a minute, the restaurant was empty except for Lehr, Blake, and another werewolf. The latter was a shade taller than both Blake and Lehr and looked like he belonged in a college fraternity more than a pack. All three men looked ready to murder Jared.

"Lehr." My voice was loud and strong, but he didn't glance my way. The last time I'd seen him was when he ambushed me at Gamecraft and Witchery. He'd used all his alpha-gene dominance to intimidate me into a seething silence. That wouldn't happen again.

"Mr. Lehr." I stepped in front of Jared, who'd stopped at the edge of the lobby. Lehr's gaze said to get the hell out of his way.

Blake moved forward.

"Don't," I said. Blake didn't look at me. Didn't take his eyes off Jared. He was all pack now. He'd kill if he had to, no hesitation. No regret.

Jared's hand clasped my shoulder, and there was movement in my peripheral vision—Garion placing his hands on the bar poised to jump. Sullens was nearby too. Even he was edging forward.

Shit. I hadn't thought about the staff getting involved.

I shook off Jared's grip, then shoved him backward. He actually stumbled, likely because it was so unthinkable for anyone to lay their hands on one of the Aged.

Well, he'd laid his hands on me first.

I turned back to Lehr and Blake. "No one is fighting in my hotel."

Lehr studied me for a long moment, then clasped his hands behind his back. It must have been some signal to Blake and the other wolf nearby. Both looked a little less likely to raze the building.

"Where are your parents, Ms. Rain?" Lehr finally asked.

"Vacation." The word came out more aggressively than I'd intended. I needed to dispel the tension here, not increase it, so I clarified. "They're out of town for a while. I'm managing The Rain while they're gone." I was using the word *manage* very loosely.

"And you've taken it upon yourself to shelter *that*." He turned his attention back to Jared. "You are a coward hiding here."

"I plot," Jared said. "I do not hide."

A strangled laugh escaped my lips. I couldn't help it. I was still a bit delirious from exhaustion and blood loss.

Blake glared, and the third werewolf's mouth tightened like he was holding back a snarl. My mom's words rang through my head: *Don't laugh around paranorms, Kennedy. Few things are more delicious than a good sense of humor.*

My sense of humor had helped me endure growing up around paranorms. Usually, it was appropriately timed.

"You are violating the treaty," Lehr said, anger invading his voice. "You have violated my daughter and my pack. If you aren't a coward, step outside."

"Killing you would hurt Nora," Jared said coolly.

"Killing me would grant you Arcuro's forgiveness." Lehr dangled the words like bait.

I would never understand paranorms' loyalty to their hier-archies, the way vampires would sacrifice for their clans and wolves would kill and maim for their packs. The other groups of paranorms would commit crimes too in order to remain included in their covens or courts or other organizations. Jared might love Nora. He might disagree with Arcuro and resent him for being declared livestock, but dangling his master's forgiveness was a temptation I wasn't sure Jared would refuse.

"You are here during the week of the full moon," Blake said from his alpha's side. "We have the right to drag you outside." His gaze cut my way. "Unless Ms. Rain plans to violate the rules again."

"He's an upper-tier paranorm," I said. "You all are allowed into The Rain no matter whose week it is."

Fury flared in his eyes. He had a reason to be angry. Last night was supposed to have ended the problem with Jared. Blake might not know details about what had happened later, but he knew I had to be the reason Jared was alive and here. "He has twenty-four hours."

"Five years," I said.

"What?" he demanded.

"Five years," I repeated, meeting his eyes. "That's how long his employment at The Rain will last."

It felt like Blake was ripping me apart piece by piece. We'd been adversaries before, but now we were something far, far worse.

"An *employee*?" Lehr sneered. Then he laughed. It was a cruel, derisive sound that bounced off The Rain's walls. Goose bumps prickled across my skin, and the hair on the back of my neck rose.

"What work could he possibly do here?"

He'd stepped closer to Jared.

I inched forward. "He's a chef."

Lehr's gaze shifted back to me. "Really?" He laughed again. "Blake, you didn't tell me how much Ms. Rain had changed."

Oh, Blake was furious. He stood there so tense he could have been chiseled from the walls of Arcuro's compound.

"I said she was perceptive and strong-willed. Not a child." It felt like he was stripping my layers away. The bite wound on my neck throbbed. A small voice in my head screamed that Lehr knew everything—the way I'd protected Deagan, the catastrophe with the police officer, my reckless trip into Arcuro's compound. Why wouldn't he know? Blake would tell him everything. Except...

Except my gut said Blake hadn't told Lehr about Nora and Jared. Lehr had found out another way, most likely from Arcuro. The master vampire wanted to destroy Jared. Why not recruit his enemy to take care of the problem?

"You will give me permission to remove the vampire from your property." Lehr said the words like I'd already agreed.

"Nope," I said. "I won't."

Lehr took another step closer. "You are dangerously close to showing bias toward vampires, Ms. Rain. You visit Arcuro, you protect vampires, you encourage my daughter to wed *that*." He jabbed a finger in Jared's direction.

"I wasn't encouraging her." At least, I hadn't been.

"Wedding dresses and cakes," Lehr said. "You've assisted her. You agreed to host the spectacle and to be her maid of honor."

Oh my god. Not that again. "I am absolutely not going to be in her wedding."

"There will be no wedding."

*Yes, there will be.* I didn't say the words out loud—I really didn't want bloodshed in The Rain—but that wedding now sounded like a brilliant idea. I should have seen it before, a way to show them they couldn't control everything in their worlds. This was the perfect scandal.

But my parents would never go for it. Stability was paramount.

"You hired the vampire," Lehr said. "Fire him."

"It's time to—"

"You came to speak with Kennedy," Jared said. "You have spoken to her. Leave."

"I came to rip out your spine!" Lehr snarled before I could tell Jared to shut up. The sudden viciousness knocked me back a step. I bumped into Jared's chest.

"Fitting that Arcuro would declare you livestock," Lehr said. "The scions you've created aren't much more than chattel either. Arcuro's disowned them. Lifted his protection. We're free to hunt them down. It will be fun to gnaw on their bones."

Shit. Lehr couldn't attack Jared without violating The Rain's status as neutral ground. But if Jared attacked Lehr…

I turned my back on Lehr, faced Jared. "You need to go."

Blake moved several paces to my left. The third werewolf stalked to my right. With Lehr, they formed a triangle.

"Now, Jared," I said, pushing, but this time he didn't budge.

"Your chattel don't get to hide behind a Rain," Lehr continued behind me. "Do you think Kennedy would still protect you if she knew all that you'd done?"

Jared stiffened.

"Does she know about the lives you've taken? The punishments you've dealt out? Does she know about—"

Jared lunged for Lehr's throat.

## 20

"Stop!" Nora's voice cut through the air, freezing Jared in place.

I'd say Nora's timing couldn't have been better, but that would be a lie. It would have been great if she'd intercepted her father before he ever reached The Rain.

"Dad," she bit out, her fury evident in each stride she took toward us. "You shouldn't be here."

"Daughter," Lehr said, deadpan. "Neither should you."

I tugged at Jared's shirt, which I'd grabbed when he'd gone after Lehr. No reaction again. His attention was riveted to Nora.

I glanced at Garion, who met my eyes briefly before refocusing on the werewolves. The only way I could force them to leave was by getting the staff involved. I didn't want to do that. I needed another way to prevent this confrontation.

My gaze locked on Blake. I'd somehow convinced him not to fight before. Could I convince him again? He'd said he'd kept knowledge of Nora's relationship from his alpha for as long as he could. They were friends. At least, they had been. He didn't want to hurt her and—

"You will return to the estate," Lehr said to his daughter. "You will be watched. You will be judged. You will fit back into your place in the pack, or you will be removed. Understood?"

What an asshole.

I must have made some noise because all eyes turned to me.

"And you wonder why she rebelled," I said.

The Rain fell more still and silent than when Jared had told Lehr to leave. The pack alpha took one slow step toward me, then another, and another. Each one deliberate. Each one measured. Each one meant to make me cower back in fear.

I held my ground. Sweat beaded between my shoulder blades.

He stopped an arm's-length away. That's when the third werewolf moved. His strides were fast and aggressive. I angled toward him, saw the look of determined punishment on his face, and—

Blake was at my side. He didn't say a word, didn't snarl or lift a fist, but the other werewolf stopped abruptly. His nostrils flared. Something passed between him and Blake. I would have sworn the former was about to take another step, but Lehr raised a hand.

"Luke," Lehr said. "Outside. Blake, a word."

Blake's gaze shifted from me to Jared. That's when I noticed the vampire's hand on my arm. Garion was now on this side of the bar, Sullens was only a few strides away, and the rest of the staff looked poised to move too. Poised to protect.

I pulled free from Jared yet again. I didn't like the way he was defending me, like I was somehow his responsibility. I didn't like the staff's reaction either.

Luke's mouth twitched into a smile before flattening out again. Then he followed his alpha's orders and left the restaurant. Blake watched until he was halfway across the lobby before he moved to Lehr's side. Lehr leaned close to his ear to say something I couldn't hear.

Blake glanced my way. His shoulders straightened, and he suddenly exuded calm and focus.

Lehr looked at me, then his daughter. Then, to Blake, he said, "Handle this," and turned away. With each step he took toward the door, my adrenaline diminished. By the time he exited, it was completely gone and I was drained.

I found the nearest chair. Pulled it out from the table. Sat.

I was going to throw up or pass out or both. Sometime in the past five minutes, I'd used the last of my energy. The adrenaline was all that had kept me upright. Everything hurt again, and I couldn't keep the world level or clear. This had to be what a concussion felt like, the pounding in my head, the nausea, the blurred vision. All I wanted was to slip back into bed. *My* bed. The one at my apartment forty-five minutes away.

I lowered my head and stared at a section of coffee-brown carpet until a pair of broken-in shoes stepped into view.

Suppressing a groan, I looked up.

Blake looked down. "I have orders to make your life hell."

"What's new," I muttered.

"You thought things were bad," he said. "You have no idea. You're going to regret helping the vampire."

The vampire was still there, standing a few paces to my left. He was looking at Nora, who had her killing glare focused on an empty chair at the bar. If she'd been a fire elemental, it would have defied the laws of the Null and burst into flames.

"Just go, Blake." I braced my hands on my knees and stood with only the slightest waver.

His eyes narrowed.

"What's wrong with you?" His hand lifted. I watched it like a snake striking out in slow motion. I could picture the coming crisis, the way he would grab my chin, angle it to the side, and squint at the should-be-invisible bite mark on my neck. He would see it, and he would *know*.

I ducked beneath his reach at the same time a voice thundered, "Don't touch her!"

Blake froze. It wasn't a shocked or worried stillness; it was more of a how-dare-you-give-me-orders cessation of movement. He looked over my right shoulder, and a few seconds later, Christian moved into my peripheral vision.

Blake *humphed* and dropped his hand.

"Christian," he said, no inflection in his voice, "what a surprise."

"You need to leave."

"You need to be careful," Blake countered. "You've been lucky to survive this long. Test me and that will change."

What *was* Christian? He stood there and took Blake's threat without so much as a blink.

"Nora," Blake said. "Let's go."

She hadn't budged since her father had left. She still looked ready to kill even when she met Blake's gaze.

"I need to talk to her a second," I said quickly, an attempt to ward off a confrontation.

"No," Blake said.

"You already got your way. The wedding is canceled. We have some things we need to call off."

It was a blatant lie, and he knew it. But if he had any respect at all for her—if they were, indeed, on some level still friends—he would give her some time.

Seconds ticked by.

"You have two minutes," he finally said. The words came out as a deep growl. If we'd been outside the Null, the air would have vibrated like thunder.

When he walked away, a second wave of relief nearly knocked me off my feet.

Holy hell, we survived. And not even a drop of blood was shed.

"Nora," Jared said. Her name—those two soft, blurred together syllables—was the first glimpse of vulnerability he'd shown since I'd dragged him inside The Rain.

"I couldn't let him break the treaty." Her voice was vicious compared to his, a blow meant to shut him up.

Maybe giving them a chance to talk wasn't such a great idea.

I cleared my throat. "Thanks—"

"I had no choice," Jared said.

"You *chose* to step out of the Null." She took the phrase *if looks could kill* to a whole new level. Her look could stake, shred, and maim, and she still wouldn't be satisfied until his broken body had been tossed into the sun to burn.

"I could not jeopardize The Rain."

"You didn't try to resist his call."

"I have resisted him for months."

"You have played your games," she bit out. "I was nothing but a pawn on your chessboard."

Something dark crossed Jared's face. "At least I was willing to fight my master."

Nora went still. It looked like there was still a chance for that bloodbath to happen.

I rubbed at the headache throbbing behind my eyes.

"You arrogant bastard," Nora said, her voice just louder than a whisper. "You won't last one week here as an *employee*."

She turned, strode past Christian and to The Rain's front door. Two minutes was, apparently, enough time for them to talk.

"Are you okay?" Christian asked.

The answer was a firm no, but I said, "I'm fine. You called her?"

Christian shoved his hands into his pockets. "It seemed like a good idea."

"I should have thought of it."

He shrugged. "You weren't well."

True.

I looked at Jared. "*You* should have thought to call her."

"She would not have answered."

"You could have used my phone, but it's probably for the best. You weren't willing to take my advice. You would have just pissed her off more."

Jared stared. "Your advice?"

"I said you'd have to break to get her back. Grovel. You did the exact opposite."

"I groveled."

"Really," I said, my voice flat. "I must have missed it."

"I spoke to her first," he said.

"That's not groveling."

My cell phone vibrated in my back pocket. I slipped it out. It was a text from my mom: *Everything okay?*

*Freaking fantastic*, I typed. Then I deleted it. They were going to flip when they heard about this—when they heard about all of it—and I was not in the right mental state to have that conversation yet. They'd be home soon, and we could talk face-to-face.

I needed a full night of restful sleep before then. I wouldn't get that here. I needed the comfort of my real bed, my regular life. I had a class in the morning that I couldn't skip and an afternoon shift at Parlay that I couldn't miss, not if I wanted to keep my job.

I fished my keys out of my pocket.

"What are you doing?" Jared asked.

"Going home."

"You are home."

"Home to my apartment. I have classes and roommates and a life away from here."

"You cannot drive."

"My parents will be back tomorrow. I'll—"

"You cannot drive." He cut me off. "You are my responsibility. I will not allow you to end up dead on the side of the road."

"I am *not* your responsibility."

"You can barely stand without wavering."

"If I'm wavering, it's because I'm sore from dragging your ass up—"

"Turn around," he ordered.

"What?"

"Quickly. Turn around."

I could do it, but I didn't want to. My *head* didn't want to. Every time I moved too quickly, the world wobbled. Which was his point.

"I'll drive you," Christian said.

I looked at him. In the past few days, I'd been in a car with werewolves and vampires. None of those rides had been pleasant. Getting into a vehicle with yet another species of paranorm didn't seem like a wise idea.

"I'll be fine," I said.

"Christian is acceptable."

I glared at Jared. "I need my car."

"I'll drive it," Christian said.

"Then how will you get home?"

He gave one of those indifferent, half-shouldered shrugs. "Friends."

The way he said that triggered a memory. It made me want to ask who his enemies were. Arcuro had said his vampires tracked an unsanctioned to The Rain. My gut said Christian was somehow involved in that.

"Christian drives or you stay," Jared said.

I wanted to chuck my keys at his face. Instead, I handed them to Christian. "Fine. We can talk on the way."

———

CHRISTIAN CRACKED THE CAR WINDOW. A late spring cold front had moved through, giving a bite to the already chilly mountain air. I didn't have a jacket with me, but he cranked up the heat, so I didn't complain. It was better to have fresh air flowing in and not just because it helped with my nausea. Christian smelled good, like leather and aftershave, and if I smelled him, then he undoubtedly smelled me.

My phone vibrated. Another message from my mom, asking again about Turnover, but this time she added more question marks.

I thought about calling her, but I wasn't sure I could handle that conversation. Not right now, at least.

*Horrible,* I wrote back.

*Oh?*

Oh? That's all she had to say? If things hadn't gone so very far into hell, I might have returned to the idea of this being a setup.

Christian pointed the air vents toward me. "Who are you texting?"

"My mom."

*Remember treaty,* Mom wrote. Like I needed another reminder of its existence.

"Where are they?" Christian asked.

I looked up. "Where do you think they are?"

His expression closed off. Figured.

"While we're talking, who was chasing you Saturday night?"

Silence.

"Was it an unsanctioned?"

He glanced at me, then returned his attention to the road. "What makes you think that?"

"Arcuro tracked an unsanctioned to The Rain."

His jaw clenched. "It's not what you think."

"Oh really? Why don't you tell me what I think."

"The vampire chasing me was… He was angry about something, but he did not enter The Rain and he did not stay in Arcuro's territory."

"Why was he chasing you?"

"He was angry—"

"You said that. Why?"

"I can't tell you—"

"Did it have anything to do with the ransacked rooms?"

"Kennedy—"

"If you don't want to answer, then pull over. I'll get out here."

His jaw clenched again, then he exited the highway.

"Seriously?"

He shook his head and pulled into a gas station.

I reached for the door handle. Stopped. This was my car. He was the one who needed to get out, not me.

I hit the button to unlock the door. Christian immediately relocked it.

I hit the button again. "Get out."

"I can't give you answers yet," he said, meeting my eyes. "It's complicated, and you don't want to be involved."

I bristled. "I'm already involved."

"You don't have to be. Your parents will be home tomorrow. You can stay at your apartment. Finish school. Get a job away from The Rain—"

"Who the hell are you?"

His mouth closed. He stared at me. I stared back, but it took an effort not to shift. We weren't in the Null, and I didn't know what he was. I didn't know what he could do. He'd never been aggressive toward me though, and I wasn't getting the typical *fear me* vibe most paranorms gave off. That didn't mean he wasn't something dangerous; it just meant he was something different.

"Wait here," he said finally.

I frowned at the gas station, then back at him.

"Please."

Curiosity edged out my irritation. I sat back in my chair and folded my arms. After a moment, he got out of the car.

The late-afternoon sun reflected off the glass door when he opened it to go inside. Was he a witch? He had a chip on his shoulder like so many of them do. I should go back to Gamecraft and Witchery. I should go inside this time and ask Owen for information. I should—

I should mind my own business and stay away from The Rain.

How did Christian know what I wanted? What else did he know about me?

Through the glass doors, I watched him walk to the checkout counter. What I wanted didn't matter anymore. Blake wasn't the type of person to deliver empty threats. He wouldn't leave me alone without an order from his alpha, and that wouldn't happen anytime soon. The only reason the wolves hadn't bothered me after I'd helped the unsanctioned five years ago was because I'd left for boarding school. They wouldn't let my interference in their world order go this time. They'd find a way to torment me without violating the treaty.

The treaty that apparently had one hell of a loophole.

Maybe Mom's advice was good. Maybe I needed to remember the treaty—to reread it—and find some way to get Blake and every other paranorm out of my life.

I texted my mom to ask if the treaty was in The Rain's safe.

*Yes everything ok*, she responded almost immediately.

*What's the combination?*

The gas station door reopened, and Christian came back to the car, carrying a paper bag. He climbed behind the wheel, dug into the bag, then shoved a sports drink into my hand.

"Drink."

I pushed it back toward him. "I'm not thirsty."

"Drink," he said again. This time, it was a command.

I rolled my eyes but twisted off the top. After a few sips, I twisted it back on, then peeked into the bag he'd set between us. There was an orange, an apple, a too-ripe banana, and a package of peanut butter crackers.

"You have the munchies?" I asked.

"You need food."

I scowled. I don't know why it bothered me so much, but I didn't like him taking care of me. It made me feel like I was in his debt.

Maybe that was why he did it. Maybe he wanted something from me. It wasn't a room at The Rain, because he obviously had that covered. So what was it?

He must have felt me staring, because he turned his head to look at me. Several seconds passed before he looked away and turned on the engine.

Reluctantly, I opened the crackers and took a small bite.

My phone dinged. It wasn't a text; it was a belated notification of a missed call from a collection agency and a voice message. I'd been getting calls about payment negotiations for more than a month. I'd thought they were scams since I wasn't behind on my credit card. Now, it was beginning to look like they were legit.

*That* problem wasn't going to go away when my parents got home, not unless Mom was telling the truth and there was a really big misunderstanding or mistake. I didn't think that likely.

"You aren't, by chance, an accountant, are you?" I asked Christian as he pulled out of the parking lot.

"Unless you count running numbers for the gym, no."

"I thought you might have a side gig." I pinched the bridge of my nose, trying to ease the headache that wouldn't go away. "My parents told you about the hidden halls, didn't they?"

After a slight hesitation, he nodded.

"And you told Jared?"

No nod this time, and he kept his eyes on the road. It made sense though. My parents said Christian was a friend of some sort, and he and Jared obviously knew each other. But the stony look on Christian's face said he wouldn't talk about it.

I huffed out a breath. "It's not right they'd tell you about it and not their own daughter."

"Maybe they knew you'd get yourself into trouble."

"I used to never get into trouble," I said.

"Really?" He glanced my way. "You never hid in a guest room to see what all the bangs and thumps were about?"

Heat leaped to my cheeks. I had. When I was eight. The couple in bed had caught me and gone directly to my parents. We'd had the whole birds-and-bees conversation after that.

"Why would they tell you about *that*?"

He shrugged, then turned in to my apartment complex. "They like talking about you."

"Yeah, but you're…"

He looked at me. I didn't know how to finish that sentence, so I asked, "Are you an incubus?"

He coughed and pressed too hard on the brake. "Do you have the overwhelming urge to throw yourself at me?"

"Not in a sexual way," I said.

He laughed. It was sudden and genuine and lit up his usually serious face.

"You wouldn't get a punch in," he said.

"I'm not as helpless as I look." I pointed out my building.

"Never said you were."

"You were thinking it though."

He pulled into a parking spot and turned off the engine. "Come on. I'll walk you to your door."

"I don't need an escort, just my keys."

"I don't trust you enough to walk up the stairs yet."

"What if I live on the ground floor?"

"Do you?"

I didn't. Dad thought it would be too easy for someone to break in.

I held my hand out for the keys. He placed them in my palm before he climbed out of the car. I got out too and shut the door.

"I can make it on my own."

"I'm sure you can," he replied, "but you don't have to." He motioned me ahead.

"Fine. But only because I've recently developed a hatred of stairs." I tried to ignore the way his mouth quirked into a smile as we headed to my apartment. Sure, I might have put more weight than usual on the rail and *maybe* I was ridiculously out of breath when I reached the third floor, but Christian didn't once have to save me from tumbling down and breaking my neck.

"Made it," I said, opening my door. It was rude to shut him out so quickly after a forty-five-minute drive into the city, but I was tired, he was cryptic, and I'd had enough interactions with paranorms that night.

"Kennedy." He flattened his hand on the door when I started to close it. "If Blake gives you trouble, call me."

"And what would you do? Fight him?" My tone said exactly how stupid that would be.

"I'd help you."

"You've already helped more than enough. I appreciate it, but I'm good. I don't need anything else."

He looked like he wanted to say something. Instead, he nodded and lowered his hand.

I shut the door, then headed for my room and my bed. I was halfway across the living room when my phone pinged. It was a text from an unknown number: *Call if you need me.*

I scowled. I'd never given Christian my number.

## 21

"Hey, sleepyhead. You've got to see this."

"What?" I asked groggily. Carrie stood at the foot of my bed, my blanket in her arms.

"It's hard to describe. Come on." She threw a pillow at my head, then left the room.

Going back to sleep sounded like a much better idea than climbing out of bed, but a glance at the clock on my nightstand said it was 7:23 a.m. I'd crawled into bed before dark and slept the whole night.

I grabbed a sweatshirt from my nightstand, pulled it on, then finger-combed my hair into a messy bun. Carrie wasn't in the living room, and the front door was open, so I padded across the carpet, then stepped onto the landing.

She stood at the rail with John and Alex, who were both peering down to the parking lot below.

Stifling a yawn, I joined them… and instantly woke up.

A pair of very familiar unicorn underwear hung from the nearest light post and others from the branches of at least a half dozen trees. The underwear adorned the bushes like ornaments and littered the sidewalk and parking lot. Nearly every car in view had a pair hooked over a windshield wiper. Only one vehicle was so completely covered it was impossible to make out the make and model. I knew what it was though. An old, blue Toyota Camry.

"I can't figure out if someone really likes you," Carrie said, "or if they really hate you."

"What makes you think this is because of me?" How the *hell* had Blake found hundreds of pairs of unicorn underwear identical to the one he'd picked up in my room? How had he gotten them here *overnight?*

"We have this," a voice said behind me.

A girl close to my age took the last two steps up to our landing, then handed me a paper. It was an invoice for 1,128 pairs of unicorn underwear with my name and address on it. The price at the bottom almost made me choke.

"This might be the best prank ever," the girl said. I was pretty sure she worked in the leasing office. Her name was Ann or Angie or something close to that.

"You have to tell us who did this," John said.

"It was… It wasn't anyone important."

"You have to clean it up," Office Girl said. "I won't tell my manager if you can do it before this afternoon."

What the manager would do, I didn't know. Evict me?

"I'll get it done," I said.

When she left, I fisted the invoice in my hand, crinkling it into a ball. I couldn't afford 1,128 pairs of underwear. The invoice better be fake. Blake must have altered it, then stuck it to the office door to make sure I was hit with the blame.

I looked out at the underwear again. It was going to take forever to clean it up.

Carrie and the guys helped at first, then they had to leave for their classes. I wasn't going to make it to mine. My grade would be docked unless I could convince my professor that this was an extenuating circumstance. But what was I going to tell him? My name had ended up on a werewolf's shit list?

Just after lunch, I fished the last of the undies from a tree and stuffed it into a trash bag. I dragged myself up the stairs to my apartment, determined to sink into a long, hot bath. I was sweaty, sore, and extremely pissed off. Climbing ladders and using broomsticks to hook underwear off branches and light posts was a hell of a lot harder than I'd expected. I still had to figure out what to do with the eight trash bags full of underwear. Maybe a women's shelter would take them.

I turned on the bath and waited for it to get hot. The tub was half-full when my phone rang. Out of habit, I reached for it. It was a university number. I swiped it on and said hello.

"Kennedy Rain?"

"Yes," I said. "Who's calling?"

"This is Sasha Norris from the Department of English. We've received a complaint of plagiarism against you, and we need to set up an appointment to discuss it. Are you available this afternoon?"

I gripped my phone hard.

"I haven't plagiarized anything," I said.

"It's a formal complaint submitted in writing with supportive evidence," Sasha said. "I can't log a protest over the phone, but your professor and the dean are both available at two o'clock today."

"Who filed the complaint?" I asked, my voice flat. I was going to *kill* Blake.

"Don't you want to ask what the complaint was filed on?"

"It doesn't matter because I haven't plagiarized."

"The complaint was from another student who claims you copied large portions of a paper on the impact of women writers on Regency England. If you gather notes and drafts of the paper, it will—"

"That was last semester."

"Students and staff have six months to formally file. Can you be here by two? The dean and Dr. Shanna are both busy. The next time they could meet would be during Dead Week."

That was more than a month away.

I rubbed at my forehead. "I have to work this afternoon."

"Two o'clock today is the only time we have available."

Damn it, my boss was going to be pissed.

"Okay. Two p.m. I'll be there," I said.

I hung up the phone, drew in three slow, deep breaths. This wasn't a big deal. I could handle it. I'd clean up this mess just like I'd cleaned up the underwear. I still had my notebooks from the previous semester, and I should have a file or two on my laptop. I could refute this.

Blake would not win.

---

I COULDN'T FIND the damn paper.

I couldn't find a draft of it on my computer or a data trail to the links I'd used for research. My laptop's full history had been deleted, and I had no freaking idea how or when. I'd come straight home after the confrontation with Lehr. I'd slept hard, but if someone had come into my room, I would have woken up. The only time the apartment had been empty was when we were stuffing underwear into trash bags.

My professor might still have a copy of the paper, but she would also have the so-called evidence Blake had manufactured. If the evidence was as convincing as the undie invoice, I was in trouble.

I glared at my laptop. There had to be some way to retrieve the history and deleted files. A tech person could probably do it. I just had to find someone who was willing, maybe an engineering student.

John. John was in the School of Engineering. I was

almost certain he was pursuing a computer science degree. Even if he didn't have the skill set to do what I needed, he'd get further than I would. Plus, he would have friends.

Someone knocked on the door while I was going through my papers one last time. I ignored it and set one notebook aside.

The person knocked harder.

It wouldn't be anyone I wanted to talk to. I was certain of that. It would be another crisis I had to fix. If I ignored it, if I didn't answer, maybe it would go away on its own.

Another knock.

My eyes closed. Whoever it was, whatever they wanted, Blake probably paid them a fortune to give me hell. They weren't going to go away.

Gritting my teeth, I stomped to the door.

I peered out the peephole. It was the leasing office girl. Sighing, I opened the door.

"Hello, again," she said, a somewhat remorseful smile on her face. Beside her stood Eli, the apartment's security guard.

Its *elemental* security guard.

Shit.

"Ms. Rain," he said. "Someone called Kelly with a noise complaint."

"What a surprise," I muttered.

"They also claimed you have more people living here than allowed," Kelly said.

I looked at Eli, who stood there too stiffly to not know who I was.

"It's just me and my roommate," I said.

"Mind if we come in and check the place?" Kelly asked.

"I'm running late for a meeting with my professor. Can you guys come back later?"

It wasn't a lie—I was already going to be late for my

meeting—but I realized belatedly that it made me sound like I was hiding something.

With a silent groan, I opened the door wide. They wiped their feet on our frayed and faded welcome mat, then stepped inside.

Our living room came furnished. It was relatively clean except for the backpack I'd emptied on the couch, searching for evidence that I hadn't plagiarized.

I trailed behind Kelly as she glanced into my bedroom, then into Carrie's.

"Looks fine to me," she said. "Someone has a vendetta, don't they?"

"Yeah. I'm sorry about this. And about the panties. I can't believe someone was able to underwear the parking lot without anyone noticing."

I looked directly at Eli when I said the last part.

"I'm one person," he said. "It's a big complex."

What a load of crap. He was an elemental, and since he hadn't started any fires or manipulated the weather and there were no large bodies of water nearby, my guess is he was connected to the earth. He should have sensed werewolves the second they stepped onto his territory.

"It was a lot of underwear," I said. "It must have taken a pack of people to get it done in one night."

He didn't so much as blink.

Kelly smiled sympathetically. "Maybe submit a police report for harassment?"

"That's a good idea," I said, though I had no intention to see another police officer any time this decade.

I walked her to the door.

"Good luck with your problem," she said, then she and the elemental headed for the stairs.

On an impulse, I called out, "Eli."

He stopped on the first step and turned.

"I'd appreciate a heads-up the next time someone suspicious steps on the property."

He stared at me a long moment, then he gave an odd nod of his head, more diagonal jerk than side to side or up and down. After he disappeared down the stairs and someone else came up, I realized why.

"Kennedy." Nora walked past me and into my still-open door.

"Why don't you come in," I muttered, then followed her inside.

She stopped in the middle of the living room and stared down at the couch. My things were still strewn across it, my backpack on the floor at her feet. She seemed to be sneering on the inside as her gaze swept the rest of the room. She was definitely judging. She'd grown up in a rich pack and had never had to rent a place to live. Lehr took care of his daughter and his wolves. They wanted for nothing.

"Can I get you a drink?" I asked half-heartedly.

"I was thinking," she said, stepping over my backpack to circle the coffee table. "Arcuro isn't forgiving. He isn't sloppy. He wouldn't have let Jared leave without a very bloody, very loud fight. The whole region would have felt the reverberations, and yet, I've heard nothing. I didn't think about it before, but someone must have convinced Arcuro to let him go."

Icy eyes met mine.

"You're just now putting that together?"

"You went to Arcuro's compound." She stepped toward me. "You begged for his release."

"I gave him a job."

"A job that didn't exist before you crawled into his compound."

What the hell was this? She should be thanking me.

"I didn't crawl, Nora. I didn't beg. I also didn't give up on him. I stumbled on a solution that gave him a chance—"

"You stumbled on a solution that should have gotten you killed."

I crossed my arms. "Is that why you're pissed? Because I survived going down into the vampires' compound when you were too afraid to consider it?"

She shoved hard.

I expected the attack, so I went with it, stumbling back to prevent bruises. I might have even stayed on my feet had I not hit the sofa chair. My momentum tipped it over.

My feet flew over my head.

I rolled a second time and came up at the edge of the kitchen.

"You didn't want the wedding," Nora snarled. "You wanted me to 'choose another groom.'"

"Forgive me," I snapped. "But I started to believe you really did love him. It's good to know it was just some postadolescent rebellion."

Her nostrils flared. Yellow flashed in her eyes. Nora was there to pick a fight. She wanted me to retreat. I wouldn't.

"You never knew when to leave me alone," she said. "You always had to provoke me. You haven't changed at all since you ran away from home."

"I learned never to back down from people like you," I said. "You and your friends and the pack your daddy assigned to protect you walked all over me. Every time I did what I was supposed to and averted my gaze, you pushed your influence further."

"I should rip out your throat," she whispered.

"That's the difference between you and me. I don't want people to die."

Her breaths were more rapid than mine now, her tentative rein on her temper so shaky I could almost see its vibrations in the air. People didn't stand up to Nora Lehr. They bowed to the princess's whims, or they got the hell out of the way.

"Why?" she asked between gritted teeth. "Why did you pull him out of the compound? He's been Arcuro's shadow for a century. He would have been fine. *Content.*"

The last word was said like a curse, like the worst part of all of it was that things would return to the status quo, and Jared would go on with his life without a hitch. She was wrong.

"You were too angry to see the truth when he walked away." I let some of the ferociousness leave my voice. "It killed him, Nora. He wasn't walking away to return to his master's side. He was walking away to die."

There it was, a flicker of weakness, of pain. Vulnerability was something werewolves didn't show. It's why it hurt her so much. She'd let Jared in, trusted that he loved her, that he would brave the sun and the moon and break the laws of the world to be with her. She'd been confident of it, and when she'd seen it slip from her control, she'd lost it. And she was hurting.

"Arcuro wouldn't have killed him," she said.

"He declared Jared livestock. He was nearly drained."

She went supernaturally still. I didn't understand why until she said, "He didn't look nearly drained yesterday."

Oh fuuuuuuck.

"That's why you looked sick." Her voice became different. Scary. Cruel.

"The compound is deep. It has a lot of stairs. I was exhausted."

"He bit you," she said, a quiet menace dripping from the words. "Did you like it, Kennedy?" She advanced. "Did you cling to him? Did you ask for more?"

My heart rate quickened. Air rasped in my lungs, and perspiration dampened my hairline. Her juju was going full throttle, and I was so damn close to doing what she wanted. So damn close to running. She had just gone terrifyingly territorial.

"It was an accident, Nora. I was just convenient."

"Convenient." It would be convenient to drive her claws into my gut, her eyes said.

I backed farther into the kitchen.

"Nora, you need to calm down."

"You want him to do it again." She backed me into the counter. "You want him to do more than bite you."

Her eyes went full yellow. Shit! If she attacked…

I had to do something, had to stop her from making a fatal mistake.

My skin grew clammy. My gaze skirted over a useless box of cereal, the empty knife block, the pot in the sink full of dirty dishwater. For once, I was grateful Carrie never washed the dishes.

I lunged for the pot, wrapped my fingers around the handle, then slung it through the air.

Cold, dirty dishwater drenched Nora's face. Her wolf's eyes flickered from yellow to a shocked amber, and the predator who had hold of her soul loosened its grip.

I kept the pot held ready. Hitting her would be a bad idea though. It would make that predator surge back to the surface.

A piece of macaroni tangled in her always-perfect hair. It hung wet and limp on her shoulders. The whole upper half of her blouse was soaked through.

"I am not a threat, Nora. I'm never going to get involved with a paranorm—any paranorm—and certainly not one who's old enough to be my great-great-grandfather."

Praying I wasn't making a mistake, I tossed the pot to the ground, a diversion and a small submission.

"He's yours," I said. "All you have to do is forgive him."

So much rage sizzled in her eyes I was surprised the water didn't vaporize into the air. But her wolf's instinct had retreated. Hers was a human anger now, an anger that could be controlled.

She squared her shoulders. I hadn't realized how concaved they had been. Her chin had been tucked, her fingers bent into barely human claws. She had been heartbeats away from shifting.

Without another word, she left my apartment.

I didn't move, not for a long time, and when I did, I stumbled for the couch. My entire body shook as the adrenaline drained away. I rubbed my palms over my face, trying to erase the chill, the numbness, but the jittery feeling wouldn't go away. I needed something to do, needed to occupy my hands. I grabbed the backpack off the floor and started shoving pens and papers inside it.

There was a knock on the door. Nora coming back because I'd ruined her silk shirt? Or some other catastrophe Blake had designed?

Exhausted, I crossed the living room and opened the door.

A werewolf stood on my welcome mat, but it wasn't Nora.

---

## 22

"Kennedy," Luke said. "Whatever did you do to Nora?"

It was the wolf who'd accompanied Lehr and Blake to The Rain. I moved in front of my door but kept it open a crack. "She had an unfortunate encounter with dirty dishwater. Blake sent you?"

He snorted. "Blake doesn't send me anywhere." He surveyed the camp chairs shoved against the wall, the dilapidated ice chest, the decor on the railing. "What did you talk about?"

"Boys." I threw the word out there, hoping he'd catch the hint and leave.

"That's right." He moved to the center of the landing, dominating the space. "You two went to high school together. I always thought that was strange, Lehr sending his daughter to play with the flock."

Flock, like humans were just a bunch of sheep. I was beginning to like the guy about as much as I liked Blake.

"Is there something you want?"

His eyes met mine, and I had to fight the urge to look away. I wasn't sure how to deal with him.

"May I come in?"

"No." I stepped into the breezeway and shut the door behind me. It was better than hiding behind it and risking him breaking it down. "If you have a question, ask it."

His pleasant smile slipped a fraction. "Have you rethought your stance on the vampire?"

I must have been numb from everything that had happened in the past forty-eight hours. Alarm bells were only now sluggishly ringing in my head. He wouldn't have just dropped by because he was in the neighborhood. He had to have been sent here, if not by Blake then by Lehr.

As if sensing my discomfort, he moved away, walking the two steps to the railing to casually lean against it.

Maybe I was overreacting.

"No," I said.

He very purposefully met my gaze. Oh, he'd been looking at me before, but the air shifted. It became denser, like it wanted to hold me in place.

I hooked my thumbs in my belt loops and pretended not to notice.

"You don't see the problem you're causing," Luke said. "Lehr and Arcuro are never in agreement, but they are on this. Every second Jared lives, resentment on both sides builds. Lehr's relationship with his daughter has suffered. It's hurting the pack. Arcuro isn't overjoyed to lose his scion either. He blames us. We blame him. It's a precipice we're standing on, Kennedy Rain. This needs to be over and done with. Fire Jared, then everyone can be on their merry little way."

Those last three words were delivered like they were the lyrics to a children's song.

"My parents will be home soon. Maybe they'll agree with you." I had no idea what they'd do. He was an employee now and under the protection of a treaty I planned to read real soon.

"Of course," Luke said. "Leave it to your parents to clean up your mess."

There was so much scorn, so much accusation in his voice he might as well have been channeling Sullens.

"Look," I said. "I'm exhausted. I'm behind on my school-work, late for a meeting, and the past week has generally sucked. If you could wrap up this whole intimidation thing, I'd appreciate it."

"You're not scared." He pushed away from the rail. "If Blake was doing his job, you would be."

"Trust me, he's doing his job."

"Oh yes. Pranks with panties. Very terrifying." He took another step toward me. "Blake is weak."

"I'm sure he'd love to know you said that." I had to turn my head to keep him in view.

Luke laughed, circled closer, then said softly, "Go ahead. Threaten me again."

"I wasn't—"

He grabbed my hair and slung me around.

My stomach slammed into the railing. Air whooshed from my lungs.

"You'll fire Jared," he snarled, bending me over the rail. "Then you'll deliver the bastard to Lehr's doorstep."

My feet came off the ground. The rail split me down the middle. He pressed his weight into me, driving my rib cage harder and harder into the metal bar.

"You have a roommate." He gripped my shoulder. "You have neighbors." His fingers dug into a pressure point. "You have people you care about."

Numbness spread down my right arm as fear shot through my body. It turned into shock. He was about to break me in half.

"The treaty—"

"Think carefully," he said. "Think about the people who would find your organs splattered on the concrete. Think about your parents when they come home and identify your broken body in the morgue. Is the vampire worth that?"

My ribs were in agony. I swear one cracked. The others felt like they concaved inward.

I wheezed, trying to find enough air to respond. Carrie's decorations fluttered down to the sidewalk below. Everything except a narrow strip of green was cold, killing concrete.

*Why isn't he writhing in pain?*

I couldn't think about that yet. I had to think of a way to survive.

"Tell me you'll fire him," he whispered into my ear.

I locked my jaw shut. Screw him. Screw all of them. I would not cave.

Fighting him was a waste of time, so I stopped trying to push away from the rail. Instead, I gripped the rails below me and pulled myself over it.

The sudden change in movement let me slip from Luke's cage. I intended to hang on, to dangle there until my feet could reach the railing on the floor below us. I was tall enough, probably strong enough too, but my hands crossed when I fell.

I lost my grip, scrambled trying to find something to hold on to.

My wrist slammed against the second-floor railing, and I kept falling.

I caught one brief glimpse of the blue sky, then the world went black.

---

"Ms. Rain!"

My scream lodged in my throat. My eyes were squeezed

shut tight. I was too afraid to open them, too terrified I'd see myself broken.

"Ms. Rain." Someone grabbed my arms, started pulling me free. "I'm sorry. I saw you fall. I couldn't think of anything softer."

Something tangled in my hair, and I finally opened my eyes. Eli pushed aside broken foliage, trying to free me from a bush that hadn't been below my balcony a minute ago. It scratched and clawed my skin, then it began to pull away from me without help from Eli's hands.

"You…" I cleared my throat, which was still tight from the scream that hadn't had time to break free. "You grew this."

He nodded once and pulled me the rest of the way out of the bush. My back and neck and shoulders—really, my whole body—hurt, but I was alive. If Eli hadn't been watching, if he hadn't been an earth elemental…

"Thank you," I said.

He pulled a branch—seriously, it was too big to be called a twig—from my hair.

"The wolf?" I asked quietly.

"Gone," he said.

"He shouldn't have been able to hurt me."

He plucked a twig from my shirt. "If I thought he'd hurt you, I wouldn't have let him on the property. None of the other wolves were aggressive."

I ran my fingers through my hair, shaking loose a few leaves. "The ones that hung the underwear?"

He nodded. "And the others who have been watching you. Ms. Lehr sent the last one away when she arrived."

"Someone's been watching me? For how long?"

"A while."

"And you didn't think to tell me?"

"I promised not to interact with you unless it was an emergency, and the wolves assured me there would be no violence."

"A wolf can't guarantee that, especially not the week of the full moon." I experimented with rising onto all fours and... Wait. "You promised? Promised who?"

He expression closed off.

"Who did you promise?"

His mouth tightened. He stood, then offered his hand to help me up.

Typical paranorm. Doesn't answer my question and expects me to trust him.

I glared, stood on my own, and smothered a million curses. Holy cow, I *hurt*.

"Who?" I demanded again.

He grimaced.

"Eli."

"Your father," he said. "He wanted to be sure you and your roommate were safe."

That wasn't the answer I'd expected. Everything had been fine before my parents left town. Why would a paranorm need to watch me?

"When did he talk to you?" I asked.

"A while ago."

"A while as in a few days or a few weeks?"

"A few months."

"Did he say why?"

Eli shook his head.

Of course he didn't.

I blew out a breath.

"Thank you," I said. "For saving my life. If another paranorm comes to the complex, I'd really appreciate a heads-up. I can give you my number."

The corner of his mouth lifted into an embarrassed smile. "I already have it. I am glad I was able to help. The property is clear now."

With a bow of his head, he turned and left.

I looked up to the railing I'd fallen from. My stomach twisted. If Eli hadn't grown the bush, I'd be dead. Luke would have killed me…

Or maybe he wouldn't have. Maybe he hadn't *intended* to.

My gaze shifted from the third-floor rail to the staircase. I needed to get my keys.

God, I hated stairs.

With a great deal of effort and no small amount of cursing, I made it back to my apartment. I shut and locked the door behind me, then headed to the kitchen. The floor was still wet with dishwater. I needed to clean it up before Carrie came home. Remove all evidence of a struggle.

I washed my hands and arms. They were scratched from falling into the bush. The worst injury, though, was my wrist. A dark purple bruise spread across it. I was lucky it wasn't broken.

I was lucky *I* wasn't broken.

Grabbing towels from the bathroom, I sopped up the water. The pot had held more than I expected. It had splashed everywhere, even up to the edge of the living room carpet. I threw the chunks of pasta into the trash can, then sprayed the floor down with a cleaner and wiped it up again. So gross.

When I'd finished, I grabbed Advil from the medicine cabinet, then went to the fridge for a bottle of water. I opened the door—

And yelped.

A deluge of thick red liquid gushed over the floor.

I backed away, my gut churning as the puddle expanded toward my shoes. It looked like blood and…

And it smelled like ketchup.

I looked closer. Our fridge was almost empty except for the thick red mess and the remnants of what looked to be popped balloons. There were pushpins too, attached to a long strip of masking tape that must have hit the balloons when I'd opened the door. The ketchup was everywhere except for the top shelf.

That top shelf was clean, and the only thing on it, sitting dead center and staring out at me, was a steampunk robot wedding cake topper.

Blake was fucking dead.

## 23

"Blake!" I yelled, slamming my car door.

I stormed to the front porch.

"Blake!" I yelled again.

The door opened when I reached the porch's top step. I fisted the steampunk cake topper in my hand, then launched it through the air.

It hit Blake in the center of his forehead.

The cocky smile that had been on his face vanished.

"It's not wise to attack a wolf in his territory," he said.

"Then stay out of my territory."

He crossed his arms over his chest and leaned against the doorjamb. "No. Not until you give me what I want."

He intentionally made that sound suggestive, and I wished I still had the cake topper in my hand so I could chuck it at his head again.

"I've spent the day cleaning up your shit. You're meddling in the human world. In *my* world. Stop screwing with me."

He chuckled and pushed away from the doorjamb. "Sweetheart, I haven't even started to screw you."

An erotic ache pulsed through my body, exactly like he wanted it to. Damn werewolf.

I shoved the feeling aside and jabbed a finger into his chest. "Turnover is in three days. The full moon is tomorrow. Back off or I'll kick the wolves out the second I get home."

He stepped forward, forcing me backward. "Empty threats? I thought you were more clever than that."

If I did it, Lehr's pack would have to handle the consequences. The wolves would feel the effects of the full moon. If some were moonsick, they might not be able to control their tempers, their thirst for blood. Blake wouldn't be able to mess with me because he'd be occupied hunting the violent wolves.

That was the problem though. I *should* kick them out, but I couldn't. I wouldn't be able to live with myself if a wolf lost his or her mind and hurt someone.

Blake's mouth curved into an infuriating smile.

"We're hosting Nora's wedding." As soon as I said the words, the weight that had been riding my shoulders these past few days shifted. It was still there, still a huge burden I didn't want to carry, but it felt right, using The Rain to do something good. Even if it resulted in me being entangled in the paranormal world for the next couple of months, I'd find a way to make it work.

Blake's expression turned cold. "That issue has been taken care of."

"They still love each other."

"You must not know Nora," Blake said. "He betrayed her. He made her weak. Werewolves don't like their vulnerabilities on display."

"He answered his master's call."

"He made a promise that he broke. She won't forgive him."

"We'll see about that."

I turned to trot down the steps. Blake smoothly jumped to the ground and cut me off.

"Don't interfere," he warned.

I copied one of his condescending smiles. "You're meddling in my world, so I'm meddling in yours."

I stepped past him, strode to my car, and yanked open the door.

Pain shot through my wrist. I gritted my teeth and fished my keys out of my pocket with my uninjured hand.

"Wait." Blake slipped between me and my car.

I made my jaw unlock, met his eyes, and said, "Move."

"What happened?"

My wrist was still throbbing. "What do you think happened?"

He sniffed. "With you, I don't know. Save any other vampires lately?"

"Get the fuck out of my way."

He moved closer. "Who hurt you?"

"Like you don't know. You're Lehr's second. You're giving the orders!" I tried to shove him out of the way with my good hand.

"Kennedy."

I launched my knee toward his crotch. He blocked it easily.

"Kennedy, look at me."

I tried to knee him again. I wanted to hurt him. Every little interference, every condescending word or grin, I blamed it all on him. Even Nora was his fault. If he'd done his fucking job, she wouldn't have met Jared. She wouldn't have fallen in love with him.

He backed against the car and dodged when I swung my fist at his face but not when I punched his chest. I punched him again then again. He held his hands out to the side, then he put his hands on my shoulders.

"Shhhh," he whispered. His touch was gentle but firm, and his eyes… I'd never seen him like that before. He wasn't angry. He wasn't alpha. He wasn't arrogant or mocking. He was the man he might have become if he hadn't been turned into a paranorm.

A million butterflies burst into flight in my stomach.

He searched my face. Maybe he was trying to discern my thoughts. Maybe he was trying to find the answer to the question I couldn't remember him asking.

His focus dropped to my mouth.

Maybe he was thinking about kissing me.

His thumb slid along my collar bone, and the butterfly wings beat faster. They were going to explode from my skin and carry me away.

Oh God. I couldn't get carried away.

I reached up to shove him again, but this time, when my hands touched the hard muscles concealed beneath his shirt, they stopped. He was warm, strong. He peered down at me like I was something to protect, and in that moment, I felt wanted. The pain in my wrist vanished, replaced by a full-bodied tingle that made my breaths turn shallow. I wanted to feel his lips on mine, wanted his hands to explore my body.

His gaze heated. The short distance between us shrank further. I wanted this, to learn what it felt like to kiss him, to kiss a werewolf.

A werewolf.

A paranorm.

Shit!

"Luke." I threw out the name like a defensive shield.

Blake retreated fast. He stopped two paces away and went still, like a wolf coiled to pounce. Or to run. I wasn't sure which, but he should know that was a line he was forbidden to cross. I couldn't get involved with any paranorm. It would show favoritism. It would start a war.

Except... I was so stupid. This wasn't us getting involved; it was him finding another way to torture me and me caving into his damn werewolf pheromones.

Blake blinked. The air between us finally chilled.

"Luke?" he said. The hair on the back of my neck rose. "He's watching Nora."

"She was at my apartment before he showed up."

"Before he touched you." He made a sound low in his throat, and the edges of his eyes glowed yellow. I didn't know what this anger was. It felt out of place. Misdirected.

"You didn't send him?"

"No."

Did he tremble? I wasn't sure. His anger had shifted into a quiet, steady rage. If he was human, I might have said he was pissed Luke had touched me. More likely, Blake's fury was about his dominance and the proper order of life. Luke had stepped out of line and played with his toy.

"Did Lehr send him?" I asked.

The glow rimming his eyes expanded. The air grew thick with the threat of violence.

I'd dropped my keys at some point. I bent down to pick them up, not taking my eyes off him because he looked on the verge of exploding.

"You're afraid," Blake said.

"I'd be stupid if I wasn't."

"You don't need to be."

I'd saved a vampire his alpha wanted dead, and I'd just promised to make Nora's wedding happen. Blake had reasons to direct his anger my way.

I sank into the driver's seat and tried to close the door. Blake grabbed it. He leaned down to meet my gaze. It was impossible to ignore his nearness, impossible to ignore the heat from his body and the scent of him, a scent that made me think of wild nights and untamed nature.

"Luke won't touch you again," he said. Then, eyes still rimmed in yellow, he closed my car door.

I COULDN'T GET Blake out of my head. I cracked the window on the way to The Rain, but I couldn't erase his scent from my memory. I couldn't forget that almost tangible connection that had snapped between us. I knew I was reading too much into those few minutes, twisting his tone from possessive to protective. It was an excusable mistake. Blake was undeniably hot, and his pheromones, his status as a strong, dominant alpha, would make it hard for any girl to keep her head on straight. But I wasn't any girl. I knew I was being chemically and magically manipulated.

By the time I parked in front of the hotel, I'd smothered the pulsating heat in my stomach. Blake was attractive and probably amazing in bed, but I would not be the stupid, weak girl who gave in to her hormones.

I drew in a slow, deep breath, then I walked into The Rain. The lobby was quiet, and Sullens didn't greet me with a new catastrophe. That was surprising given the glares I received from three guests seated at a table in the restaurant. Two days had passed since the wolves cornered Deagan at the edge of the Null and one of their own had been killed. They weren't over it.

Neither was I.

Ignoring the chill bumps that scurried down my arms, I went straight to my parents' office, shut the door, and closed the curtain. Then I took out my cell phone and crouched in front of the safe. The combination Mom had sent worked on the first try. The door swung open.

A handgun sat atop a small stack of papers.

I'd seen inside this safe before. There had never been a gun.

There were other firearms on the property, a few rifles, and a couple of really old flintlock pistols from my ancestors. We didn't have ammo for them, and they were basically relics shoved somewhere into storage. This handgun was modern.

I carefully shifted the papers out from underneath it and left it in the safe. The stack contained the usual household documents—our birth certificates, Social Security cards, my parents' will, and a few other boring papers. I almost overlooked the treaty on my first pass-through. I'd expected an old, slightly yellowing paper stored in a larger-than-normal page protector. Instead, I found an 8.5 x 11 photocopy. I thought my parents had the original, but maybe I was wrong or they kept it somewhere else.

I turned and laid the papers on the desk, then pulled out the duct-tape-covered chair and sat. The copy of the treaty was black-and-white and hard to read since it had been forced onto a page smaller than the original document. It was dated 1665 and signed by a representative from the four largest paranormal species—the vampires, the werewolves, the fey, and an elemental—and magically bound and enforced by a full coven.

The copy quality, the old language, and the handwriting made it impossible to skim, so I read it slowly and more than once, especially the paragraph pertaining to the Rains. Unfortunately, there wasn't a line that said *Thou shalt not harass a Rain.* Most of it was about the paranorms and the importance of not entering a conflict that resulted in "irrevocable revelations." I focused on the final paragraph.

*IT IS HEREBY AGREED to bestow upon the family Rain a void of magic, bound by bloodsong and fused in earth and stone. The undersigned shall solicit mediation and counsel of the line, and whosoever possesses the purpose to eliminate an heir shall writhe forevermore.*

. . .

WELL. That sure cleared things up. *Possesses the purpose.* It confirmed what Jared had said. The treaty's spell or curse or protection—whatever the hell it was—only kicked in if someone *intended* to kill me. Nothing stopped a paranorm from threatening or hurting me. Nothing stopped them from biting me.

What a freaking useless piece of paper. For me, at least. Sure, it went into detail about the blessing of the Null. Vampires and werewolves must be permitted entry in equal numbers with equal treatment and equal respect. All other paranormal species could request entry as well, and no entry could be prohibited without just cause. That was the only thing I might be able to twist. The treaty didn't define "just cause," and nowhere did it say that one Aged vampire and one alpha werewolf could block access to The Rain.

But that's what they did for the oh-so-altruistic reason of keeping us from being overrun by too many guests.

I placed the copied treaty back on the stack of papers and straightened them. One page didn't want to cooperate. I pulled it free, and my forehead wrinkled.

It was a picture of me and Astrid, one of my closest child-hood friends. We were seven or eight in the photo. Her mom and mine had been friends, and I was able to be myself around them. They were witches and spent nearly every summer at The Rain. Then, the summer I turned twelve, they'd left in the middle of the night two weeks earlier than they'd planned. And I'd never seen or heard from either of them again.

I hadn't thought of Astrid in years. I'd been first worried then hurt then angry about their sudden abandonment. Mom had said that sometimes happened with paranorms. They changed and moved on. After a few summers without so much as a phone call to say hello, I'd decided my mom and Astrid's must have had some falling out.

Why was this in the safe? It was just a photo.

I flipped it over. Scrawled on the back in my mom's neat handwriting were twenty names. Some were scratched out, nine had check marks beside them, and three had question marks. I didn't recognize any of them.

Someone knocked on the door.

"Just a second," I called out. I returned the papers to the safe, relocked it, then walked to the door and opened it.

"The kitchen," Sullens said, apparently back to his two-word conversations.

I looked toward the hallway that led to its back doors. "What is it?"

"Your new employee." Three words this time, and I hated every one of them.

"Okay," I said. "I'll take care of it."

He didn't look convinced, but he stepped aside to let me pass.

During the week of the full moon, we had more staff prepping food. Werewolves had voracious appetites, and even though their metabolism mellowed out to human levels in the Null, they'd developed the habit of eating five to six times a day. Fortunately, they weren't picky eaters. We didn't have to buy pricey ingredients or train the paranorms to cook; we bought easy-to-prep entrées like fish and chips, chicken Alfredo, burgers, all things that were quick and cheap.

When we walked in, Joash slammed shut an oven. The only time we'd interacted was when the wolves had cornered Deagan at the edge of the Null. He'd had my back then. Now, he looked like he wanted to light the world on fire.

I approached him like I'd approach a bear in the wild, remembering what my parents had said when they'd hired him a couple of years ago. It had been for his protection and the protection of others. His control issues had led to at least three major wildfires that blasted through California in the past decade. A witch had identified him and set a West Coast wolf pack on the hunt. He'd fled here, and my parents had given him a job.

They kept extra fire extinguishers around just in case.

I looked for the source of his anger, the vampire who had taken over an entire corner of the kitchen. Jared sat in a chair with his elbow propped on a stainless steel counter next to stacks of books and printouts and scribbled-on sticky notes. His eyes scanned the pages of the book open in front of him, and without looking up, he said, "He is angry."

"This is my kitchen," Joash bit out.

"I am certain it belongs to the Rains." Jared flipped a page.

"He needs to leave." A vein in Joash's neck pulsed. "I've been in charge of this kitchen for two years."

"Being *in charge* does not qualify one as a chef." Another page flipped.

"We have a library," I said. "You can read your"—I squinted at the titles—"cookbooks in there."

"Culinary books," he said. *Flip.*

*Well, thank you, Mr. Snooty.*

"Books harbor dust and mold," I said. "This can't be sanitary."

Jared looked up. "You wish to speak of The Rain's sanitation practices?"

"Um, no." Hiring Jared might go down as one of my worst decisions ever. "Look, Joash has been here longer than you. He's going to remain in charge of the kitchen."

"No." *Flip.*

"Your position here isn't final. My parents might throw you out on the street."

"They won't." Jared set one book aside to pick up another.

"*I* could still throw you out."

"You have a conscience, Kennedy. I am not concerned about being thrown out. If you want to discuss Joash's position, we may do so. I would point out the cooling units filled with expired foods and the inefficiency of this kitchen. I would point out the very bland and uninspired menu. I would also point you to the internet."

My eyes narrowed. "The internet?"

"Read The Rain's reviews. It is a wonder this place remains profitable."

I snorted. Profitable? Apparently not.

Jared's eyebrows raised a millimeter.

"It's nothing," I said. "But you need to get out of here. You need to get *this* out of here." I motioned to his mini library. "We can talk about your position later."

He closed his book. "Very well, Ms. Rain."

I helped Jared move out of the kitchen, and by *helped*, I meant I carried the thirty-two *culinary* books to the library while he made himself comfortable in an upholstered armchair and continued reading. He didn't even say thank you, so when I came back with the last stack of books, my bruised wrist aching, I slammed them down on the table beside him.

He didn't deign to look up.

Yep. I definitely should have left him in Arcuro's compound.

Sullens was waiting when I returned to the lobby. Instead of the distaste he usually wore written across his face, he just looked resigned as he pointed to my office. The camo curtain had been pushed to the side, and I could just make out the top of the head of someone seated in front of the desk.

Ugh. I should have locked my door on the way out. There wasn't a chance this would be good news.

I walked to the office, then rapped on the door as I entered.

The woman looked up from her tablet, then stood.

"Ms. Rain." She held out her hand. Tall and thin, she was both elegant and competent-looking, with dark skin and a closely shaved head. She had a kind of self-possession I envied, and I felt out of place in my blue jeans and T-shirt. At least I'd ditched the bandage on my arm in exchange for a much more discreet Band-Aid.

"Who are you?" I asked.

She reached into a pocket of her suit jacket and held out a business card. "My name is Dana Mersier. I represent In Sight, Inc. We're a merger and acquisitions company."

"Merger and acquisitions?"

She waited until I reached my parents' duct-taped chair, then sat when I did. "Yes. We understand you're having financial difficulties, and we would like to help. The buyer I represent would like to offer you a fair price for The Rain and its surrounding property."

"We're not for sale," I said. My gut had been right. I wasn't going to like this conversation.

"You will be in thirty days."

"If this is about the late notices, it's a misunderstanding. My parents are handling it." That better be what their trip was about.

"Unless you come up with a substantial sum of money," she said, "you will be foreclosed on. My client is prepared to offer fair terms now so that you will not have to go through that process. Your family will be able to stay involved in The Rain's day-to-day operations."

I tried to read the emotions beneath her professional exterior. Was this Blake's doing? Dana had the self-possession of a werewolf, and he'd proved the lengths he would go to in order to piss me off. My parents had assured me everything was fine. I definitely didn't believe that, but I also didn't think things were foreclosure bad.

"Who is your client?" I asked.

"That's confidential at this point," Dana said. "I'm here to assess the cost of renovations and to determine a fair market value for the property."

"We really aren't selling," I said. "We have a few creditors to pay off. My parents and their accountant will work that out next week."

"It's not that simple."

"People do it all the time." I'd heard the commercials on the radio. They told everyone listening they might not have to pay off their credit cards. It was practically an invitation to overspend.

"You have a substantial amount of debt and a substantial asset." She tapped on her tablet. "I don't want to take up too much of your time, but I need to ask questions about The Rain's finances."

"That's confidential at this point," I said.

She smiled in a professionally neutral kind of way. "The alternative is to let The Rain go into foreclosure. It will be put up for auction, and my investor will acquire it that way. If you sell to us now, you may retain a percentage of ownership."

We weren't going to lose The Rain. My parents might have stumbled into a financial hiccup, but we would fix this.

"I'm sorry you drove out here for nothing."

She lifted her shoulders in an apathetic shrug. "I can still conduct an assessment."

"No, that's not necessary." The last thing I needed was someone snooping around The Rain. Last week's inspector had been nuisance enough.

"This was a six-hour drive," Dana said. "I'll be quick and won't get in the way of your guests."

"Let me rephrase my objection. No, you don't have permission to conduct an assessment. You need to leave the property." I tried to keep my tone polite, but the past few days had worn me down. Patience was something I didn't have anymore.

"You're making a bad decision, Ms. Rain. I urge you to reconsider."

I stood. "I'll walk you to the door."

Her lips narrowed into a thin line. Then she slipped her tablet into her shoulder bag and left the office.

I followed, wanting to make certain she didn't take a detour on the way out. She didn't. She headed straight toward the exit and the…

The police officers.

They waited by the door, and every ounce of blood my body had replenished rushed to my feet. Officer Tanner was one of the two men. He looked at me with the grimmest face I'd ever seen.

My bruised ribs hurt. My lungs were too tight to expand. I glanced to my right, scanning the restaurant for Jared, needing his confirmation that this wasn't possible, that there was no way Tanner could remember me or Deagan or The Rain. Jared wasn't in sight though. The restaurant was empty except for a werewolf named Thad, cleaning the tables, and Garion wiping down the bar.

The two officers walked in my direction.

Running would be stupid. They would chase me down. I wouldn't make it out the door, and it would make my arrest so much worse.

Shit. I was going to be arrested. I'd never come close to that before. Before I'd met Tanner, I'd never even been pulled over for so much as a ticket.

"Ms. Rain," Officer Tanner said, his voice hard as steel. He *remembered*. How the hell did he remember?

Suddenly light-headed, I had to remind myself to breathe.

"Yes." The word sounded foreign and distant.

"Can we speak in private?"

I couldn't find my voice a second time, so I just nodded and waved them into the office.

Garion caught my eye. He raised an eyebrow, a silent question asking if everything was okay.

I gave my head a little shake. I meant it to be dismissive,

but I'm not sure how he took it. Like an automaton, I walked into the office, moved behind the desk, then sat in the camo-and-pink monstrosity of a chair.

Neither officer sat.

"Can I help you with something?" Sandpaper filled my mouth. I swallowed and tried to re-center myself. They couldn't arrest me without evidence. Maybe this was just an investigation, a search for a clue or a bluff to make me talk.

"Ma'am," Officer Tanner said. "The bodies of Derrick Smith and Sarah Rain were found near Hot Springs yesterday. There was an incident. It's still under investigation, but I'm sorry to report that both your parents died at the scene."

## 24

*Tick, tick, tick.* The clock on the wall had never sounded so loud.

"What?" I said.

"Your parents have passed away, ma'am."

I stared at Tanner. He continued talking, but only some words stood out: mauled, animals, wolves maybe. I kept listening for something that made sense. Nothing did. My mom had texted me last night. She'd given me the combination to the safe. She was alive and well and would be walking in the door any minute. She and my dad definitely weren't dead.

"Ma'am?"

He'd asked me a question. I had no idea what.

"This... this isn't true. It's a prank."

"No, ma'am. Do you have someone you can call?"

"When did this happen, sir?" I asked, my voice steadying.

"Last night. Late evening."

"Where?"

"North of Hot Springs."

Right. He'd said that already.

"My parents are fine."

His mouth tightened with a sympathy I wanted to slap away. My parents *weren't* dead.

"Their driver's licenses were with them," Tanner said, "and their car was found on a dirt road nearby."

"Fabrications." Blake had gone too far this time. This was cruel.

"It would be helpful if you could identify the bodies. Can someone drive you into town?"

"No one needs to drive me. I have my own car."

"We would prefer someone drive you, ma'am," the other officer said. "We can take you if needed."

I blew out a breath. "Everything is fine. Really. But if you insist, I can take a look."

I didn't want to take a look—I'd seen too many bodies this past week—but I would *prove* my parents weren't dead. Then I'd go back to Blake's. This time I wouldn't throw a robot at his head. I'd drive my car through his front door.

———

IT WASN'T real during the twenty-minute ride into town.

It wasn't real when I was escorted into the morgue's flower-laden waiting room and handed a clipboard with two face-down photos.

It wasn't real when I flipped those photos over and saw the gored faces of a man and a woman who looked similar to my parents.

No, it didn't become real until a woman handed me a clear bag containing items that had been found with the bodies. Dad's wallet was there. It had fallen open, and a picture of me smiled up through a photo sleeve.

No one carried photos in a wallet sleeve anymore. No one but my dad.

The moment repeated in my mind, replaying over and over

like a video that wouldn't fully download: a woman handed me a bag. I saw my photo in the wallet. My back hit a wall, and my parents' belongings hit the floor.

Woman and a bag.

Photo in a wallet.

Back against a wall and belongings on the floor.

Bag. Photo. Floor.

Bag. Photo. Floor.

"Ma'am." The woman squeezed my shoulder.

I was shaking my head. I didn't know how long I'd been standing there, how long the woman had her hand on me. She spoke words. They were in English, but I couldn't understand them.

I looked at my photo in the bag on the floor.

"Do you have family you can call? Close friends?"

"I…"

I had no one. No brothers or sisters. No aunts or uncles who could know about The Rain. My roommate… Carrie would be sad and sympathetic, but I couldn't talk to her either. I couldn't tell her that my parents had been murdered.

My parents had been murdered. Killed by paranorms.

Killed by wolves.

"Do you have a car service app? You shouldn't drive," the woman said.

I stared at her. Nodded.

She handed me a card for grief-counseling services.

I took my phone out of my pocket, a signal to her that I intended to call a car. She gave me her condolences one last time, then I turned and walked out of the morgue. It had started to rain while I was inside. Numb, I stood under an awning and unlocked my phone to open the app. A message popped up on the screen.

*Did you find the treaty?*

My hand shook. Nausea slipped over me like a coat of

slime. My mom lay on a slab inside the morgue. Her purse was in the bag in my hand. Her cell phone was with her killer.

I became so brittle a breeze could have cracked me into pieces.

I tapped to my favorites, then selected "Mom" from the list of contacts.

The phone rang once, twice, then clicked over to voice mail.

A new message popped up.

*Sorry sweetie. Bad reception you checked the safe?*

Every breath I managed sliced at my lungs. It felt like air escaped through those slashes. I wasn't getting enough oxygen. The world became more unbalanced than when Jared half drained me.

How long had I been texting with my parents' killer? Had their killer given me the combination to the safe?

What had the cops said? Their bodies were found yesterday.

I vomited behind a giant potted plant until nothing was left in my stomach. Nothing was left in me except emptiness and the distant, dull agony striking through my center.

This shouldn't have happened. My family was untouchable. We kept the peace between paranorms, and we helped them. We gave vampires the sun and freed the wolves from moonsickness. We helped restore their sanity. And my parents were *good*. They were kind. They followed the rules.

This wasn't possible. I'd read the treaty an hour ago. I'd heard Honcho's screams and seen him collapse to the ground. Our lives were *protected*.

A silent sob wracked through my body. I wouldn't let it fully escape. I couldn't. If I did, I'd fall completely apart, and this wasn't the time for that.

I wiped the back of my hand across my mouth, then stood, gripping my cell phone tight. I scanned the dark, drenched parking lot. I needed someone who could track a phone.

The police station was three blocks away. I'd go there. Tanner would help me. I'd tell him what had happened to my parents, tell him what had happened to *him*, and I'd make him remember.

I stepped out from under the canopy.

A pair of bright headlights glared through the pouring rain, driving straight for me. The driver turned and braked hard, then threw open the door.

"Kennedy!" Nora called.

I walked down the sidewalk. Three blocks. Then I'd get help.

"Kennedy, wait!"

I couldn't outrun a werewolf. I couldn't outwalk them either. Nora caught up and cut me off.

"It wasn't us, Kennedy. I swear it. My father swears it."

Rage crawled out of a cave deep inside me and clawed its way into my chest.

"Get the fuck away from me!" I yelled, my voice as vicious as any wolf's.

"We don't kill like this."

"I've seen your kind kill."

A line appeared between her brows. It smoothed out, and she said, "We protect the Rains. We don't hurt you."

"My parents weren't hurt. They were *slaughtered*. Their faces were slashed open and stitched back together. The cops said it looked like wolves. You know it's true, or you wouldn't be here denying it. Lehr knows it's true!" I screamed the last words in her face.

She backed up a step. For a werewolf, that was like retreating to the opposite side of a battlefield. I didn't fucking care.

I brushed past her.

"A pack member works in the medical office," she said. "He called my dad. My dad sent me. I know my father, Kennedy. He respects the treaty. If he didn't, he would have ripped Jared's throat out."

I kept walking.

"Where are you going?"

My phone chimed. My steps stuttered then stopped.

*are you okay?*

My mom was a stickler for grammar. She couldn't *not* use the proper punctuation. I should have noticed it before, should have figured it out. Maybe I could have helped—

No. I couldn't go down that path right now.

I scrolled through the messages. The last call from my mom's phone had been on Monday, right before Jared erased Tanner's memories. I hadn't answered, but it had to have been Mom, not her killer. The killer didn't want to talk. He or she wanted me to spill the location of the treaty.

That's what the last few messages had been about—the treaty that should have made their killer writhe in agony.

"Who are you talking to?" Nora asked. Rain ran down her hair in rivulets and plastered her white button-up to her body. Mascara smeared across her face where she'd rubbed a hand over her eyes. I'd never seen her look so human and never been so aware that she wasn't.

I lowered the phone and continued walking.

"Kennedy." She cut me off again. "Give me the phone."

"Get out of my way."

She held out her hand. "Now."

I felt the pull of the command. Her dominance pushed in around me, and I had to fight the urge to do what she wanted.

I met her gaze, squared my shoulders, and let my body language tell her to fuck off.

"Give me the phone or tell me who it is." She was barely clinging to control.

"Take it," I challenged.

Yellow flashed in her eyes the same moment lightning struck nearby.

Deafening thunder crashed through the air. She grabbed my wrist. I swung my free hand at her nose. Missed. Then I punched again.

She kept her hand locked on my wrist but stumbled back, more shocked than hurt.

I pulled my fist back a third time.

With a snarl, she flipped me over her hip.

My back slammed into the concrete, and my skull hit hard enough to eclipse the pain screaming through my wrist and ribs. I didn't let go of my phone though. She wasn't going to get the damn thing.

She knelt beside me, her eyes fully yellow now. She let me see them, see how close to the edge I'd pushed her. It was a warning not to push further.

Her gaze shifted to the phone one second before tires screeched to a stop a few feet from my head.

A door swung open. A pair of shoes stepped onto the wet pavement.

The way Nora raised her head to look at the newcomer was all wolf.

"I'm taking her home."

That was Garion's voice, but...

I twisted out from under Nora. She let me, shifting back into a crouch before she straightened with an inhuman grace.

It *was* Garion. He shouldn't be there. Our employees had to stay on Rain property.

"You'll keep her there," Nora said.

I pushed myself up to my knees, saw Garion nod.

"She's texting with someone. I want to know who."

Garion reached down, grabbed my arm, and lifted me to my feet like I was as hollow as I felt.

"We'll take care of her," he said. He maneuvered me behind him, then gently pushed me toward the car.

*My* car.

I opened the passenger door. Looked inside.

No keys. He'd hijacked it.

The bubble of laughter in my chest would have been maniacal if I'd let it out, so I swallowed it down and dropped into the passenger seat.

"It wasn't us, Garion," Nora said. "You have to convince her."

"I don't have to convince her of anything. Stay away from The Rain."

I closed my door as Garion opened his. He climbed behind the wheel, then turned the heat up and pointed the vents at me.

I was shivering.

Garion drove out of the parking lot, his jaw set in the grimmest look I'd ever seen.

"You're outside the Null," I said.

He nodded.

"Are you in trouble?"

"As long as no one is actively scrying for me, I should be okay."

The windshield wipers swished back and forth, slinging aside the rain except for a streak across the passenger side of the window. I should replace the wipers.

"I don't know what to say, Kennedy."

"How did you find out?" I asked.

"Lehr. He called five minutes after you left."

"He knew before I did."

"I don't think he would have called if the pack did it," he said. "And if the pack did it, I don't think they would have been so obvious about it. They would have covered their tracks."

He was choosing his words carefully. It didn't matter. My parents were found near Hot Springs. That was in Lehr's territory. He monitored every paranorm who entered the region. If he hadn't given the order, he knew who did.

"Someone's been texting you?"

I looked down. I still had a death grip on my phone.

"It's my mom's number."

His head turned sharply. "Today?"

"Yes."

His nostrils flared. He looked at my phone like he could crush the killer through the digital signal.

"He's been asking about the treaty. He wants me to find it. And he said, or I asked, that it was in the safe. He told me… he… he told me the combination." I barely had the air to get out the last words. The killer had forced the combination from my parents. How? My mind jumped from one horrific scenario to another, each one worse than the previous.

Garion put his hand on my shoulder. "Shh. We won't talk about it."

"But he's *here*." I held up the phone. "He's talking to me. Asking questions. And I don't know what to write back. I have to write back. I have to know…" I had to find out who he was.

I forced my raw throat to swallow. "I need… a witch. Take me to Owen. I can give him something of my parents. He can scry for the killer."

"I'm taking you home," Garion said.

"Then someone at The Rain can do it."

"No one at the hotel will step out of the Null."

"You did."

"You're the last Rain." Those words sucked the oxygen out of the car. "And my contract expires soon anyway."

I didn't want to be the last Rain. I wanted to be a college student. I wanted to go to class, hang out with friends, date, then get a job on the other side of the country. I'd always known I'd come back to The Rain, but it was supposed to be decades from now, after I'd lived my life and my parents were old and gray.

My jaw ached, I was squeezing my teeth so tightly together. My thoughts were so fucking selfish.

"I would have come to get you anyway," Garion said.

"If there's a witch at The Rain, they have to help. It will be a condition of them staying employed."

"They have contracts, Kennedy."

"I can fire them."

"People need stability. You can't change——"

My phone pinged, and chill bumps prickled down my arms.

*Yoohoo. Kennedy.*

*Sneaky girl.*

"Give me your phone," Garion said.

*If your lying about the treaty I'll find out you'll scream louder than your parents*

I chucked the phone onto the center console like it was a striking snake. Garion picked it up, scowled at the messages, then silenced it and stuck it into the storage sleeve on the side of his door.

"I should have replied." I turned down the heater. I was still wet and cold and felt like I might be sick again, but I needed to be numb.

"It wasn't anything you did or didn't do. Word is spreading."

We were almost to The Rain. I leaned my head against the window and watched the rain cut through the headlights. It wasn't even nine, but I was so tired. So drained. I'd poured all my energy into tears I hadn't cried.

Garion's hand went to my shoulder again, and he squeezed. "I'm sorry, Kennedy. This shouldn't have happened. Your parents should have been safe."

I didn't respond; I just kept staring into the rain-drenched night.

He let go of my shoulder to run his hand over his face, a rare display of emotion. He'd worked at The Rain for half a decade. My parents had given him sanctuary from whatever he was running from. They'd been his friend, and he was hurting too.

I swallowed down my own pain, then asked, "Are you an elemental?"

He drew in a breath, re-centering himself, then said, "No."

"Banshee?"

He shook his head.

"Leprechaun?"

A small smile played across his face. "You aren't even trying anymore."

I tried to smile too, but my mouth didn't remember how.

"Are you a necromancer?"

His smile faded.

"No," he said quietly. There would be no raising anyone from the dead.

He turned down The Rain's drive. The lights were dim, the windows dark and haggard, as if the building itself mourned.

The lobby went quiet as soon as I entered the doors. The staff and guests filled the big room and the restaurant. Only the crackling of the flames in the fireplace disturbed the silence.

I didn't want to be there. I didn't want to provide the para-norms shelter or let them have any place in my life.

I walked to the fireplace. Two women sat on its stone ledge. They moved out of the way and I watched the flames shimmer and dance. I needed to wrestle my thoughts into order, figure out what I was going to do, how I was going to make it through the rest of the night and the weekend and the funeral that I'd need to schedule.

Sullens approached, his face more pinched than usual.

"I'm sorry," he said. He shook out a blanket, then placed it around my shoulders.

I didn't know what to do with a Sullens who wasn't judging me.

Someone moved in my peripheral vision, another employee who would give me condolences.

I met his eyes and shook my head in a way that said "back off."

He retreated. That signaled the others to move. I watched the guests—the strangers, the werewolves.

"Why don't you go upstairs," Garion said. He stood close behind me, a protective shadow.

He wanted me to go upstairs to the empty residence. I couldn't, especially not with a hotel full of werewolves. Tomorrow was the full moon. If I kicked them out, they'd be at their most aggressive level. Those who had been moonsick before arrival might be moonsick again. They needed to stay at The Rain through a full moon to push away the madness. It would be irresponsible and dangerous to make them leave now.

It would be stupid to let them stay.

*Animal attack. Wolves.* That's what someone at the morgue had said, and Dad's face had looked gnawed on…

My throat closed up. I was going to be sick again.

I needed to get out of here, to be alone, but not upstairs.

I looked at the downstairs office, saw the closed curtain, and remembered the pink-and-camo-taped desk chair.

Not there either.

My heart rate kicked up. I was surrounded by paranorms. I scanned their faces, and my gaze caught on a familiar were-wolf. He'd been part of the group that had cornered Deagan at the edge of the Null. He'd wanted to kill Sullens because Sullens had killed Honcho, ending his screams. He'd demanded a life in return for the life Sullens had taken. He didn't look sympathetic. He looked unhappy, like it was an inconvenience to be in the same room as me.

My loss was an inconvenience.

"Get out," I said.

He remained seated on the couch.

I strode toward him.

"You. Leave."

His eyebrows rose when I stopped in front of him. "The moon is full. I have a right to stay until Turnover."

"My parents had a right to live."

"Ms. Rain," Sullens said gently. "Allow me to escort you to your room."

"Not before I escort him out the door."

The wolf stood. He stared me down.

I didn't look away or retreat despite him being a good half foot taller. His posture challenged my authority.

I wanted all of them out. I wanted to hurt the person or persons who had killed my parents. The only evidence I had pointed to the wolves. Until they proved otherwise, I would ban them from The Rain.

"They will stay," a quiet voice said from behind me.

I faced him fully. "You are not in control here."

"Neither are you."

I could have taken those words wrong, could have interpreted the softening of his tone as a condescension, but I felt the tremble of weakness in my hands, the brittleness in my heart. I didn't have it together, and I had no one to turn to for help.

Jared rearranged the blanket around my shoulders. Belatedly, I realized why. I'd touched up the makeup covering the bite mark on my neck that morning, but that had been eons ago, and I'd been standing in the rain outside the morgue.

"We will discover who did this," Jared said, "and we will kill them. Go upstairs now."

I shook my head. His expression darkened. He wasn't used to people disobeying him.

Stepping around him, I walked out the back door.

I didn't know what I was doing; I just knew I had to go. Rain needled the terrace. A strong wind misted it beneath the overhang and made my blanket billow like a cape behind me. Instead of staying under the covered walkway, I cut across the pentagon's center, veering to the left of the rippling pool.

Someone called my name. I kept walking. Reached the rain-puddled garden path.

"Kennedy!" Christian grabbed my arm and turned me toward him. His bright blue eyes searched my face. I searched his, my heart rate increasing, the blood in my veins heating.

"It's true," he said, horror bleeding into those two short syllables.

"Let. Go," I bit out.

Immediately, he released me.

"Who are you?" I demanded, stepping back onto the paved walkway. "*What* are you?"

He retreated. "Kennedy, I—"

"What do you know!" I shoved him. It was like shoving a boulder. Rain plastered his shirt to his rock-hard chest and his chiseled arms. He raised his hands in a placating manner.

"Let's talk inside." He'd backed toward the Catalan.

"Who killed my parents?"

"Please." He opened the door. "You'll freeze out here."

"Why have you been so interested in what they were doing?"

He stepped into the small building. "They're friends."

"Spare me the bullshit!" I advanced on him. "You know what happened. You're involved in this!"

"No. God, no. I wouldn't h—"

I launched a fist toward his face this time. He blocked it easily.

"I'm sorry," he said. "I…"

He clenched his teeth together and took a deep breath. When he let it out, his expression closed off. That's when I realized how open it had been, how raw and different from his usual quiet restraint.

"I need to talk to a few people," he said. "I'll find out who did this."

"You know who did this."

"Give me a few days." He opened the door beside him, and I realized he'd continued to back up. We were standing beside the Catalan's ransacked suite. It was clean now, but it had been his.

He left the door open and moved a few steps away. "You need to rest, Kennedy. You still haven't recovered—"

"If you don't start talking, you're banned from The Rain."

"Kennedy—"

"Stop saying my fucking name! You don't know me!"

He ran a hand through his drenched hair. It was such an unguarded, human gesture, my mind stuttered. I couldn't get a good read on him. He didn't fit into any of the boxes I'd laid out for paranorms, and he wasn't like Garion. He wasn't a friend. He was an entity that didn't fit into any world.

"Talk," I ordered.

He lowered his hand and met my gaze. "We were helping someone. A vampire with an abusive master."

I stared at him. Was he lying to me? I don't know what I expected him to say, but it wasn't that.

"My parents don't interfere in paranormal matters."

"They… they regretted what happened with the unsanctioned five years ago. They said you were right to help, that they should have helped a long time ago."

"No. Stability is paramount. They wouldn't do that. They…"

"No one deserves to be abused," he said.

"The police said it was a wolf attack."

A muscle in his cheek twitched. "I'll look into that. Just stay at The Rain. You'll be safe here."

"I don't care about being safe."

"Ken—" He grimaced and backed away. "I know. I'm sorry. I have to go. I…" He shook his head. "I have to go."

He turned to the door. If I'd had the energy, I would have launched myself at him. I would have hit and scratched and pounded him into oblivion, but when he left, the last remnants of my strength and composure abandoned me too.

An ugly sound ripped from my throat. Then another. And another.

I leaned a hand against the wall, trying to choke back the sobs, but my knees gave way. I slid to the floor and wrapped my arms around my legs.

This couldn't be real. My parents couldn't be gone.

## 25

No matter how much I slept or how many times I woke up, reality didn't change. My parents were dead. Murdered.

I cried alone, falling in and out of consciousness on the floor of the Catalan. At some point, Garion found me. He carried me into the ground-floor suite and tucked me into bed.

Time passed. Minutes. Hours. It didn't matter. I felt cored out. Empty.

Garion and Sullens took turns bringing me meals. Garion sat beside me in the room's wingback chair. Sullens didn't sit. He placed the tray on the nightstand and stood with his arms folded, looking less judging than usual and more worried.

They both had watched me push around food with my fork. The thought of eating had made me queasy.

I texted a few times with Carrie, letting her know I wouldn't be home for a few days. I didn't tell her about my parents. I didn't tell her that The Rain was supposed to be my home again.

Two days after I identified their bodies, my phone rang. I stared at it on my nightstand. My parents' killer hadn't texted again. I'd scraped up the courage to call the number once. It had gone straight to voice mail.

Heart thumping, I grabbed the phone, swiped it on, and listened. After several seconds passed, a male voice said, "Hello?"

"Who is this?" I made myself ask.

"This is Ed Silverstein at the city impound lot. May I speak to Kennedy Rain?"

I blew out a breath. "This is me."

"We have property that was removed from a vehicle belonging to Sarah Rain. It's ready for pickup. Can you come by today to get it?"

The crackers Sullens had forced me to eat churned in my stomach.

*Breathe. Focus.* Maybe I'd find some clue in whatever property they'd removed, something that would help me figure out where my parents had gone and what they had been doing.

"What time do you close?" I asked.

"Soon, but if you leave now, I can wait for you."

"Give me about thirty minutes."

"Sure. Drive safe." The call clicked off.

I'd changed into dry clothes Garion had brought. He'd left a sweatshirt too, so I threw that on, then grabbed my shoes. I didn't want to go to the main building—I wanted to avoid the staff who would watch me too closely—but I needed my car keys. I was pretty sure I'd left them in the office.

Maybe I could slip in the side entrance.

I opened the suite door and stopped.

Jared sat in a chair in the small rec area, an ankle crossed over his knee and a cookbook in hand.

"What are you doing here?" I asked.

"Learning." He closed the book. "You are going somewhere?"

"A walk."

He set the book aside. "I will accompany you."

"No, thanks," I said. "I just need some fresh air."

"So do I." He stood. The Aged didn't get subtlety very well.

"I want to be alone."

"Your parents were murdered," he said. "You will not be alone."

"I'm not your responsi— Never mind." I turned my back on him and left the Catalan. He followed a few steps behind me. Fortunately, he was comfortable with the silence. I didn't want to talk, and he wasn't exactly a chatty vampire. He was serious and somber and…

And he was a killer. If anyone other than my parents had been murdered, he would have no concerns at all.

I wanted to kick him off my property. I wanted to kick them all off.

I looked at the eaves of the lobby, the curved roof rising up into the late evening sky. I wanted to burn the whole thing down.

Shoving open the back door, I strode inside.

Sullens looked up from the reception desk. He opened his mouth. Closed it. Other staff members looked my way. Overall, the lobby was mostly empty. Even the restaurant looked deserted.

"They're gone," I said.

Sullens nodded once and clasped his hands behind his back.

"The wolves," I clarified.

He seemed to relax a little. "Yes, Ms. Rain. They were sent away after the full moon."

"They're not welcome back." I walked away before he could respond to that. He said something to Jared. I didn't catch what it was. I shoved open the door to my parents' office and grabbed my keys off the desk.

My eye caught on the camo-and-pink chair. My throat closed up. I struggled to suck in air.

*No. No!* The paranorms would not see me cry.

Fisting my keys in my hand, I left the office and headed straight for the front door.

"Kennedy," Jared called.

I didn't break stride.

"Don't let her leave," he said.

Isaiah, the vampire who'd bitten Melissa Geary a millennium ago, stepped toward the door. I threw a vicious glare his way, and he hesitated, his gaze shifting between me and the Aged vampire who'd given him an order.

I took advantage of that pause and yanked open the front door.

"Kennedy," Jared called again, but I was already outside. The staff couldn't follow me without breaking their contracts.

*Garion broke his.*

My throat burned. I hadn't seen him inside. I hadn't seen him since that morning. He hadn't said anything about leaving.

Would he have said something? All my life, others had left. Few had said goodbye.

I pulled open my car door. I couldn't worry about that right now.

The engine started. Cool air blasted from the vents. Though the night was cold, I didn't turn it down.

A light mist dampened the pavement. Without the stars and moon lighting the foothills, the roadsides were deep, black abysses. But I knew this path, the hills and turns, the most likely places for deer and other animals to cross. I'd become even more familiar with it in the future. My parents were gone. The Rain had to be my life now.

I bit my bottom lip, trying to keep my eyes dry. My lungs felt like they were filled with glass. This shouldn't have happened. It shouldn't have—

Someone shot out in front of my car.

I swerved. My tires hit the gravel on the side of the road, then hit something else.

The night spun and blurred. My headlights slashed across the person again. I slammed on the breaks and *boom*.

———

I DON'T KNOW if I lost consciousness. I didn't remember the airbag going off, but it lay deflated in front of me. My ears rang with the sound of the crash, my chest hurt from the seat belt strap, and my face was wet with blood.

A tree trunk replaced the passenger seat, caving in the entire right side of the car. Smoke rose from the engine that was somehow still running. At least, the battery was still running. A commercial played on the radio, crackling out of one speaker.

Out. I needed to get out.

I tried the door. It didn't budge.

Smoke began to burn my eyes. The air grew hotter, denser. I fumbled for my seat belt, got it undone.

Something moved outside the car. Someone.

"Help—" I coughed and squeezed my eyes shut, trying to clear my vision.

I spotted the person again. I was hurt—I likely had a concussion—but why would I see *her*? Melissa. Why would she be out on the road at night?

Suspicion crawled through me as smoke clawed at my throat. I tried my door again. When it still didn't open, I punched at the already broken windshield. Glass cut my hand. I had an opening, but it was *hot*.

Something in the engine popped. The already buckled hood whooshed up, and flames shot toward the sky.

I couldn't get out that way.

I screamed and rammed my shoulder into my door. I pounded my fist against the window, attempted to roll it down.

Think! I had to think!

The glove box. Dad had bought me a window breaker tool when I first received my license. It was there. Problem was that entire side of the car was crumpled like a tin can, and I could barely see.

I fumbled in the smoky dark. Metal and plastic cut my hands and arms. I ignored it. I had to find that window breaker.

My fingers brushed against it. Barely. It felt wedged between the pages of an auto manual I'd never looked at. I almost had it. I just needed a few more millimeters.

Metal groaned behind me, followed by a rush of air.

Hands grabbed me, pulling me backward out of the car and billowing smoke. My eyes stung so badly I couldn't keep them open. I felt the air around me cool, heard the flames fade, felt the rough gravel beneath my dragging legs. By the time I regained enough coordination to almost get to my feet, my rescuer lowered me to the ground.

Wheezing, I focused on him. On Deagan.

"You are having a most terrible week, Ms. Rain," he said.

"Jared—" I coughed.

"Yes, he called me. He said you were, quote, 'An idiotic fool of human who will destroy herself and the Null.'"

"Idiotic fool?"

"I pointed out the redundancy. The phone line went very silent. Best not to mention it when you see him again. Now." He helped me sit up. "Do I return you to The Rain or take you to an emergency room?"

"I was headed to the evidence lot," I said, taking careful breaths. If I stayed still, I didn't feel like I would throw up. I might not need an ER.

"At this time of night?" Deagan asked.

"They were waiting…" I faded off. It was a Friday night. No one but me cared about my parents' property. Why would the guy offer to stay late?

"I was lured out here."

"Lured? By whom?"

Melissa. I didn't know who she was, but I was certain I saw her outside my car. Maybe I had seen her at my apartment complex a few days ago too. She had something to do with my parents' deaths.

"How good are vampires at finding people?" I asked.

"We have resources," Deagan said. "Who do you need to find?"

"Melissa Geary. It's probably a fake name."

"That's hardly helpful."

"I think she is a vampire."

"Ah," he said sagely. "Would that be the vampire who was here moments before I pulled you from your car?"

"You saw her?"

"I felt her. Briefly. I thought she was young, but then she vanished. Only the Aged can disappear that quickly."

"Would you recognize her if you were near her again?"

"I am not certain." His brow furrowed. "If she is one of the Aged, she masked her aura too thoroughly to identify. If she is young… Well, they all tend to feel the same."

Great.

"Can you stand?" Deagan asked.

"I think so." I shifted to my hands and knees. It fucking hurt. I waited for the pain to fade.

"A small amount of blood would fix you up quite quickly."

I turned my head, intending to glare. Instead, I squeezed my eyes shut and tried not to pass out.

"I really do think it would be best," Deagan said. "We need to get off the road—"

My car exploded.

Heat and a wall of air rocked me backward. Instead of collapsing to the ground again, I rose into the air, held in Deagan's arms. The vampire moved fast, sprinting to his car so quickly the night blurred.

Or maybe he strolled and it looked like a blur because my head and vision were so screwed up.

He opened his car door, placed me in the passenger seat, then he stared back toward the burning wreck and *hmmed*.

"What?" I asked.

Firelight danced in his eyes. "In all my many years, I have never seen a car blow up in person before. I thought that was a myth."

If I hadn't been on the verge of throwing up, I would have rolled my eyes.

———

THE MOMENT I sat in Deagan's car—a slick BMW—my eyes drooped shut.

Deagan promptly woke me. Then it happened again. The third time, he changed his mind about taking me to The Rain. He turned around and drove to the nearest emergency room instead.

I had a concussion, three broken ribs, and a sprained wrist. The wrist might have been from hitting the railing in my apartment, not from the wreck, but the doctor wanted to keep me overnight. I didn't argue. Deagan did. Or rather, Jared did via Deagan. While the nurse talked to me, I watched the vampire pace outside my room, cell phone held to his ear. Deagan was trying to convince his master that I was perfectly safe here.

My parents should have been perfectly safe.

"Ms. Rain?" my nurse said.

It took a lot more effort than it should have to bring my attention back to her. "Sorry. What did you say?"

"Is that man next of kin? Visiting hours are over."

She was talking about Deagan. He looked out of place in his long, embroidered coat—purple this time—and he moved wrong. His steps were too smooth, too deliberately contained.

"He's…" I didn't want to call him a friend. I wasn't sure if it was true, and it would likely get him kicked out of the hospital for the night.

But did I want him to stay? Trying to think—to concentrate—hurt my head.

The nurse turned to Deagan. "Sir, visiting hours are over. You need to go."

Deagan slipped his phone into a pocket inside his coat. "I will stay."

The nurse nodded like that was the smartest idea she'd heard all day, then she left the room.

My already sensitive stomach churned. "That wasn't necessary."

He cocked his head. "What wasn't?"

Paranorms could be so oblivious. He didn't even realize he'd used his power on her.

"I don't need a babysitter," I told him.

"Fantastic," he said way too loudly. "I do not sit with babies."

"You don't have to yell."

"I am not."

"Then don't talk." I closed my eyes and rubbed at the center of my forehead.

"I wish you would allow me to give you blood. This inconvenience would instantly be resolved."

"You're still talking."

"Yes, well, fair warning. You may want to cover your ears. A wolf is approaching. Blake, I believe."

My eyes shot open. "No."

Deagan's mouth tightened. "Very well."

He removed his coat and turned toward the door.

My mind was slow to catch up with what his actions meant.

"Wait!" I sat up too quickly. "It's okay. It's fine," I said. The last thing I needed was a fight between Blake and Deagan in the middle of the hospital. "Just tell him to be quiet."

I lay back against the pillows. Before I could close my eyes again, Blake appeared in the doorway.

Deagan blocked his path. "She has a concussion and has requested silence."

"Get out of my way," Blake growled.

"That's not silence," I said. "You can move, Deagan."

After a long hesitation, Deagan moved aside.

Blake stepped into the room, filling it with a torrent of strength and fury and *him*. The wreck had really screwed up my head because I felt safe. I shouldn't, not with a wolf stalking toward my bedside.

"Kennedy," his voice rumbled over me.

"Unless you're here to tell me who killed my parents, you need to leave." My voice was the only steady thing in the room.

"It wasn't us."

He towered over me, and I hated it. I hated him and his ability to manipulate emotions. He wanted me to be calm. I wanted to rage. I wanted to hit him and hurt him and force him to apologize for… for everything that had happened.

My parents had been killed sometime Tuesday night. That was after Lehr had come to The Rain. Blake had given wolves orders to hang underwear from trees and fill balloons with ketchup. He'd scraped up a plagiarism accusation. He could have sent other wolves to track and kill my parents…

Except murder was a big leap from the pranks and harassment. It didn't seem likely.

Lehr could have ordered it though. Luke could have.

Or my parents could have been killed by other paranorms or by humans.

Did the treaty even apply to humans?

I didn't have answers, and all Blake had were denials.

I funneled my anger into my glare. "Get out."

Blake's eyes darkened. A muscle in his cheek tightened. He drew in a breath.

Then he lowered to a knee.

The move put him level with me, a gesture of equality that trapped the air in my throat. Dominant wolves didn't kneel. They didn't quiet the world or fight back the fire in their veins.

This wasn't the first time he'd held himself in check though. I'd calmed him outside The Rain, then he'd calmed me outside his house. What was this? A manipulation? Sensing the emotions of others was one of the powers of an alpha wolf. They knew when someone was too enraged to submit. They knew when they needed a cold command to push through a challenge. They read people.

"Stop werewolfing me," I said.

A smile bent the corner of his mouth. "None of my tricks work on you." He reached up and brushed my hair behind my ear.

It's strange how the softest touch can cause the hardest hit of lightning to ricochet in your stomach. It's a tangible thing, a physical feeling that can shift realities and confuse the senses. My thoughts tangled in my head. I was hurting. I wanted comfort, and there was a strong, powerful man kneeling in front of me.

A powerful *paranorm*.

I stiffened away from him. "What are you doing?"

He cocked his head slightly, and his brow furrowed as if he was asking himself that question. His gaze traveled over me in a way it hadn't before. It wasn't possessive. It wasn't dominating. It wasn't assessing or searching for weaknesses. But it was searching for something.

Deagan coughed loud enough to rattle my brain. Maybe he

rattled Blake's too because he gave his head a little shake, then quickly stood.

"We will help you hunt your parents' killers," Blake said. His tone had shifted. This was Lehr's second in front of me now.

"I can't trust your help." I kept my voice level.

"You trust theirs." He meant Jared and Deagan, or vampires in general.

"They haven't threatened me."

"No?" I swear he glanced at my neck. I had so many scratches and bruises he shouldn't be able to see the bite from three days ago, but it was hard to keep my hands in my lap and not to rearrange my hair.

"What happened tonight?" he asked.

"When you tell me what happened to my parents, I'll let you know."

Oh, he didn't like that at all.

"I'm going to sleep," I continued. It was easier to be on the attack. "If you want to be helpful, you can leave."

He was like a steel chain twisted too tight. It shouldn't be possible to snap the metal, but any more pressure and the link would break.

"Nora was right about you," he said. "You have an almost suicidal need to test our patience."

"Goodbye, Blake." I ignored the flare of gold in his eyes, ignored the way his shirt clung to the tight muscles of his arms and chest.

He kept himself under control, then turned toward Deagan, who watched us from the doorway. A handful of seconds passed, neither vampire nor werewolf breaking eye contact.

"You will watch her tonight," Blake ordered. "I'll send wolves at dawn."

"Other arrangements have been made for her daytime safety."

"They'll be here at dawn," Blake growled as he strode forward. He paused beside Deagan, silently emphasizing his point, then he disappeared down the hallway.

I collapsed against my pillows, exhaustion flooding my body.

"You are quite adept at aggravating him," Deagan said.

"Paranorms killed my parents." I struggled to keep my eyes open. "I don't care if I offend him."

Deagan pulled the room's single chair closer to the door. "You don't really believe it was Lehr."

I stared at the whiteboard on the opposite wall, seeing but not reading the nurse's illegible name. "Believing it's Lehr motivates him to prove otherwise."

Deagan chuckled. "Clever and cutthroat. I like you, Kennedy."

The nurse's name blurred and disappeared as I lost focus. I clung to consciousness a moment longer, debating if I should kick the vampire out of my room. Before I could settle on a decision, I lost the battle with my eyelids.

## 26

FUNERALS SHOULDN'T BE AT MIDNIGHT.

I stood in the gazebo a few dozen yards away from where the staff had arranged a perfect square of white plastic chairs. The center aisle straddled the Null line and pointed toward the family cemetery. The mausoleum and the surrounding area were lit by portable floodlights. Practical of them. Only the paranorms outside the Null would have been able to see well in the dark. Those on the inside would be as visually impaired as me.

By some unspoken agreement, the wolves were the ones clustered outside the Null. The vampires gathered nearer to The Rain. I watched the two groups ignore each other.

I wondered if there would be a bloodbath.

I wondered if I cared.

"This thing could use painting," a voice said behind me.

Deagan strolled up. He'd switched his purple coat for a long red one with leather patches covering his shoulders. His version of formal wear, maybe.

"Didn't Jared tell you to go?"

"Oh yes. Gave me a direct order to be far, far away when

Arcuro arrives. Funny thing though. His commands aren't binding when he issues them from the Null." He dropped his voice to a conspiratorial whisper. "He's not entirely happy with me."

"Why risk coming here?"

He lifted a shoulder. "You saved Jared's life." He rested his forearms on the gazebo's rail. "And tonight should be interesting."

My parents' funeral would be *interesting*.

I glowered at him, then followed his line of sight back to the gathering. Tonight was technically Turnover. Arcuro hadn't sent his list of approved vampires though. Instead of the usual guests, there was an eclectic mix of vampires, wolves, elementals, and a scattering of other paranorms, all of them powerful.

"You need to know the important players in the paranormal world," Deagan said.

"Do I?" My voice was flat.

"Many are here," he said. "See the woman in the pretty red dress?"

"The dress that matches the color of your coat and is totally inappropriate for a funeral?"

"That's Satine. She is in line for the kingship should the current one croak. So is Arcuro. Naturally, they despise one another."

"Naturally," I echoed.

"And the trio in the center of the aisle? The man's name is Grant Everett. He's a powerful witch from New York."

Grant Everett. The name sounded familiar, like I'd heard it recently.

"And outside the Null," Deagan continued. "Do you see the dominant wolf? The one who isn't Lehr?"

I did. He'd arrived before Lehr and his wolves. "They don't look friendly either."

"They aren't," he said. "It's difficult for wolves to tolerate another pack alpha in their territory. Viktor's little empire slices along the east side of the Appalachians. It bumps up against Lehr's not very far from the place where your parents' bodies were found. A coincidence, I'm sure."

I faced him straight on. "You know something I don't?"

"No," he said, still unfazed despite the ice in my voice. "I'm merely pointing out that there are many people who could be responsible for your parents' murders."

"Or it could be the obvious person."

"Not even Arcuro thinks Lehr is responsible for this."

"On good terms with him, too, all of a sudden?"

"People talk, Ms. Rain."

"What are they saying?"

"That Derrick and Sarah had been acting differently lately. Arguing more. That finances were tight because money was disappearing. That they were getting involved in something they shouldn't."

"Something?"

"There are many rumors. Most of them are ridiculous. Regardless, your parents were murdered by someone who was willing to risk the wrath of the treaty."

Or they had utilized a loophole.

Deagan's head turned slightly, focusing past my right shoulder. "Ah, here approaches another reprimand."

Jared strode toward us, wearing his black slacks and shirt and a confidence that said he owned the earth he walked on. He was either brave or stupid to show his face. Arcuro wasn't there yet, but Marco was. Gloria was. Two other vampires I recognized from the compound were.

And then there was Lehr. He stood at the edge of the Null with a few of his wolves.

Jared walked up the gazebo's three steps, bringing with him a dark, brooding anger. I didn't have to worry about him offering condolences or sympathies or empty words of comfort.

He wasn't one to waste his breath on placations that wouldn't help, and I appreciated that.

"My lord." Deagan gave him an overexaggerated bow.

"They will follow you." Jared's voice was cold enough to shatter steel.

"I am prepared," Deagan said.

"You are a fool."

"I'm not the one who fell in love with a werewolf."

Jared stared. That was it. He didn't move, didn't blink, didn't say another word, and it was terrifying.

A muscle in Deagan's cheek twitched. He lowered his head. "Forgive me."

"Perhaps your well-being should not trouble me."

"I was out of line."

"Perhaps I should not be concerned if another overrides our bond."

"I would not like that, my lord."

"Perhaps you would like to take ownership of my clan."

"No, my lord."

Deagan looked properly chastised, shoulders concaved, chin tilted toward the ground, but his eyes were still raised and meeting his master's. It would have been submissive enough to appease most people. Jared wasn't most people.

"You still have a clan?" My tone was just sardonic enough to lure Jared's cold gray eyes to me. If my sense of self-preservation hadn't *poofed* to dust since my parents' deaths, I might have been afraid.

His expression remained frigid when he slipped a folded piece of paper from his pocket. He handed it to Deagan. "I want security doubled day and night. Arcuro should not know I own it, but he may discover its significance. I am to be contacted at once if there is an issue."

Deagan opened the paper, grimaced, then, with an exasperated little sigh, said, "All right."

Jared had a way of punching the air with his silence.

"It will be done, my lord." Deagan lowered his head in a bow, then turned to me and bowed farther. "Ms. Rain, if you need help eliminating the loathsome bastards who did this, call me. I am in your debt."

Jared snorted, and Deagan's mouth quirked into a smile before he trotted down the gazebo's steps.

"I'm surprised you put up with him," I said.

Jared watched his scion stride toward The Rain. "I am too."

"It could have been you," I said.

Jared gave me a stony look that said explain yourself.

"You could be the loathsome bastard. Maybe you worried my parents would kick you out when they returned. You killed them so you could stay. So you could have influence at The Rain and over me."

"I am not Lehr." Jared's gaze cut into me. "And you are not easily manipulated. If you were, it would be far easier to keep you safe. You need to be careful, Kennedy. Someone found a way around the treaty's magic. They may attempt to do so again."

"How could they get around it?"

Jared looked at the gathering of paranorms. "I drank from you without repercussions."

"Because you didn't intend to kill me."

"Yes. Perhaps your parents were not intended to die."

"You didn't see their bodies."

He dipped his head, acknowledging the truth of my words.

"The treaty is old magic, Kennedy," Jared said. "And magic can be broken."

"You've thought this through, haven't you?"

He looked at me. "I have no reason to kill your parents, nor am I willing to risk ending the Rain line."

Because if we died off, the Null might die as well. The risk of that alone should have kept us safe.

Jared motioned toward the gathering. "It is time."

With my injuries, my concussion, and the general stress of the past week, I was done. The last thing I wanted to do was put on a mask and pretend that my parents' killer—or at least the killer's accomplice—wasn't among the paranorms. I scanned their faces again, looking for signs of guilt, signs of scheming, signs of something. I also searched for Melissa. She had to have something to do with their deaths. Maybe she was the person behind it all.

Jared didn't follow me down the gazebo's steps. I walked alone, my gaze locked on the two coffins waiting at the front of the arrangement of chairs. Half the seats were filled. Paranorms began to move in to fill the empty ones.

Someone stood from the section on my right, then stepped into the aisle.

"Kennedy," Owen said, facing me.

I wanted to ignore the witch, to brush by him and get through this before my composure gave out, but he blocked my path. Owen looked like a cross between a stage magician and a bartender. Despite the chill of the night, the sleeves of his black button shirt were rolled up, revealing the tattoos that crawled up both his arms. He was a smidgen shorter than me but made up for the lack of height with broad shoulders and hard muscle.

"I am sorry it's taken a funeral to meet again," he said. "My condolences. I had deep respect for your parents."

*But not for me.* I almost said those words out loud. He hadn't called my parents when Lehr walked into his store, and he hadn't given me any indication my plans were at risk. He was all about information and profit.

"Did you know they were in danger?" My question was direct enough to raise his eyebrows.

"I would have warned them if I'd heard anything."

"Really."

"You still think I betrayed you," he said after a long pause.

"You were the only one who knew what I was doing."

"Outside of the unsanctioned paranorms you helped."

"They didn't turn me in."

"How do you know?" he asked. "I'm not the only one who trades in information. Lehr and Arcuro could have granted someone clemency in exchange for your name."

I should have told him to leave. I should have told all of them to leave.

He blew out a breath. "This is the wrong time for that conversation, but we should talk. Stop by the store sometime. It's not too far from your work."

I almost laughed. My work. I'd missed a shift again. I was sure my boss had fired me by now. I could probably use my parents' deaths to get my position back, but it didn't matter. The Rain was supposed to be my job now.

"If I find out you knew something," I said, "I'll destroy you. I'll make sure you're shut down and forced out of town, and any paranorm who has any dealings with you won't be allowed to set foot into The Rain."

He'd maintained a semipleasant expression during our conversation, but witches were touchy. They had an inferiority complex that made them reject being threatened or pushed around. His mouth turned down.

"I understand perfectly, Ms. Rain," he said. "And I did not betray you five years ago."

He moved out of my way and retook his seat. That's when I noticed the woman beside him had been watching us.

Goose bumps prickled across my skin. All the paranorms had been watching. When I swept my gaze across the crowd, they pretended to look at other things, but I felt their gazes return as I moved down the aisle. They didn't know how to treat me. Many of them were so old the loss of a couple of lives didn't faze them. They were here because they had to be. They'd been ordered to come by their clan, their coven, their pack, or their court. No one truly cared. No one understood.

I kept my shoulders back, forced my raw throat to swallow, and focused on my parents' shining coffins. When I felt lost like this, I'd call my mom. I couldn't call her anymore.

Someone dropped into the empty seat on my left.

Nora.

I stared at her. She stared right back, practically daring me to send her away.

"You are not alone," she said.

Someone else approached.

"Kennedy," Carrie said, her eyes red and teary. "I'm so sorry." She gave me a hug, then sat down on my right. Alex was with her. John too. Both leaned down to hug me before they sat.

"How did you find out?" My throat closed up.

"She called." Carrie nodded to Nora.

Nora kept her gaze locked on the pastor as he took his place between my parents' coffins. I bit the inside of my cheek. I would *not* cry in front of the paranorms.

The paranorms. A midnight funeral. God, how was I going to explain this to my friends? How would I explain the strange behaviors of the crowd? The groups that had formed? The overconfident stances of the wolves and unnatural stillness of the vampires?

My friends weren't stupid. I saw their frowns, the quizzical glances they tried to hide. Excluding anomalies like Nora, vampires and werewolves were made, and they tended to target attractive humans. The number of strong, masculine men and lithe, gorgeous women seated around us was impossible to miss.

The pastor began to speak. I'd met him before. He was

human but aware of the paranormal world. Someone must have told him my friends weren't. He spoke carefully, alluding to differences, to the darkness people had to walk through. He talked about common interests and the goodness of God. That God can make good things come from the trials we endure.

There wasn't anything good about my parents being murdered. Perhaps he was alluding to something good coming from the continued existence of vampires and werewolves and other beings who hid from the human world.

Carrie looked at me more than once during the eulogy. I kept my gaze straight ahead so I didn't have to meet her eyes. I noticed some of the paranorms glancing our way though. That's when I realized they, too, knew my friends were human.

*Oh.*

Nora was smarter than I gave her credit for. She might have called Carrie because she thought I needed the support, but she'd also called because it forced the paranorms to be on their best behavior.

When the pastor finished and the coffins were lowered into the ground, Nora stood. She walked out of the Null and joined her father. Never once did she look in Jared's direction. He looked in hers though. He tracked her movements, appearing like a vampire who thirsted for her more than he thirsted for blood.

"How are you doing?" Carrie asked.

I pulled my attention back to my friends.

"I'm…" Devastated. Angry. "I'm glad you're here. Thanks for coming."

John dropped into the seat Nora had vacated. "Is this why you ran off the other day? You knew something was wrong?"

God, that felt like eons ago. "I'm sorry about that. I should have called."

"Hey." He bumped my shoulder. "Don't worry about it. Is there anything we can do?" His gaze wandered at the end of the sentence. Satine and her red dress walked by. I couldn't figure out if her smile was sympathetic or threatening.

"No, I'm all right."

"Good," Carrie said. "Then it's okay if I'm mad at you for holding out on us."

"What?" My mind wasn't functioning well enough to work out her meaning.

"This isn't a quaint little hotel. It's practically a resort. It's beautiful and eclectic and weird."

I smiled. Carrie always knew how to lighten the mood.

"I grew up here. It just seemed normal to me." That might have been the biggest lie I'd ever told in my life.

She gave me a playfully scolding look, then, after I assured her again that I didn't need anything, she and the guys left without pointing out the other beautiful and eclectic and weird things about my parents' funeral. Either they were too polite to say anything or they thought me too fragile to handle intrusive questions.

Or perhaps they just thought I was part of a cult.

"You okay?" Garion stood in the aisle to my right. I thought about rising, but gravity pushed me down. Even though the night was cold, it felt stifling, like there wasn't enough air to fill the atmosphere. The Rain was a heavy pressure at my back, a huge boulder I had to lift or it would crush me.

"What happens now?" I asked.

"Your parents would want you to finish school. They would want you to have a life."

"The Rain…"

"You'll have to stay close, but the staff can handle the day-to-day operations."

"Like it was handled these past two weeks?"

"We only needed you at Turnover and the few times when there were hiccups."

"You don't know how bad some of those hiccups were."

What would he say if I told him about Tanner? About Jared biting me? What if I told him about The Rain's debt and the business card I'd been keeping in my pocket? What if I told him that I'd briefly considered selling everything?

"You can handle college and the hotel," he said. "As long as we have stability, things will be fine."

I didn't respond; I stared at the graveyard fence that had been removed and set aside for the funeral. The coffins had been lowered into the ground beside my ancestors. Behind the mausoleum, an excavator waited to push the dirt into the grave. Ruhl, The Rain's groundskeeper, leaned against it, waiting to repair the earth.

"I'm opening the bar," Garion said. "I can make you a drink. Maybe Jared can cook you something to eat."

"*That* issue hasn't been resolved yet," I said. "Go ahead. I need a few minutes."

He scowled but said, "Don't stay out too long. The night is cold."

Normally, I would have retorted with a sarcastic "thanks, Dad."

Aside from Ruhl, I was alone. He wasn't the talkative type, though, and he kept his distance. I walked to my parents' graveside. I should have said something, should have placed flowers or dampened the earth with my tears. But I was empty. Nothing felt real anymore.

Sometime later, with my face and fingers numb from the cold, I left, taking a longer route through the garden and around the terrace in an attempt to avoid as many people as possible. I stared at the ground while I walked, not wanting to make eye contact, so I didn't realize Luke stood in front of me until he peeled away from the column he'd been leaning against.

He didn't offer condolences, and there was no sympathy on his face.

"This doesn't change things," he said.

"Get off my property." My voice was cold and quiet.

"Fire Jared."

I didn't snap all at once. It was a slow, gradual cracking, like a can of Coke crumpling or a branch bending in a strong wind. My hand fisted at my side.

"You almost killed me," I said.

"You almost killed yourself."

I wished I'd taken the gun from my parents' safe. "You found a loophole in the treaty. Convenient timing."

He stepped closer. I didn't back up.

"Are you insinuating something?" he asked.

"My parents' killers found a loophole."

"You're right. That is funny timing."

Someone caught my arm before I launched my fist at his face. I didn't have to look to know who'd stepped to my side.

Luke's upper lip curled.

"Fuck off," Blake said.

The other wolf didn't move, not for a long time. Something passed between the two of them, something dark and vicious.

Luke was going to make a play for power. I knew it in my gut. Lehr had ordered him to watch Nora. He wouldn't give that assignment to a weak wolf, and Luke had been at Lehr's side when the alpha came to The Rain the other day. He might not challenge Blake tonight, maybe not tomorrow either, but at a time of his choosing, he would strike. He'd try to rip holes in Blake's flesh and replace him as Lehr's second.

With one final sneer, Luke turned and strode off.

"You'll tell me if he touches you again," Blake said near my ear. The quiet promise of protection curled in my chest. I wouldn't turn toward him. I wouldn't let myself remember the heat in his eyes when he'd knelt by the hospital bed or the disastrous kiss we'd almost shared outside his home.

"You'll let go of my arm."

He did. Immediately. Then he stepped to the side and looked at me. His eyes held a mix of anger and violence and something else, something that might have been remorse.

"You can leave, too," I said.

"We didn't kill your parents. If we had, I would know. I'd tell you."

"Even if your alpha forbade it?"

His mouth pressed into a thin line. Answer enough for me.

"Goodbye, Blake." I climbed the porch steps.

"Kennedy," he called.

I stopped but didn't turn around.

I felt him move closer. He was tall, so even a step below me, he could see over my shoulder.

"You want evidence," he said near my ear. "I'll bring it to you. You don't need to search for answers yourself. Stay at The Rain. Keep it running smoothly. I won't interfere again."

He wanted things to be the same as they had been before. He wanted stability.

"Ms. Rain?" Sullens said from the terrace door.

The air behind me remained warm for several seconds, then the night chilled when Blake walked away.

"What is it?" I asked, climbing the steps.

"I'm sorry." He handed me a paper.

It was Arcuro's guest list. He wrote one line of condolences and another line about the significance of The Rain in the paranormal world. He was certain I would continue in the tradition of my parents and that I should demonstrate that intent by returning a signed copy of the letter.

I stared at the list of sanctioned vampires for a long time. Then I crushed the paper in my fist.

Screw stability. I was going to change everything.

Kennedy takes on the paranormal world in **Bound by Bloodsong**.

**Turn the page for a sneak peek**

OR

Do you want to know how Nora and Jared hooked up?
Subscribe to my newsletter at https://www.sandy-williams.com/avoidofmagicLP to read their story as I write it.

## SNEAK PEEK: BOUND BY BLOODSONG

## CHAPTER ONE

*You're needed.*

Those two words were officially my least favorite words in the world, especially when voiced with Sullens's British accent. That phrase had started this nightmare a little over a month ago, and it had preceded a hundred more mini catastrophes in the following weeks. I'd had a short respite since my parents' funeral, but I'd known it wouldn't last.

I stepped off The Rain's antiquated elevator and scanned the lobby until my gaze locked on Sullens. He nodded toward the closed front door. The thick wood prevented me from seeing who stood on the other side, but that didn't matter. Tomorrow was Turnover. I knew who was there.

Putting on my best go to hell look, I strode across the lobby, gripped the curved iron handle, and pulled.

"Hello, Blake," I said when the door swung open.

"Kennedy." His expression was hard too, an indication that he was there in his official capacity as Lehr's second-in-command. He stood at the edge of the porch, right inside the invisible Null zone that extinguished his werewolf magic. Unfortunately, it did nothing to extinguish his good looks. He had a perfect five o'clock shadow going, and his dark hair was mussed up and just long enough to catch a bit of the breeze. Add in a fitted T-shirt that hugged the muscles in his shoulders and chest, and he would go viral if I snapped a picture of him.

I leaned my shoulder against the doorjamb, an echo of postures he'd used on me in the past to show how easy it was to be in control of a situation.

His glower deepened. Then he held out an envelope.

I kept my arms crossed.

"It's important," he said.

"So is finding my parents' murderers."

"I'm working on it."

"Are you?" I tilted my head. "Because all I've heard are denials that the wolves are involved."

"We aren't."

"Where's the evidence?"

He lowered the letter. "I can't prove a negative."

"You haven't tried."

"I am trying." His voice lowered to something just above a growl. "More than I should."

Asshole. I pushed off the doorjamb and turned to go inside.

"Wait," he said quickly. "That came out wrong. What I meant is that I have other responsibilities. One of those includes supervising moonsick werewolves. They need The Rain, Kennedy." He held out the envelope again. "And Lehr has promised it."

Slowly, I faced him again. "What do moonsick wolves do in other places?"

"What do you mean?"

"The Rain is the only Null zone on the planet. I assume there are werewolves across the globe. What do they do?"

"They're sent here," he said. "Or they're killed. Is that what you want to happen?"

He knew it wasn't. He knew how much it weighed on me that he'd killed a moonsick wolf and her brother a month ago.

"They will hurt people if they don't find peace in the Null."

I held his gaze. "Sounds like you're going to have a busy week."

"Kennedy." His voice changed. Without saying more than my name, he let me know how this wasn't me. I wasn't cruel or apathetic about people's lives.

I kept my tone hard. "My parents were murdered. My parents who enforced your rules, who preserved your peace, who willingly gave up any chance of a normal life to make *your* lives better. They did everything right."

"It shouldn't have happened," he said. "I'm sorry that it did. I've promised that I will find out who killed them, and I will. Accepting this list doesn't change that."

I stared at the envelope he held. It was a return to normalcy, a return to the way things had always been, with Lehr the gatekeeper for the werewolves and a vampire named Arcuro the gatekeeper for his people. No one made it to The Rain without their permission.

Well, mostly no one.

I took the envelope. Blake's expression relaxed at what he saw as a submission.

Keeping my eyes on his, I gripped it between my fingers. And ripped it in half.

His gaze locked on the torn envelope.

I ripped through it again.

His mouth dropped open.

The envelope and folded page inside were too thick to rip a third time, so I let all but one of the pieces fall and removed the torn letter from the last section. I unfolded the small square and proceeded to rip it into tiny pieces.

Then I threw them into the air and let the wind swirl them to Blake's feet.

He looked up. I expected clenched fists, a snarled threat, an aggressive step my way.

Instead, he blinked and said in the most stunned voice I'd ever heard from him, "I can't believe you did that."

"Come back when you find out who killed my parents."

He still looked shocked, a fact that was pretty damn satisfying. I was just about to pivot back toward the door when he removed another envelope from his jacket.

I paused. Raised an eyebrow. "Is your paper shredder broken?"

The corner of his mouth tightened into something halfway between a smirk and a smile. "This is the envelope I should have handed you first."

My gaze shifted between his wood-dark eyes and what he held. When I recognized the return address stamped onto the white paper, I reached for it.

Blake held it higher.

The satisfaction I'd felt seconds ago vanished, replaced by the rage Blake should have shown when I ripped the first envelope apart.

"You're the reason they haven't given it to me!"

"No," he said, too damn calmly. "Bureaucracy is the reason they haven't given it to you. I just cut through it."

I lowered my hands to my hips. "Hand it over."

He studied me. I didn't bother to hide my anger. I'd been trying to get my parents' cell phone records for weeks. The company had made me call the police station, which made me call the court house records, which sent me back to the cell phone company because they should have given me a form to fill out to begin with, only the company claimed a form didn't exist. I spent more time on hold than I did talking to a human being, and the only progress I made was deciding I needed to talk to a lawyer.

"Blake," I warned.

"Turnover is tomorrow," he said. "You'll let the wolves in."

"You'll give me the fucking envelope."

Those dark eyes took me in. He still wasn't angry. He was something else, and I had to remind myself that he was there at his alpha's bidding. He didn't actually care about me or my parents; he cared about the pack and its strength and position in the paranormal world.

"They'll be here tomorrow at dusk," he said. A statement of fact.

"I will lock every damn door." Also a statement of fact.

"Fine. They can sleep under the stars." He held out the envelope.

"I—" I shut my mouth. Werewolves didn't need a roof over their heads to find peace in the Null. The magic-free zone stretched over a quarter of our hundred-acre property. The hotel occupied only a small corner of that.

I eyed the envelope. I wanted it, but I didn't want to make the compromise.

"You already called the numbers," I said.

"You wanted me to find the people responsible."

"What have you learned?"

He lowered the envelope, again analyzing me with those eyes that seemed to see more than I wanted him to.

"May I come in?"

That was different, Blake asking permission for something.

"No," I said.

Annoyance flickered across his face before he opened the envelope and slid out the stapled pages inside.

He moved to my side. "These are incoming and outgoing calls for the past three months. Almost all the calls were to you or area businesses for the first two months, then, about three weeks before they died, the pattern changed."

He flipped the page. He'd taken surprisingly meticulous notes. His neat handwriting trailed down the left side, noting the dates he called, if he made contact with someone, and what the outcome of the call was.

"A lot of people don't answer unknown numbers," he said. "Those are highlighted yellow. These"—he pointed to almost a dozen numbers with circled area codes—"are all from the same place."

"Where?"

"Cincinnati." He looked at me. "Do you know anyone there?"

He was standing close and was only a few inches taller than me. If I looked up, the small distance that separated us would become even smaller. So I didn't look up. I deliberately locked my gaze on the paper and said, "No."

I could practically feel his smirk. He knew exactly why I wouldn't make eye contact. My body didn't always listen to my head when I was around him.

"I didn't think so," he said. He handed me the papers. "You should call the highlighted numbers. If the call goes through with The Rain listed on caller ID, they might pick up."

I nodded, half listening as I continued to look over the records.

"I want to know who you talk to," he said.

I stopped my agreeable nod and finally looked up. He'd inched slightly further away, and his expression was serious again.

"Sure," I said.

"I mean it, Kennedy. Someone found a way around the treaty when they killed your parents. They can find their way around it again."

"They kill me, they kill the Null."

"That's what we think would happen," he said. "I'm not willing to risk your life based on an assumption."

I smiled at him. "My life isn't yours to risk."

"It's mine to protect." His voice turned rough.

I rolled my eyes. "Thank you for the phone records. You can get lost now."

"There's something else," he growled when I turned toward the door. I deigned to glance his way.

"I went to the site where Sarah and Derrick were found," he said. "I couldn't pick up a scent."

"That was three weeks ago."

"I went straight there after I saw you at the hospital. Their deaths were violent and bloody. I should have smelled the excitement of the paranorms who did it."

My stomach churned.

"It was deliberately camouflaged."

He said that like it was significant. "You're not talking about dirt and branches."

"It was like walking into an electronics store with static on all the screens and the volumes turned up to max. Chaotic. Loud. Impossible to identify a single scent."

Goose bumps darted up my arms. They were more from the discomfort in Blake's posture than from his words. Few things unsettled Blake, but the camouflage had him agitated.

"That's convenient," I made myself say.

His expression darkened. "You're so determined for us to be the villains you won't see any evidence proving otherwise."

"You haven't shown me any evidence."

"We've circled back to this. Fine." He crumpled the empty envelope in his fist. "I'll be your enemy, but Turnover *will* happen tomorrow."

He paced down the porch steps.

"You forgot the *or else*," I called after him.

He glared over his shoulder, but didn't say anything. He continued on to our small parking lot and climbed into an old Ford truck that was more battered than the cracked and potholed cement beneath it. It creaked when he open the door, shuddered when he closed it. The engine squealed twice before it rumbled on. I watched him drive out of the lot, side beds swaying, just in case I got to see the damn thing fall apart.

No luck.

Sullens was waiting when I walked inside The Rain. I'd known he was there, known other staff members would be nearby too. They acted like they just happened to be walking by or, in the case of one woman, rearranging fake flowers, but ever since my parents were murdered, they'd been discreetly keeping tabs on me.

And I'd been keeping tabs on them—studying them—because I didn't 100% trust the staff.

"He's right," Sullens said.

"About what?" I stared down at the phone records as I walked toward my parents' office. My office now.

"You being so sure the werewolves are responsible," he said.

"You don't think they are." I faced him when we reached the door. His gray eyes had lost the contempt they'd held when we first met, but he still viewed me as a foreign thing, a stranger to be treated with caution. That might be due more to the fact that he was a witch than anything else, though. I'd read his file—I'd read all the staff's files—and witches were notorious for carrying chips on their shoulders. Individually, they were dismissed as being inferior to other paranormal species. They had human strengths, human weaknesses, and human life spans. Their magic was mediocre at best until they formed covens, but due to their oh-so-pleasant personalities, those covens rarely stayed together.

"Lehr controls his wolves," Sullens said, "and he had no reason to want your parents dead."

I just hmmed and reached for the doorknob. Before my fingers touched it, something shattered in the kitchen. Probably something expensive. I didn't want to know what it was—I couldn't afford to replace a paper plate—so I ignored it and pushed open the office door.

Another shattering sound, this one followed by a thunderous boom.

"Damn it." I tossed the phone records onto the desk then strode to the hallway that cut between the office and the kitchen. By the time I reached the swinging door, another boom rattled the air.

Since The Rain hadn't had guests in three weeks, the restaurant hadn't been serving food. The paranorms cooked for themselves in the Barn, a literal barn that had been converted into a surprisingly nice residence for the staff. Only two people occupied the kitchen now—Jared, who stood unruffled near the center island, and Joash, who'd crashed against a now dented metal cabinet.

Joash snarled something unintelligible before he leapt back to his feet. He reached to the counter behind him and grabbed the fire extinguisher.

I would have commented on the irony of the fire elemental's choice of weapon if he hadn't rushed Jared, swinging the extinguisher like a baseball bat.

Jared didn't budge other than to casually lift his arm to block the blow.

The crack of bone echoed through the kitchen.

Jared looked down at his dangling arm. He blinked. Then his nostrils flared.

My stomach churned. Arms should not bend in more than one place.

Joash readied for another hit.

"Don't!" I darted forward and grabbed the extinguisher just as he started his swing. The momentum pulled me off balance, but Joash froze as soon as he registered my presence.

"He changed the order," Joash ground out.

"Let go of the fire extinguisher."

"This is my kitchen."

"Actually, it's mine. Let. Go."

Fury flared across his face, but he released the extinguisher. I set it back on the counter.

"Jared," I said. He still stood there staring at his grotesquely broken arm as if he were offended by it.

When I repeated his name, he looked at me. Then he looked at Joash.

Three steps, and Jared grabbed the fire elemental by the throat.

Pre-order **Bound by Bloodsong**

OR

Do you want to know how Nora and Jared hooked up?
Subscribe to my newsletter at https://www.sandy-williams.com/avoidofmagicLP to read their story as I write it.

# ACKNOWLEDGMENTS

This would be the worst book ever written if not for the help of Nevada Martinez, Renee Sweet, and Yvanca Wensing, who read the really ugly version of Kennedy's story.

Thank you also to the beta readers who helped make this book (hopefully) not suck: Rachelle Morrison, Vicki Fanibi, Corrie Lavina Knight, Christy Georgen, Wilda Sowell, Shelli Richard, and Wendy Trujillo.

Have I mentioned I'm a feedback junkie? I need lots of opinions and thoughts to convince myself a book is good enough to be published, and I am so grateful to each and everyone of you! Seriously.

I'm also super excited to be working with Jessa Slade again, who made me look deeper (and deeper!) for my character's motivation.

I am incredibly happy with how A Void of Magic turned out, and I couldn't have created this story without the team of people who support me. Thank you!

# ABOUT THE AUTHOR

Sandy Williams writes urban fantasy and science fiction, both with a strong shot of romance. She's a fan of the enemies-to-lovers trope and loves books with high stakes and fantastical settings. When she's not being a bookworm, she loves playing board and card games like Dominion, Quacks of Quedlinburg, Dungeon Pets, etc (but not Goblins because she ALWAYS loses that damn game!).

## ALSO BY SANDY WILLIAMS

### The Anomaly Novels

Shades of Treason

Shades of Honor

Shades of Allegiance

### The Shadow Reader Novels

The Shadow Reader

The Shattered Dark

The Sharpest Blade

### Kennedy Rain

A Void of Magic

Bound by Bloodsong (Pre-order)

A Void of Magic

Print ISBN: 978-1-7360157-5-9

Ebook ISBN: 978-1-7360157-2-8

Made in the USA
Coppell, TX
14 November 2021

65752964R00194